Touch Me Not

A Manwhore Series Novel

By Apryl Baker

Touch Me Not

Limitless Publishing, LLC
Kailua, HI 96734
www.limitlesspublishing.com

Formatting: Limitless Publishing

ISBN-13: 978-1-68058-285-7
ISBN-10: 1-68058-285-2

Dedication

For Sofiane

Chapter One

The student union of Boston University was packed, inside and out. The first day of moving into the dorms was always hectic, and by lunch, everyone wanted to just find a seat and sit down. Late August in Boston, while not hot, wasn't cool either, so most wore shorts, tanks, skirts, and various other summer paraphernalia. A Dr. Dre Beatbox on one of the outside tables blared some upbeat playlist, and lots of the people assembled outside moved to the music. A veritable feast of hormones.

At least that's how Nikoli Kincaid saw things. His gaze moved over the mass of bodies, categorizing all the women there. He couldn't find a single one outside the newly arrived freshmen he hadn't bedded over the last three years. Well, there were some, but he simply wasn't attracted to those few. He never had sex with the same woman twice. It was a strict rule of his, and one he refused to break for anyone. He sat there and debated if he should pick up the cute little redhead who looked lost or the brazen blonde who eyeballed him with open lust.

Nikoli smiled at the blonde. He knew the effect he had on women and used it to his advantage daily. His grandmother called his good looks a curse; he called them facilitators of a good time. Hair the color of rich, dark chocolate and onyx eyes pulled women to him. His eyes were always full of the promise of mind blowing sex. His Russian accent only added to his allure. He'd had a woman twice his age tell him that once. He'd been a little grossed out at first being hit on by a woman who could be his mother, but he'd accepted a long time ago what his looks could do for him.

No better way to christen the beginning of his senior year than…his mouth dropped open, earning him a questioning look from the guy sitting beside him. Luther Conway had been his best friend since freshman year of high school and was the only person who really knew him. Hell, some days Nik didn't know himself, but he could count on Luther to keep him grounded.

"She is *not* a freshman."

"Who?" Luther sat up and scanned the crowd, his eyes coming to land on what caught Nik's attention so thoroughly. Hair so black it glinted blue in any kind of light was held up in a high ponytail. Warm blue eyes rested on the guy she spoke with. Her small, delicate face radiated laughter. She was a stunning beauty who had no idea how beautiful she really was. Lily Holmes really had no idea the effect she had on men.

"Don't even think about it, Nik," he warned.

"That's Lily Holmes."

Ah, the fabled Lily Holmes. He'd heard her name often. She tutored most of the football team and several members of his own frat house. How had he never laid eyes on her before?

"They'll break every bone in your body if you hurt her," Luther growled at him.

"It'll be worth it." He grinned and jumped up, the lusty little blonde forgotten as he sauntered over to meet Miss Lily Holmes.

Lily smiled, but inside she grimaced. All she really wanted to do was go find a quiet corner and sit for a bit. Not that that was even a possibility. She sighed as several of Adam's football buddies came over. They all had to say hello, and then more people wandered over, the small crowd around the maple tree in front of the Student Union growing by the second. She'd promised to meet Adam here for lunch, but if he didn't show up soon, she was going to bail. She needed to check with the bookstore to see if her lit book was in yet. As of yesterday, it still wasn't in stock, but they were hopeful it'd be in today.

She scanned the crowd and sighed in relief when she spotted Adam heading her way. He looked so all American, boy-next-doorish with his sandy blond hair artfully spiked, laughing at his friend Mike Craft as the two of them pushed their way through the crowd. Lily smiled softly as they approached. Adam Roberts had been her best friend since third grade. She only wished he would wake up and realize how much more they could be, but she'd given up on that hope a long time ago. Now

3

he was engaged to be married to Susan Williams, and she had to pretend to be ecstatically happy for him when all she wanted to do was cry. It sucked to be her, but then that was nothing new.

For two seconds, she wanted to growl in frustration. Sue and her little posse of sorority sisters were firmly attached. Adam had been so busy over the summer working for his dad and then spending what time he had left with Sue, that Lily had been put on the back burner. She'd been busy herself, interning at a literary agency in New York most of the summer. While she didn't hold it against him—well, not much—she would like to sit down and eat one meal with him, just the two of them. She missed her best friend.

"Lily." Adam grinned and wrapped her in a bear hug, but only for a second. He knew about her phobia.

"Hey." She grinned right back at him. "Hi, Sue."

"Lils, you gonna be too busy to help me with my economics class this semester?" Mike asked.

She loved Mikey dearly. He was the only other person besides Adam who she trusted. Mike's curly brown hair and big old green eyes were always gentle. Now, put him on the football field, and people ran from the terror those eyes inspired. It always made her laugh.

"Mikey, I've never taken an economics class."

"What? Why haven't you taken the class?" He frowned at her.

"Um, because I'm not a business major?"

"Well, hell, Lily, what am I gonna do?"

"Hell if I know." She laughed at his chagrined

expression. Somehow, over the last three years, she'd become the unofficial football team tutor. She blamed Adam for that. It had started with him asking her to help out a friend or two, and before she realized it, she was tutoring most of them in one subject or another. Now she found it hard to say no. They depended on her. As a result, she was friends with the entire team, their frat houses, and several of their girlfriends and their sorority houses. She'd gained tons of "friends," but really, she could count her friends on one hand. Sad, but true. She had major trust issues.

"He can go sign up for a tutor." His girlfriend, Janet, shook her head at him. Janet was a tiny little thing. She always reminded Lily of Tinker Bell with her gamin features and pixie cut strawberry blonde hair.

"Hey, can I borrow you for a sec?" That was the only thing Lily heard before someone grabbed her hand and she was running to keep up. What the hell?

She ran straight into him when he stopped. They stood about a hundred feet away from the crowd she'd just been in. Yanking her hand free and taking several steps backward, she turned furious blue eyes up at him and nearly stopped breathing. The inky black depths she stared into were alight with amusement.

"That was rude," she told him in an attempt to regain a bit of her composure.

"I thought you needed rescuing, Lily Bells."

"That's not my name," she seethed. The nerve.

"I know who you are."

Lily knew exactly who he was too, and what his reputation was, but damn, why was his voice like silk with his sexy Russian accent? She had no intention of ending up on his list of one-nighters, though.

"And I know who you are, Nikoli Kincaid, so you can just march yourself back to wherever you came from. I'm not interested."

"Aw, now, Lily Bells, don't get your panties all in a twist. I never once asked you out."

Lily narrowed her eyes. She could see Adam and Mikey staring at them, a frown on both their faces. "I'm just saving you the trouble."

He smiled, which caused things south of the border to clench, and Lily gasped slightly. "What if all I wanted was a tutoring session?"

"Your GPA is as high as mine."

He reached up and traced the outline of her lips with a finger, and she flinched back. She did not like to be touched.

"That's enough," she told him a little more forcefully than she'd intended. "I'm going back to my friends now. And even if you did just want a tutoring session, the answer is still no."

His words stopped her retreat.

"I don't give up that easy, Lily. I always get what I want."

"Then get used to disappointment."

Nikoli watched her stomp back over to her friends and smiled wickedly. He hadn't had a challenge since the ripe old age of seventeen when he'd set out to seduce one of his uncle's newly divorced friends. She'd held on to her morals for all

6

of a week. Lily was going to be a challenge he'd relish.

Yes, indeed, Lily Holmes and he were going to be on intimate terms, and soon. This was going to be fun.

Chapter Two

Lily was fuming by the time she returned to her friends. The nerve of the cheeky bastard. She was mad at herself too. Nikoli's touch had not inspired the same type of fear everyone else's did. The fear was still there, just lessened a bit by something else she didn't understand. Something that made her stomach clench deliciously. He wasn't going to know that, though, not ever. She had no intention of ever being one his *girls*.

"What was that about?" Adam asked as soon as she returned.

"Nothing," she said dismissively. "So how was your summer, Mikey?"

Mike laughed at her obvious attempt to change the subject. "You need us to go explain a few things to old Nik?"

"No, there's nothing to explain," she said, exasperated. "He needed a tutor, and I told him I didn't have time to take on anyone else."

"Tutor, my ass," Adam grumbled. "Lily, you…"

"I know exactly who he is, Adam," she

interrupted. "I already told him no."

Adam frowned at her, before turning his eyes back to where Nik still stood under the tree where she'd left him. Sue, who up until now had not said anything one way or the other to Lily, reached out and tugged Adam to her, reminding him she was there. He looked down and gave her his one hundred watt smile. Lily died a little inside at the sight, but she kept her bland expression firmly in place. Wouldn't do to give Sue any more ammunition against her.

"So, did you guys watch the news last night?" Janet piped up. "There was another woman reported missing."

Lily *had* been watching the news, and it disturbed her. Three women had gone missing in the Boston area over the last three months. The bodies were recovered exactly a week after their disappearance. All three had been brutally raped, tortured, and severely beaten before being strangled. The police were finally admitting they had a serial killer on their hands. This latest disappearance had occurred six days ago. If the serial killer stuck to his pattern, the poor woman's body would show up tomorrow.

"Janet, you worry too much." Sue rolled her eyes. "We're perfectly safe on campus."

Lily wanted to roll her eyes at the little blonde tart. She honestly thought they were safe just because of a college campus? Psycho killers could stroll through campuses as easily as they could through a mall. There was no major security when it came to monitoring who was and who was not supposed to be on campus. Colleges were just as open to the public as the local McDonald's. Sue grew up in a bubble. She had no idea of the big bad wolves out in the real world, right in your own backyard. Stupid.

"Don't worry, ladies." Mike flexed his muscles. "We'll protect you."

Lily did roll her eyes at that. Mikey, for all of his six feet, two inches, still behaved very much like a little kid showing off. It was one of the things she loved about him, though.

"All right, Michelangelo, I feel soooo much safer now," she said. She and Mike had bonded over Teenage Mutant Ninja Turtles reruns last year when Janet broke up with him. They were both addicted to the new TMNT cartoon series, despite the fact they were both technically adults. Who said adults couldn't watch cartoons?

He smiled and threw a fist in the air. "Who else is gonna save your ass?"

"Campus security?" Lily asked dryly.

He stuck his tongue out at her. So mature. Lily turned her attention back to Adam, who was still nose deep into Sue. They looked so happy. It was one of the reasons she was so supportive. She didn't really like her, but Sue made him happy, and that was all that mattered to Lily.

"Lunch?" she asked Adam pointedly.

A contrite expression appeared. Oh, no…the little Barbie struck again.

"Lils, we had something come up, and I have to go to lunch with Sue and her Mom. Wedding plans."

"No worries." Lily laughed good-naturedly, even though she was cursing six ways to Sunday inside. "You go do what you need to do. We'll get dinner or something later in the week."

"You could always come with?"

Sue glared the promise of death at her from behind him. She was tempted to say yes just to piss her off, but shook her head instead. "No, I'm good. I'm gonna go grab a bite, then head to the bookstore to check on a textbook I'm waiting for."

"You sure?" he asked again, a hopeful expression on his face. Lily knew for a fact he detested Sue's mother. His bed, he could lie in it.

"Yeah, I'm sure. You two go make your wedding plans."

"He's a blind fool, Lils," Mike whispered sympathetically as they watched Adam and Sue walk away.

She sighed, not bothering to deny anything was wrong. Mike knew her too well, almost as well as Adam. Instead, she changed the subject. "What are we gonna do about that economics class of yours?"

"Did you have to remind me of that?" he grouched. "You know I'm doomed, and I won't graduate."

She rolled her eyes at him. Despite being a jock, Mike was exceptionally smart. He just needed a little prodding in the right direction sometimes. "You know I'm not gonna let you fail if I got you through statistics."

They both grimaced over that statement. Statistics and Mike were not things that should ever be said in the same sentence. Lily had almost given up on him before she found something that made sense to him. Thank God she had, or they'd both have failed. She'd spent so much time trying to teach him the basics, she'd fallen behind herself last year. It hadn't even been a class she needed, as she was an English major. She'd only taken it to help him, but she refused to do that again. Her GPA meant to much to her.

"I'll find you a tutor," she promised. And she would. God help her if she'd let him fail after all the time and effort she'd put into him so far.

"How was your summer?" Janet asked, bringing Lily's attention back to her.

"It was great." She smiled. "I spent most of the summer interning at a literary agency in New York."

"You were in New York all summer?" Janet's eyes lit up. She wanted to move to New York after graduation to become a journalist, and Mike wanted to work on Wall Street. The two of them had been together for almost two years now. Lily was expecting Janet to show her a ring soon. Mike was over the moon for her.

"I can't believe you were in New York all summer and didn't think to call up and say, 'Hey, Mikey, I got a pad in NYC!'" He looked seriously injured. "Do you realize the epic parties we could have had?"

Lily laughed at his outraged expression. "Sorry, Mikey."

"Dude, not cool." He glared. "Not cool at all."

She laughed "I'll catch you guys later. I do need to check and see if my book is in before all the new freshmen swarm the bookstore."

Every time Lily was around Adam and Sue, she got so frustrated it was all she could do not to scream. She honestly couldn't figure out what Adam saw in the little tart, aside from her being a blonde, blue-eyed Barbie doll. Adam had always been a sucker for blonde hair. There was no substance to Sue. All she cared about was herself. There wasn't a kind bone in her body. She had even attempted to stop Lily and Adam from being friends, but that was where Adam had drawn the line. He'd told her in no uncertain terms that Lily was family, and if she pushed, she wouldn't like the outcome. Sue had shut up, but she still did little things to try and separate them. Like lunch today. Lily would guarantee the emergency was nothing but a ruse to get Adam away from her.

*Sighing, she shook her head and headed for the bookstore. Maybe at least something would go right today and her book would be in.

Nik watched Lily walk away from the crowd gathered under the tree and debated following her. She was going to prove to be a challenge. He couldn't think of a single time he'd ever had to work for a woman. They usually fell all over him, but not Lily. She had outright told him she had no interest whatsoever in him. Maybe she was just playing hard to get? Something told him that wasn't her game, though. She had zero interest in him, and it rattled him.

Luther joined him under the tree, and the disgusting grin across his face irked Nik almost enough to punch his best friend. Not that it wasn't warranted; it just rankled he could wear the grin at all. This was a new experience for him, and he didn't like it one bit.

"She shut you down in less than a minute!" Luther crowed.

"Shut the hell up, man," he grouched.

Luther laughed. "Hell, no. This is a first, and I am going to take extreme advantage of all the ribbing I can do."

"Not for long," Nik said darkly.

"Leave it alone, Nik." All the laughter had gone out of Luther's voice. "Lily is not the kind of girl you just fuck."

"Then what kind of girl is she?" Nikoli's mind was already plotting how to get her into his bed.

"She's the kind of girl you marry," Luther told him.

"That's bullshit, man," Nik scoffed. "They're all the same, just have to figure out the right notes to hit with her."

Luther shook his head. "Your funeral."

Nikoli knew Luther was only looking out for him, but Luther's warning wasn't going to deter him.

He always got what he wanted.

Chapter Three

The bookstore was just as crowded as Lily suspected it would be. All the new freshmen were eager to get their things sorted quickly. At least this was her last year here, the last year she'd have to deal with seeing Adam and Sue together. He was her best friend and she loved him, but being around him hurt a lot. He never saw what was in front of him. He preferred the blonde airheads.

With a sigh, she fought her way to the front counter, only to discover the book had not yet arrived. Class started on Monday, and they didn't expect it in until sometime next week. Well, that was just flippin' great. Dejected, Lily made her way back to the cafeteria. At least she might be able to grab a bite to eat before she needed to go check on the girls at the dorm. She was in charge of one of the floors and got a steep discount on her room and board because of it. The do's and don'ts speech she had to give later this evening was not something she looked forward to. Inevitably, each semester someone just had to try sneaking either booze or their boyfriends into their rooms after hours. College kids were college kids, no matter the school.

Lily snagged a salad and a Coke before heading into the main lunch room. She nodded to people as she passed. Several waved her over to their tables, but she wasn't in the mood for chit chat. Depressed over Adam's deciding to bail on lunch, she refused to try to be sociable with anyone else. Instead, she found an empty table and sat. If people came over, she'd just excuse herself, but most people knew to leave her alone when she sat by herself.

Stabbing a piece of tomato, she imagined it was Sue's smiling face. What she wouldn't give to be able to tell that woman what she really thought of her, but Adam loved her, and that was that. Lily had been determined to put her feelings for Adam behind her, but how could she when he was there all the time?

Boston was supposed to be Lily's escape from everyone and everything from her past, but Adam found out she was going here and decided to tag along. She'd specifically chosen Boston because he wanted to go to LSU. He'd been given a full football scholarship there. Who knew he'd go and change his mind? Boston offered him a full scholarship too, but their team was nothing compared to LSU.

At first, she'd taken it as a sign that maybe she meant more to him than she'd first thought. The man *had* followed her to Boston over LSU. She later found out he didn't think she could handle it on her own, and his big brother instincts had kicked in, trying to protect her like he always did. He'd never see her as anything but a little sister. Then he'd met Sue in their sophomore year. Nail—coffin.

New York was her new out. She'd worked her ass off over the summer, and it paid off. The literary agency where she'd interned told her they'd be willing to take her on as an assistant to one of the agents when she graduated. Lily loved books, and the opportunity to work where she could one day represent authors who wrote awesome books was amazing to her. She, herself, was polishing up a manuscript to start sending off to prospective agents. Now that she'd had the opportunity to understand what agents looked for when reading query letters and partials, she had a better grip on how to present her own work to them.

"So is it just me, or men in general?"

Lily's head snapped up to see Nikoli sitting down at her table. Her eyes narrowed. He gave her a grin designed to melt her bones—and it did—but she refused to let him see how much he affected her. Right now, she just needed to get up and get out. She'd come over here to sulk in peace and quiet, not listen to BU's self-proclaimed connoisseur of women attempt to hit on her for the second time today with that sexy Russian accent of his.

"I think it's just you," she told him with a sigh. There went her lunch. Maybe she'd be able to grab a bite after her floor meeting with the girls.

"Aw, now, Lily Bells, that's not very nice." Nikoli's smile widened when he saw the flush creep up her face. "Everybody says you're the nicest girl around."

"Did we, or did we not, already have this conversation?" she asked. "I have no plans to sleep with you, so go find some other poor, unsuspecting girl to play with."

Nikoli laughed outright at that. "Sweetheart, I don't do poor, unsuspecting females. They know what they're in for right up front. Sex. That's *all* I want, and if they delude themselves into thinking anything else, it's not my problem. I want to make sure you understand that right up front too. It's just sex. Mind blowing sex, but still, just a one-time deal."

Nikoli watched her roll her eyes at him. It irritated him, but it fascinated him as well. She seemed to be insulted that he'd decided to have sex with her, which didn't sit well with him at all. There wasn't another girl in this cafeteria who would turn him down, and he knew it, so why was he bothering with Lily Holmes? Because she didn't want him, dammit. That rankled.

"Why don't you want to sleep with me?" he asked curiously, not sure if he wanted to know the answer or not.

She wrinkled her nose and screwed up her eyes. "God only knows what diseases you have."

"I use condoms, or we don't do shit," he told her, offended. "I get regular health checks too."

"The very fact that you need to get checked for STDs regularly is a complete and total turn off." Her voice dripped with disgust.

"No, it just means I'm smart," he countered. "I won't apologize for liking sex. It's nothing to be ashamed of." Oddly, though, looking into her blue eyes full of scorn and disdain, he *was* just a little bit ashamed of how many partners he'd had over the years, and that made him mad. "Is that why you're so uptight, Lily Bells? Do you need to get laid and are just too ashamed to admit to your own needs?"

He watched her face go pale and frowned. *Was* she ashamed of sex? When she shot out of her seat and prepared to storm off, he grabbed her wrist, and she yanked it back with a look of terror on her face for a fraction of a second. He could almost think he'd imagined it if he hadn't been looking directly at her.

"Don't touch me," she hissed. "Don't you ever fucking touch me!" Her voice was barely above a whisper, but all eyes in the cafeteria settled on her. She had no idea how beautiful she looked with her ivory skin all flushed and her blue eyes flashing. It made him want to do some very naughty things to her, but he ignored his own lust for a minute. Something was wrong here. Very, very wrong.

"Calm down, Lily Bells," he said softly. "I didn't mean any harm. I just didn't want you to run."

"I wasn't running," she said hotly. "I just didn't want to suffer your unbearable ego one more minute."

He stared at her, his eyes sweeping from those luscious lips to her perky breasts, to her trim waist, and down to her petite feet. Color flooded her face, and it made the blood rush downward to settle right where he didn't need it to right then. "Mmm...I was hoping you'd run so I could chase you."

"Problem here, Lily?"

Nikoli wanted to shout in frustration. No less than six members of the football team, two of whom were from his own frat house, stood behind Lily. How the hell was he going to wear her down if he couldn't get five minutes alone with her?

"No, Jimmy." She smiled up at the guy who'd spoken. "Nikoli and I were just discussing his STD status."

His mouth fell open. She did not...the little...oh hell *no*. He stood up himself, ready to...damn, he didn't know what he wanted to do.

He heard laughs all around, some not as concealed as others. Fury radiated from him in the next second. The laughs stopped as fast as they'd started when he rolled his shoulders, muscles rippling. Football player he wasn't, but he fought with the best of them and had beaten all the guys standing across from him bloody at one time or another over the last three years. They knew better than to cross him. He gave them his best hard-ass stare, and several took a step back.

"You know what?" Lily shook her head and started walking away. "I don't have time for the testosterone showdown. I have more important things to do."

"Let me buy you dinner, at least." Nikoli leapt after her, ignoring the snickers behind him. He wasn't letting her get away that easily. He made sure not to touch her this time around, though. "You didn't get to eat your lunch."

"Will you go away and leave me alone if I let you buy me dinner?"

He gave her his patented cocky grin. "Trust me,

Lily Bells, you won't *want* me to leave you alone."

She gave him a long-suffering look like someone would give a child and resumed walking back toward the dorms. "I am not sleeping with you now, or tomorrow, or a year from now. What do I need to do to get it through that thick skull of yours?"

"*Milaya*, there are so many things I can think of you doing to me."

"What does that mean?" she asked, frowning.

"It's Russian."

"But your last name is Scottish."

"My mother is Russian, but my father's family originated in Scotland before they moved to the United States. When he joined the army, he was stationed in Russia, where he met my mother."

"Did you grow up in Russia?"

He had her talking, and he let out a little sigh of relief. He didn't normally ever talk about anything personal with a woman, but this one was different. She wasn't falling for his usual BS. There were also her football players following them at a discreet distance. Luther was right about one thing. Lily was not one to be used and abused lightly with so many would-be protectors waiting in the wings. Even knowing he could get the shit beat out of him, he didn't care. He wanted her.

"Until I was fourteen. Then Dad sent me and my brothers to live with my Uncle Brian in Virginia the summer before I started high school. He wanted us educated in the States where he grew up. My parents still live in St. Petersburg, though."

She smiled. "I've seen photos of the city. It looks beautiful."

"It is," Nikoli agreed. "I miss it sometimes. There are so many places I used to roam when I was a kid. My brothers and I used to play in old ruins and pretend we were great knights fighting for Mother Russia." He let out a laugh. It had been years since he'd thought of that.

"How many brothers do you have?"

"Five." They always brought a smile to his face. All of his brothers, except Victor, were older, and he'd been their punching bag until he was old enough and strong enough to beat them black and blue.

"No sisters?"

He laughed. "Thank fuck, no."

She gave him a curious look at that. "My brothers and I are all very much alike, and if we'd had to defend a sister against guys like us…" He shook his head. "We'd never have had any fun."

"So they're all jackasses too?" She looked up at him, her tone innocent, but her eyes danced with mischief.

Nikoli grinned, thinking about his brothers' reactions to that statement. They'd like his Lily Bells, indeed they would. Hold up…*his* Lily Bells? What the hell was he thinking? He had to bag this chick quick before they got around to more talking.

He saw the dorms up ahead and frowned, glancing at his watch. Damn. He'd spent fifteen whole minutes talking to a woman. His longest conversation began and ended with 'your place or mine?' Definitely had to get her in the sack fast and be done with it.

"So, dinner?" he asked as they came to a stop

22

outside of one of the East Campus Brownstones, one of the smaller dormitories on campus. He liked it and the area where it was located. There was a lot of old world charm to the dorm, not like all the modern ones built in the last couple decades. The architecture screamed colonial, and the feel of it reminded him of some of the buildings in Russia. It was also located close to Kenmore Square. He rubbed his hands together at the thought of how quickly they could have access to a bed or couch— or anywhere, really. He wasn't that picky when it came to sex. The floor did the job as well as a bed.

"I thought you might have forgotten that." She let out a long-suffering sigh. "You do realize if I go to dinner, we are not having sex afterward? I'd just be going so you'd leave me alone the rest of the year?"

"I might change your mind." He watched her shiver at the smoldering look in his eyes.

"No," she said, "you won't. I have more self-respect than some of the women I've seen you with. Besides, I've had to clean up after you before, and it's not a situation I'd ever put myself in."

"Clean up after me?"

She laughed harshly. "Remember that spiel you gave me about women knowing it was just sex, and if they had other thoughts, it was on them?"

Nikoli nodded slowly, a sinking sensation creeping into the pit of his stomach.

"I've had to sit and listen to some of those girls, let them have a good cry, and then tell them you're nothing but a jerk and not worth their time. Why would I ever do that to myself?"

"You wouldn't," Nikoli replied quickly. "You know the deal up front. Just sex."

She sighed like he'd missed some big point. In her mind, he probably had, but Nikoli was clueless as to what. He didn't speak girl.

"Why the hell not?" she muttered. "Not like I have other plans anyway. If you'll go away, then yes, I'll go to dinner with you, *but* you have to promise you'll stay away from me for the rest of the year."

She just waved a red flag in front of his face, and she didn't even know it.

"You've got a deal, sweetheart."

Chapter Four

She smiled coyly at him, and he threw her dress at her. The brazen blonde from earlier today frowned at him. Nikoli was not in the mood to deal with her. He'd worked his frustration out with her, yeah, and the sex had been good, but not great. She just needed to get dressed, and then get the hell out.

He threw the used condom in the trash and started the shower. He could hear Luther in the other room explaining to her she needed to leave. She was a clinger. How had he missed that? Luther would take care of it, though. He always did. Nikoli sometimes felt bad about putting him in that position, but not enough to keep from doing it again. Luther knew him, accepted him for the asshole he was, and never judged him. They were like brothers. He loved him as much as he did his own brothers. Luther knew that too. It was why he put up with so much shit from Nikoli.

"Nik, get your pearly ass out here!" Luther called through the door. "I got a line on a '69 Mach 1, fully modded."

Those last two words almost caused Nikoli to slip as he got out of the shower. Luther and his dad had introduced Nikoli to cars, and his very own love affair had been born. Luther and he both did rally and off-road racing. Luther's dad frowned on it, but didn't say much else. That old man had bailed them out of more than one scrape because of racing. If Nikoli's father had known some of the shit the two of them got into on the racing scene, he'd personally drag Nik's ass back to Russia and put him under lock and key. Those boys in the Miami scene were heavy hitters and pulled no punches. You either survived or you didn't, and Nikoli loved it.

They'd been looking for an old American muscle car that already had the modifications they needed for the upcoming race in Miami, or one that could be modded. The race they wanted to enter had a few hitches, and not having to worry about getting the car's electronics knocked out was the key. They'd entered the race last year, only to die three hundred yards from the finish line from a tech bomb attached to the car. Nikoli had bashed a few heads, but couldn't do much else.

"We could still overhaul your Fiat," Luther offered as Nikoli exited the bathroom. "It's smaller and lighter."

Nikoli shook his head. "No, we don't want any repeats of last year. What's the payout this year, you heard?"

"Four hundred grand, last count. Entry fee went up to twenty thousand."

Nikoli nodded. "That'll bankroll the new

programmers." He and Luther had started their own business at the age of seventeen. They'd both been huge gamers and took that love to a new level. They'd designed and programmed a shooter game that eventually blew up once it was released. They hadn't wanted to sell the game, so they'd tried to figure out how to manufacture, promote, and distribute it themselves. Getting a bank loan just wasn't possible for the two of them at seventeen. So they found an alternate route—fast cars and underground races.

Luther found the first race thanks to a buddy he played Call of Duty with online. The entry fee had been harsh, three thousand dollars. They bankrupted their savings and begged and borrowed from everyone they knew. Luther's dad donated a thousand, as had Nikoli's uncle. They'd driven down to Miami and won that first race, and came away thirty thousand dollars richer.

All they'd told Luther's dad and Nikoli's uncle was the money came from an investor who believed in the game. After that, Nikoli's uncle had gotten them in touch with the right people, and their game had gone into production. They'd hired a business manager and a marketing manager who'd made deals with all the major players in the world of video games. A year later, that thirty thousand dollars turned into three million. After that, it'd just been an upward climb. The two of them owed no money to anyone and were able to bankroll any new projects by winning races. Eventually, they'd give it up, but not for a while yet. Luther loved working on the cars, and Nikoli loved racing them. Perfect relationship.

"Show me the car." Nikoli grabbed a beer out of the fridge and sat down on the bar stool next to where Luther was engrossed in the computer.

"Dude's selling it on eBay," Luther said with a laugh. "Stupid."

Nikoli let out a low whistle when the car's specs came up. Stupid wasn't the word—fucked up insane better described the ass selling it. The original 351 motor had been replaced with a 428 bored out big block. Custom three-inch dual exhausts with Flowmaster mufflers, Offenhauser Port O Sonic intake manifold, Barry Grant 1000 CFM Silver Claw carburetor, and the list just went on and on. This car was still street legal, but it had the heart and soul of a racer under the hood. They would have to do very little to it.

"Email the seller. Offer him twice what he wants for it, and we'll pick it up tomorrow, cash in hand," Nikoli said, his eyes gleaming as he finished reading all the specs. "He's a first class dumbass. There's no way he built this car just to sell it for not even a tenth of what it's worth."

Luther snorted before checking his phone. His brow furrowed, and then he looked at Nikoli, perplexed. "What the hell? Is it true?"

"Is what true?" Nikoli asked, not really paying attention. He was still too focused on the car. The deep burgundy color set off the chrome nearly as well as black could.

"Did you ask Lily Holmes on a date?"

Nikoli's head snapped around. How the hell did Luther know? "Who told you that?"

"Mac just texted asking if it's true."

"It's not a date."

"So you didn't ask her to dinner?" Luther frowned at him, then looked back down to his phone.

"Well, yeah, I did, but…"

"Then it *is* a date," Luther crowed, and then burst out laughing. "Oh, God, I never thought I'd see the day when Nikoli Kincaid had to resort to asking a girl out on a real live date."

"Do you want a beating?" Nikoli growled. How in holy hell did the fact he asked Lily to dinner get out? "Tell Mac to shut his mouth or I'll shut it for him."

Luther wheezed he was laughing so hard, and all it managed to do was piss Nikoli off even more. He swung, and his fist collided with Luther's face. He went down, cussing a blue streak. "What the hell, man?"

"This is not funny," he bit out. "I can't handle her like I do everyone else. She isn't falling for it. If I have to take her to dinner to get her naked, then that's what I'll do."

"Whatever you say." Luther laughed. "I told you to leave her alone. If you don't listen, then I am going to enjoy every minute of your domestication."

"That just ain't right, man." Nikoli glared down at his friend before extending a hand. "Nikoli Kincaid doesn't do domestication. Never have, never will."

"Whatever you say." Luther chuckled and sat back down at the computer. "Whatever you say."

Nikoli gave Luther one last glare and stomped

out of the room. No way in hell would he ever be *domesticated*.

***

"You did what?"

Lily winced and held the phone away from her ear. How did Adam find out she'd agreed to go out with Nikoli? Less than two hours had gone by, and he was shouting from her phone.

"It's not a big deal," she murmured while she unpacked the groceries she'd bought at the market. Cereal, milk, pop, and some snacks had her set. Her little mini fridge was overflowing with cans of Coke and bottles of water.

"Not that big a deal?" She could hear the frustration in his voice. "Lily, this is Nikoli Kincaid we're talking about. Do you even *know* who he *is*?"

"Yes, Adam, I know very well who he is, as I already told you," she said. "I'm not stupid."

"Right now I'm not so sure about that," he snapped.

She pulled the phone away and glared at it, imagining Adam's head. *How dare he?* "Did you call just to insult me?" she demanded. "Because if you did…"

"Lils, I'm just worried about you." Adam sighed. "I know Kincaid. He's a douche with only one thing on his mind."

"I'm perfectly aware of that." He had no right to call her and start trying to dictate what she could and couldn't do. He was her best friend, but she was not his sister or his girlfriend. It was about time he figured that out. It's not like he had time for her anymore either. She'd agreed to go out with Nikoli more because she was mad at Adam than anything else. He'd blown her off one too many times for Sue, and today's latest ditching session had grated more than she'd realized.

"Then why the hell did you agree to go out with him?" Adam exploded.

"Because I wanted to." She could hear the irritation in her own voice, but she didn't care.

"Lily, there are things you don't know," Adam stressed, "rumors about the kind of stuff he's into…"

"Adam, I am not having this conversation with you," she interrupted him.

"Well, you obviously need to have it with someone!" He paused to speak to someone in the background, and Lily heard him mumble Sue's name. She groaned inwardly. He was talking about this with her there? Lily's face flamed up, and she felt mortified.

"Look, I gotta go," she said. "People are lining up outside, and I have to give them the speech."

"Lily, this conversation isn't over," he warned. "You are way out of his league…"

"I'm not good enough for him?" she shouted into the phone. "And why exactly is that, Adam? Am I not as pretty as some of his girls? Am I too boring? Too lame? What? Explain it to me." Her voice had gone softer with each word.

Complete silence greeted her. He knew exactly how pissed she was in that moment.

"I'm waiting, Adam."

31

She heard him take a deep breath. "That's not what I meant, Lily."

"No?" she asked softly. "I hate to break this to you, Adam, but just because you don't see me, doesn't mean other people don't. Now if you'll excuse me, I don't have time to listen to you piss and moan about something that is *none of your damn business!*"

She ended the call and threw the phone on her bed. Honest to God, he confused her sometimes. Like just then, he got all jealous and territorial, but other times, it was like she wasn't even there. It could be the big brother complex he had, but that tiny spark of hope inside of her jumped up and down. Maybe he was jealous. In the end, it didn't matter, though. He'd never seen what had always been in front of him, and he never would.

She had to get over it. Adam and Sue were getting married, and she needed to accept it. Once she graduated, she could move to New York and forget all about her problems. If Adam wasn't in her face twenty-four-seven, she might be able to mend her broken heart.

A loud knock on her door interrupted her silent frustration. One of her returning girls from last year stood in the doorway, twisting her hands. Something was up.

"Mandy, what's wrong?" she asked, concerned.

"It's Stephanie," she said. "Something's wrong. She's in our room crying, and I can't get her to tell me why."

With a sigh, Lily closed her door and followed Mandy down the hall to the room she shared with

Stephanie. They were sophomores this year, and Lily tended to look out for them. Both were young and had made a lot of bad judgment calls last year. She'd even had to bust them once for drinking in their rooms. God only knew what Steph had done now.

The girl in question was curled up on her bed, her old stuffed bear held tightly against her chest as she sobbed brokenly. Her blonde hair was matted to her head and her dress wrinkled.

"What's wrong, honey?" she asked, sitting down next to the girl.

"Go away," she cried. "I'm too ashamed to talk about it."

Lily's instincts went on alert. "Did someone do something to you, Stephanie?"

She hiccupped and nodded her head. "I was so stupid, Lily. I knew better, and I did it anyway, thinking it'd be different with me. That he couldn't be as bad as everyone said he was."

Lily's gut clenched. She had a feeling she knew exactly what happened. "Tell me," she said slowly.

"I was going to eat lunch and he caught me before I went in." She sniffled. "I couldn't help it, I wanted to say no, really I did, but ohmygod, he's so hot."

"Nikoli Kincaid?" Lily asked, resigned.

Stephanie nodded. "Yeah. After, he just threw my dress at me and left. His friend told me to leave and not bother leaving my phone number. I'm so stupid, Lily. Why did I think I could make him look at me any differently? I know his reputation."

Lily sighed. She'd heard all this before. "Every

33

girl thinks that, Steph. They all think they'll be the one to finally catch and hold his attention for more than a couple hours."

"It wasn't even that long," she said forlornly. "It was only an hour, and he didn't even bother to say good-bye. He had his friend throw me out."

"Just check it off your bucket list," Lily told her. "You had sex with BU's very own manwhore. Everyone else has, so why not you?"

That caused Stephanie to giggle. "He *is* hot, and the sex was *really* great."

"See, it's not the end of the world, is it? Now you know what all the hype was about, and you can go on and find a nice guy this semester to fall for, yeah?"

Stephanie smiled before lunging up to hug Lily, who went completely still, fighting the scream that rose in her throat. "You're the best, Lily. I'm glad you're our dorm mom!"

"Just promise me you two won't have any more beer parties this year, please." She gave Stephanie a strained smile and disentangled herself as fast as she could. She winced at the conspiratorial look Stephanie and Mandy gave each other. Dear God, they were going to give her white hairs before she was even twenty-two.

"We promise to try to behave as long as it doesn't get in the way of our fun." Mandy gave Lily a grin and pulled Stephanie to her feet. "Come on, Steph, you need to wash your face before we join everyone."

Lily sighed and followed them out. They were good girls, just a little too mischievous for their own

34

good. And they did ridiculously stupid things in the name of fun, like having sex with the slutty manwhore.

She and Nikoli had a lot of things to talk about, and if he had any thoughts of seducing her, they'd die as soon as she told him in no uncertain terms she'd never be a throwaway he forgot in less than five minutes. She refused to be the one on the bed crying because she let her guard down.

No way in hell was she sleeping with him. He just didn't know it yet.

Chapter Five

Lily glanced at herself in the mirror and grinned. Worn, baggy jeans and one of Adam's jerseys over her black tank top was probably not what Nikoli had in mind when he asked her to dinner. Comfortable sandals completed her outfit, her toes shining from the pink nail polish she'd put on yesterday. Nikoli probably expected a dress and heels. She pulled her hair back in pigtails and then slipped on her 1950's style black rimmed glasses. She screamed nerdy geek going to a high school football pep rally. So not Nikoli's style.

"Well, you certainly aren't going to inspire any lustful thoughts." Janet laughed from the open doorway of Lily's room.

"My point," Lily said with a grin. "Plus, I'm going prepared to wage war."

Janet arched a brow in question.

"You remember Stephanie and Amanda from last year? The ones who had the beer party that nearly got us all kicked out?"

Janet laughed. "Oh, yeah, I don't think I'd ever

seen you that mad."

"Well, seems our boy accosted Stephanie and left her in tears." Lily shook her head. "Why will they never learn? Women are just his toy of the hour."

"He's too pretty for his own good," Janet agreed. "I love Mike dearly, but if Nikoli gave me one of those sex filled stares of his..." She shrugged. "I don't know what I'd do, honestly. I know how bad that sounds, but he is just one of those men..."

Lily sighed. Nikoli was a man who could potentially destroy a woman without a second thought and she'd go into it with her eyes wide open. He never gave them any expectations. They did bring it all on themselves.

"Speaking of Mike, he said Adam put his foot in his mouth."

Lily rolled her eyes. "Yeah, he went into over-protective big brother mode and tried to forbid me from going out with the manwhore."

"Oh, God, I never thought about him like that," Janet giggled. "Now every time I hear his name, I'm going to think manwhore."

Lily laughed herself. "Just imagine it...Nikoli dressed in black strappy heels, a mini-skirt, and a slutty top, hooking on the corner."

"Stop," Janet gasped between laughs. "That image is going to stay with me now, damn you! How am I supposed to indulge in sex fantasies about him if I keep seeing him posed on a street corner in trashy prostitute gear?"

Lily performed a mock bow. "My job is done, and the only man you'll be having sex fantasies about is Mikey."

Janet took several deep breaths and then walked over to Lily's bed and collapsed. "I needed that laugh. Mike has been grumpy all week."

"Everything okay?" Lily asked and started cleaning up the nail polish she'd left scattered on her desk.

"I think so." Janet frowned. "He's being very secretive. I'd almost think he was cheating if I didn't know him better."

"Cheat?" Lily turned and looked at Janet. "Mike wouldn't do that to you, Jan. He respects you too much. He'd break up with you before he went out with someone else."

"I guess." She sighed.

"I *know*," Lily said firmly. "Trust me. He loves you. When you broke up with him last year, I got the full-on Mike meltdown. If you'd seen what that did to him, you'd never doubt him again."

"I'm surprised he didn't go cry on Adam's shoulder," Janet said ruefully.

"Oh, he went there first," Lily confessed, "but Adam and Sue had just gotten engaged the week before, if you'll remember. Not the best place for poor, jilted Mikey to get some sympathy. Besides, he and I bonded over Teenage Mutant Ninja Turtles."

"So is that what you guys did that whole week?" Janet asked, curious.

"I supplied him with beer, chips, and cartoons." Lily smiled. "Then he got drunk, laughed at Michelangelo and Donatello, and told me all about why you broke up with him, how much of a jerk he was, and his cockamamie scheme to win you back."

"Which consisted of him storming the sorority house drunk, busting out his Ninja Turtle moves, and confessing his undying love for me." Janet giggled. "He promised to try not to be such a jerk, emphasis on the word *try*."

"Mikey's a good guy," Lily said.

"He is," Janet agreed and flopped over on her side. "Why are you going out with Nikoli, anyway? Adam is really freaking out."

Whiplash on the subject change, Lily thought to herself. "He said if I went to dinner with him, he'd leave me alone for the rest of the year. Apparently he thinks a little alone time with me will be all he needs to charm his way into my panties. And Adam can go piss off. This is none of his business."

"He's only worried about you, Lils," Janet said softly. "He's over at the frat house beating himself up right now because he thinks he hurt you with some idiot thing he said."

Lily sighed. "Did he send you over here to try and get me to cancel my date?"

"Maybe," Janet hedged.

"No offense, Jan, but…butt out," Lily told her friend. "Adam has no right sending you over here to try and do what he couldn't."

"What was the idiotic thing he said, anyway?" Janet asked.

"Didn't tell you that, did he?" Lily bit out. "He insinuated that I'm not good enough for Nikoli, that I'm too far out of his league to ever even catch his eye."

"Well, dressed like that…" Janet grinned.

"Shut it," Lily snapped. "I don't need you reminding me I'm not worth his time too."

"That's not what I meant." Janet sat up. "Lily, if anything, *you're* too good for the manwhore. He doesn't deserve anyone like you. I'm sure Adam didn't mean…"

"Can we not talk about Adam?" Lily asked, tired all of a sudden. "For once, I'd just like to forget Adam exists and have some fun."

Janet gave her the pitying look Lily hated with all her heart. Mikey knew how she felt about Adam, and Janet knew because Mikey knew. Why the hell had she let herself get drunk and confess to Mikey she was in love with Adam?

"Look, I just want to get this over with. He should be here in a minute. I told him I'd meet him out front. You can tell Adam to mind his own damn business."

Lily grabbed her purse and pointed to the door. Janet frowned, but followed Lily out the door. "Want to come wait with me so you can see his face when he gets a load of this?"

Janet grinned and nodded. The two of them laughed as they took the elevator down to the first floor and outside to wait on the front steps for the manwhore of the hour.

They didn't have long to wait, and when he pulled in, Lily gasped in delight. It had nothing to do with Nikoli and everything to do with the car he got out of. It was a black 1970 Plymouth Barracuda. She hadn't seen a car like that since the one her dad owned when she was a kid. He'd loved it. She gave a squeal of delight, much to Janet's chagrin, and ran over to the car. Nikoli gaped at her as she lovingly ran her fingers just above the body of the car as she examined it. You didn't touch them with your fingers. Luther shook his head as he pulled himself out of the passenger seat.

"Are you running a 440 or a 426?" she asked as she squatted and inspected the rims.

"You know cars?" Nikoli asked incredulously.

She ignored him and looked at Luther. "What's it running?"

"Let me pop the hood for you, and then you tell me."

Lily waited impatiently and then dived to put the hood up when it popped. There, in all its glory, sat an original 426 engine running 425 horsepower. The car could run, and run fast. There were only a limited number of the 'Cudas manufactured. Her dad had one of the first ten off the factory line, and after he'd died, her mother sold it to help pay the bills.

"426." Lily grinned like an idiot at Luther. "It's gorgeous."

"How do you know about cars?" Nikoli stepped closer to Lily, his arm brushing hers. She took an instinctive step to the side to keep distance between them.

"My dad taught me," she explained as she examined the engine more closely. "I could put a carburetor back together by the time I was nine, and rebuild an engine before I turned twelve. I used to live under the hood of a car when my dad was racing."

"Your dad was a racer?" Luther frowned and

41

then gasped. Lily figured he probably just put her last name together with her dad's.

"Martin Holmes," she muttered and stepped back out from under the hood. Her dad had been one of the biggest NASCAR drivers on the circuit, but his real love had been rally or strip racing. He'd never let her go to any of those, though. Said it was too dangerous for a kid. She'd grown up on NASCAR tracks instead. "He died in a crash down in Daytona the summer I turned twelve."

Luther let out a low whistle. "Did he teach you to drive?"

"'Course he did," she laughed. "I was driving before I could reach the pedals. I used to sit in his lap and steer the wheel until I grew enough so my feet actually touched the gas pedal."

"Who would have thought sweet, innocent Lily Holmes was a car junkie?" Luther laughed.

"I can still be sweet and innocent *and* be a car guru," she said with a wink and turned to Nikoli. "Can I drive her?"

Nikoli frowned. This was not what he'd expected. She knew cars. She knew them enough to know the engine model under the hood of the limited edition car he drove. It threw him slightly.

"Well, can I?" she demanded impatiently.

"I don't know," he said slowly. "I don't even let Luther drive my baby. She's…"

"A limited edition 'Cuda, only six hundred sixty-six made in 1970," she interrupted him. "I know what kind of car it is, Nikoli. My dad owned one. He had the seventh one off the assembly line. I promise to be careful."

He blinked and shook his head. "Maybe on the way back," he said finally.

She pouted. It was a full-on lip pout, and he didn't even think she was aware she was doing it. Her lips were beautiful when she pouted, and he took a step closer, noticing she took another step back. He was going to have to get to the bottom of this. He had no chance if he couldn't touch her.

"Don't feel bad, Lils," Luther said. "I've known him for years and he barely lets me ride in it."

"Why don't I know that you know about cars?" Janet asked from behind them. "You think Mike or Adam would have mentioned it."

"Mikey doesn't know," Lily said, "and Adam wouldn't say anything. He gets embarrassed when he has to call me to fix his car."

Janet laughed. "I'll bet. Well, I'm off to find Mike. He's supposed to take me go see some new scary movie." She shuddered. "Why I let him talk me into these things is beyond me."

"Hey, can you drop me off at my frat house on the way?" Luther asked. "Nik refused to stop on the way over. We were running late."

"Sure," Janet said. "Lily, call if you need *anything*."

Nikoli snorted at Janet's very obvious innuendo. Frankly, he was sick of it. For the last three hours, his phone had been blowing up with texts from people he knew telling him to leave Lily alone and not to hurt her. You'd think she was Mother Theresa the way people rallied to protect her.

She was still eyeballing his car with lust when he finally focused his attention on her. Her barreling

43

down the steps toward them and straight for his baby had sidetracked him. Now he gave her a good once-over and laughed outright at her obvious attempt to make herself look awful. Unfortunately, Nikoli didn't think the woman could look awful in a burlap sack. The pigtails made her look cute, and the baggy clothes she had on only added to her comfortable appearance. She looked adorable, and it made him all kinds of curious to see what she had on underneath them.

"Alone at last, Lily Bells," he murmured salaciously.

She gave him a startled look and took another five steps back.

"Shall we go?" he asked mildly when she looked ready to bolt at the desire in his eyes.

She was the prey dancing with the predator. The predator fully intended to win this hunt.

Chapter Six

"So, where to?" Nikoli asked as they pulled away from the dorm.

"Doesn't matter," she said, distracted, her fingers caressing the interior of the car.

Nikoli grinned. She was too busy examining the car to be nervous with him. If she only knew what watching her fondle his car was doing to him, she'd put her hands under her rump and sit still for the rest of the ride.

"Joe's okay?" he asked her.

"Sure," she said. "They've got the best Reubens in town, and I'm starved."

"Didn't get to eat?"

"No." She shook her head. "I had too much to do, speaking of which…"

Nikoli glanced over at her and grew slightly alarmed at the pissed off look on her face. "What?" he asked cautiously.

"You made one of my girls cry today."

Nikoli groaned inwardly. He'd only had sex with one girl today, the lusty blonde from check-in. She

45

was in Lily's dorm? Damn.

"Lily, we've already been over this," he warned. "Every girl I have sex with knows up front what to expect. I already told you this."

"Oh, I know." She nodded. "Stephanie knew it too, but she assumed she could make you feel differently."

"Her mistake," he put in quickly. "Not mine."

"Agreed," Lily said. "What I'm talking about is the fact you had someone, I'm presuming Luther, throw her out instead of having the decency to do it yourself. Do you even realize how used that makes a woman feel? Especially a nineteen year old girl?"

Well, hell. Who knew the blonde was going to land him in a morality lecture from Ms. Sweet and Innocent herself? Lily needed to stop trying to think of him as a decent guy. He wasn't, and he knew it. He was a selfish bastard on the best of days.

"What's your point, Lily?" he asked. "She knew what she was in for when she came back to my place. I was done and needed a shower. I figured she had the good sense to get gone. Not my fault Luther had to kick her out."

"You really don't care how your actions affect the women you sleep with, do you?" Lily asked, appalled.

"First, there's no sleeping involved," he grinned wolfishly at her, "and second, no, I don't care. We both get mutual pleasure out of the deal. Why should I care about anything else?"

Lily opened her mouth, but he interrupted her. "Look, we could argue about this forever and we'd never agree, so let's drop it, okay? We're here, and

I actually want to eat. I didn't get lunch either."

He'd brought her to Joe's because he thought it would be the one place he wouldn't run into many people she knew. Joe's was a little hole-in-the-wall that specialized in Cuban cuisine, and most of the BU students specialized in pizza, burgers, and beer. Nikoli had been surprised Lily knew it. She kept surprising him the longer he was around her.

"Nik!" Joe boomed when they walked in the door. He found himself tucked into a huge bear hug. Joe owned the place and treated the regulars like family. Nikoli loved it here. He'd sat here for hours programming a new game before, and Joe supplied him with food and beer for as long as necessary. Most people did coffee shops; Nikoli did Joe's.

"Hey, man." Nikoli grinned when he got loose. "Got a free table?"

"Always for you, my friend." Joe smiled, and then looked past Nikoli to where Lily stood watching, amused. "And who is this?"

"Joe, this is Lily Holmes."

Joe frowned, and then he brightened. "Original Reuben?"

Lily smiled and nodded, causing Nikoli to frown.

"I do a lot of takeout from here," she explained. "Mikey and I found the place last year, and I fell in love with the food. Mikey eats here too."

"It is good to put a face to the name." Joe smiled at Lily. "A beautiful face for a beautiful name."

Lily blushed and Nikoli laughed. Leave it to Joe to try to schmooze his date. "Down, Casanova, she's here with me."

"You've never brought a girl in before." Joe

winked at him. "She must be very special."

Lily laughed, but refrained from saying anything, much to Nikoli's astonishment. He assumed she'd make some wisecrack about their date, but she didn't. Much to his chagrin, he was *glad* she didn't. He sighed and ushered her into the dining room.

"We're starving, Joe," Nikoli said. "Where's the table?"

Joe led them to the back of the small eatery where an empty booth sat. Lily slid in, and Nikoli debated about sitting down beside her. Remembering her earlier reaction, he opted for sitting in the opposite seat. As much as he would have really liked to trap her, he would give her some space for now. The small sigh of relief she let out told him he made the right decision.

"The usual for you both?" Joe asked, and hurried off when they both agreed.

"Pigtails?" Nikoli smirked. "Going for the cute schoolgirl look?"

"Nope," she said. "I was going for comfortable. Your jeans and t-shirt make me glad I didn't go all out for a dress and heels."

"I figured you'd pull something like this," Nikoli admitted. "I came prepared for war."

"War?" She laughed. "It's just a fast dinner so we can go our separate ways and not have to think about each other again."

Nikoli frowned. Fast was not going to cut it. He needed to get her talking again. "So, your dad was Martin Holmes?"

She nodded, her expression sad. She must miss him a lot.

"What was that like, growing up on the racetrack?"

"Awesome. There is nothing like being in the pit on race day. My dad had a special headset made for me so the noise wouldn't hurt my ears. I lived for those days. We'd always get there early and talk to some of the other drivers. Dad liked to go over his car himself before the start of the race, and we'd run through the checklist together. Then I'd get to watch the race from the pit. Seeing them fly by lap after lap, it's the most *amazing* rush."

"You were allowed in the pit?" Nikoli quirked an eyebrow. He and Luther had tried to sneak into the pit at one of the smaller tracks once, and security had escorted them right back to the stands.

"My dad was Martin Holmes. What do you think? I lived in that pit thanks to my dad's crew. They always snuck me in. Being there, feeling the rumble of the ground beneath my feet as the cars sped by, the rush of the trail of wind they left behind them…there is no other feeling in the world like it."

She sounded like him, Nikoli realized. That was exactly how he felt every time he got behind the wheel for a race. The adrenaline rush was almost better than sex. Almost.

"You never thought about driving yourself?" he asked, curious.

"No. I was there the day my dad crashed. I saw them have to cut him out of the car. I haven't been behind the wheel of an actual race car since that day."

"I get that." He nodded. "Do you still like racing,

though?"

"Sure, I grew up on it. I'm still a huge NASCAR fan. My dad loved rally racing too. He used to build cars just for those races. He never took me to any of them, but it was his passion."

"I don't think I've ever met a girl who knew so much about cars." Nikoli shook his head. "It's new for me."

"Well, that might not be true." Lily smirked. "You admit yourself that you don't talk to the girls you sleep with, so how do you know they didn't know cars?"

"Well, I've never had a girl completely ignore me to lust after my car, either." He laughed. "I'm guessing that's a dead giveaway."

Lily blushed. "I think lust is a strong word."

He grinned. "You were caressing the car like a lover, Lily Bells. I know lust when I see it."

"You *are* going to let me drive her, aren't you?" Her eyes lit up with excitement.

"That car is my baby, Lily." He frowned. "You said yourself, you haven't driven a racer…"

"She's a racer?" Lily burst out. "I didn't see any mods."

Nikoli stopped breathing for a second. Before him now sat the sexiest woman he'd ever known, even dressed like a high school teeny bopper. She knew cars, she knew racers, and her eyes lit up like Christmas when she talked about them.

"I removed them last year. She's street legal now, but there are still a few modifications that aren't noticeable at first glance. She'll run faster than the average 'Cuda."

"Maybe not drive, then," Lily hedged. "Could you take me for a ride, show me flat out how fast she runs?"

"Yeah, I can do that." He grinned, his own excitement shining through. He loved to drive fast, and he sensed a kindred spirit across from him. For the first time all night, the thought of being just friends crossed his mind. Then she shifted and her breasts bounced slightly, and the thought flew out the window. Nope, sex, and then maybe just friends. Or friends who have sex a lot? He'd never done the friends with benefits thing before. Hell, he'd never done the female friend thing in his entire life.

Lily was gentle and shy at a deep level, and an enigma. She had the courage to stand up to him, but blushed and looked down at the smallest compliment. Her innate tendencies were calling to all sorts of his own dominant ones, including some serious protective ones. Very few women had ever struck that cord in him, and Lily was the only one he'd ever contemplated keeping. He frowned. When had he started to think about keeping her?

His phone buzzed and he pulled it out. Luther wanted to know how the date was going. He made a face at the phone, well aware his friend couldn't see it, but it made Lily chuckle.

"So you race cars?" Lily surprised him by asking.

He nodded. "Yeah. Luther and I got into when we were seventeen. Been racing since. We do a lot of rally races, as well as a few underground ones."

"Underground? Can't you get into a lot of trouble for that if you get caught?"

51

Nikoli grinned. "That's the point, Lily Bells. It's all about the risk you take."

"You do seem like a risk taker," she said, her smile infectious.

"You have no idea." He winked at her and leaned back, letting his leg touch hers. She immediately scooted over. He frowned at her, and she glanced away and then looked relieved.

"Food's here," Lily murmured as Joe and a server came trudging over.

"Here we go." Joe beamed at them as he set Lily's plate down. Nikoli laughed at Joe's obvious attempt to impress Lily. He never brought food out himself.

"Thank you." Lily smiled shyly up at him. "It looks wonderful."

"Only the best for Nikoli and his lady." Joe grinned. "You let me know if you need anything at all, beautiful lady."

"Go on back to the kitchen." Nikoli laughed. "You'll end up stealing her before I even have a chance."

Joe turned to look at him, and the censure in his eyes made Nikoli very uncomfortable. Joe was well aware of his one night stands, as well as his other peculiarities when it came to sex. The two of them ran in the same circles. It's how he'd met Joe.

"Be careful with her," Joe warned. "Slow, my friend, and you'll keep her. She's worth keeping."

Nikoli nodded his understanding, aware Lily took an entirely different meaning from that statement. "I'll keep it in mind."

"If you don't, I might," Joe warned him.

Nikoli bristled and actually stood up.

"Just warning you, friend to friend." Joe may have said it with a smile, but the warning was clear in his voice. The man was only twenty-six and handsome. If he wanted to charm Lily, he could, Nikoli realized. He didn't like the thought of Joe with Lily, not one little bit.

"Stay the hell away from her, Joe," he growled. A wave of rage he didn't quite understand hit him hard. "She's mine."

"Uh, girl sitting right here," Lily piped up, "and I don't belong to anyone except myself."

"Things change, Lily." Nikoli's voice had gone cold, and Joe finally got the message. He backed off and left them alone. Nikoli refused to let Joe anywhere near her, especially knowing what he did about him. If that meant Nikoli letting Joe believe Lily belonged to him, then that's what he'd do.

"Care to explain that?" Lily asked once Joe had left.

"Joe is worse than I am," he said after a minute. "I just wanted to make sure he left you alone."

"So, protecting me from the wolves, huh?" she asked mildly. "Pot, kettle, black?"

Nikoli laughed, aware of the irony. "I'm the only wolf getting into your bed tonight."

"You wish." She grinned at him. "I'm remaining chaste tonight."

"That remains to be seen," he told her, his eyes full of the promise.

Lily picked up her sandwich and took a bite. A look of utter joy crossed her face. "Ohmygodthisisgood." The words came out all

53

strung together between mouthfuls of food.

"You are hungry. I don't think I've ever seen anyone shovel food like that."

"You don't know our Lily then."

Nikoli watched Lily stiffen up and then turn to see Adam glaring down at her, Sue beside him. How the hell had he found out where they were? Anger and frustration played a tug-of-war inside him. He knew Adam was Lily's best friend, so he had to be careful here, or she'd get mad and leave.

"What are you doing here?" Lily demanded, obviously pissed. Maybe he wouldn't have to do anything. Nikoli forced his face to remain calm as he watched the two of them.

"We came to grab something to eat," Adam said carefully. "We saw you and decided to come check on you."

"*You* wanted to come check on her," Sue said petulantly. "*I* wanted to go get pizza."

Nikoli frowned at Sue. He'd never liked the woman. What Adam saw in her was beyond him. It was obvious she despised Lily from the death glare Sue leveled at her.

"Adam, you hate Cuban food." Lily's voice was velvety soft, and Nikoli realized just how mad she was. "So why are you here? I didn't think you even knew about Joe's."

"Luther mentioned that Nik loved this place, and I knew you loved Cuban food, so…"

"So you decided to stop by and what, exactly? Demand I go home? I'm not your sister or your girlfriend, Adam. You can't tell me what to do. You don't have that right."

"Lily, you're my best friend, I have every right…"

"You know what? I'm not going to ruin my date by arguing with you. I was having fun before you showed up. Why don't you go and find a table and shovel food into your own mouth before you put your foot in it…again!"

Adam looked like he wanted to say more, but his very angry fiancée hauled him away. Nikoli studied Lily as she glared at their departing backs. It wasn't until she looked back at him that the truth of it hit him. He'd seen it in her eyes before she could conceal it.

Well, hell.

"You're in love with him!"

Chapter Seven

Lily gaped at Nikoli. How had he figured that out? "Awesome skills there, Sherlock, but you couldn't be more wrong."

"I saw how you looked at him."

"Does it really matter?" She sighed.

"Of course it matters," Nikoli said. "Does he know?"

"What do you think?" She focused her attention on the people walking along the sidewalk outside. "He's getting married in four months."

Nikoli stared at her, and it made her squirm. She couldn't quite read his expression, and it made her nervous. As long as they'd been talking about cars, she'd been fine. She adored cars as much as some women freaked out over shoes. To her surprise, she'd been having fun before Adam showed up. There weren't many people she could sit down and talk shop with. He'd surprised her.

"Why don't you tell him?" Nikoli asked her after a long moment.

"Because he thinks of me as his little sister," she

admitted bitterly. "He's never seen me that way."

"Oh, I think you might be surprised there." Nikoli gaze swept to Adam and Sue's table. "The way he's glaring at me right now smacks of jealousy."

Lily forced herself to refrain from looking in Adam's direction.

"Again, you're wrong," she told him. "He's only looking out for me. I am, after all, going to dinner with Boston U's very own manwhore."

Beer spewed, and Lily laughed out loud. Nikoli looked at her, aghast.

"What did you just call me?" he demanded, his eyes smoldering.

"A manwhore," she replied sweetly.

"I am not a manwhore!" he denied hotly, which only made Lily laugh harder. He looked so shocked.

"Yes, yes, you are," she wheezed. "You sleep with a different woman every night, sometimes several a day. You define the word *whore*. It's your nickname with most of the girls."

"I am a connoisseur of women," he growled. "Yes, I enjoy sex, but that doesn't make me a whore!"

Lily giggled, thinking about her earlier conversation with Janet about him hooking on the corner. She wondered what he'd say to that, but he looked so upset she decided to hold that little tidbit for later.

"I'm not sure I want to sleep with you anymore," he told her petulantly.

She only laughed harder. Gods, she hadn't laughed like this in ages. Her sides ached from it.

She caught Adam staring at her from the corner of her eye. He looked bewildered and alarmed. It was almost as comical as the outraged look on Nikoli's face.

"This is a situation I've never been in before." Nikoli leaned back. "The girl I want to sleep with is in love with her best friend, who's getting married."

"It's not your average quandary," Lily agreed, trying to stop laughing.

Nikoli stared at her, his look calculating, and it made her nervous, drying up her laughter. "Why are you looking at me like that?"

"I'm thinking, here, Lily Bells," he said softly, his eyes measuring.

Lily's sense of self-preservation went on high alert, DEFCON two, to be exact. Her eyes narrowed. "There's nothing to think about here, Nikoli. Adam's getting married, I'm moving to New York when we graduate, and you're not sleeping with me tonight."

"No, I'm not sleeping with you tonight," he agreed, shocking her. "I have other plans for you, Lily. Things we can't really discuss here, though."

"We can discuss anything you want right here out in the open." No way was she going anywhere private with him. That might not bode so well for her.

"Let me ask you a question." Nikoli leaned forward, shifting his legs so they were touching hers. He'd essentially trapped her, because she couldn't scoot anywhere else. So she pulled her legs up underneath her. Nikoli raised his eyebrows. "Question answered."

58

"What was the question?" She pushed her food around on her plate nervously. She had an idea of where he was going with this.

"You don't like to be touched." It came out more of a statement than a question. He'd answered it himself so she saw no point in denying it.

"No, I don't, but that's really none of your concern."

"Oh, but it is, Lily Bells, especially if I'm going to help you."

"Help me?" What was he talking about now? "If you think your sexual prowess is going to instantly cure me, you're dead wrong."

He smiled, but it was a smile full of danger. Lily shrank a little against the booth she sat in. That smile made all sorts of things inside of her clench in a not unpleasant way. She didn't understand how a smile could do that to her, but she was beginning to see how so many different girls had succumbed to it.

"Do you want Adam?"

"That's a moot point. He loves Sue *and* he's getting married. Once we graduate, I can escape like I tried to before. He'll go off with Sue, and I'll go to New York and move on."

"Escape?"

"I decided to come to Boston because Adam was going to LSU," she admitted. "He changed his mind and came here instead."

"So he followed you to Boston?" Nikoli's gaze became more calculated by the second.

"Yeah, but not for the reasons you're thinking," Lily put in quickly. "He only wanted to make sure I was okay, that I could handle it."

"Why wouldn't you be able to handle it?"

That was not something she wanted to get into with him. "Doesn't matter."

"Does it have something to do with why you don't like to be touched?" he asked softly.

Her nostrils flared defiantly. Why was he getting so personal?

"You realize if you want to stand any chance of winning him away from the blonde model, you're going to have to let him touch you."

"Adam is aware of my sensitivity to people touching me," Lily hissed. "Why are we even talking about this?"

"Look over at Boy Wonder, see how he's holding her hand? Would you let him do that? *Could* you let him touch you like that?"

Lily peeked over at Adam's table. Sure enough, he was holding Sue's hand, his thumb idly brushing the back of her palm. Lily wanted to be able to let him do that, but the thought alone sent her into panic mode.

"You don't stand a shot at winning him if you can't let him touch you, Lily Bells," Nikoli whispered so only she could hear. "You need to be able to tolerate it if you want Adam. He needs someone he can touch, caress, kiss, and make love to. Right now, that's not you."

"Do you think I don't know that?" Lily seethed. "I have wondered so many times how different things might have been if I could let him touch me."

"Then let me help you."

"How exactly can you help me?" Lily asked

suspiciously.

"For starters, you said he only looks at you like a sister, but the looks I've been getting since he got here say something else entirely. He's jealous, and it's working the blonde up into a full on rage. You need someone to show real interest in you, to spend time with, someone he can't stand."

"Let me guess, that someone would be you?" Sarcasm dripped from each word.

He gave her a devilish smile. "Of course. Who better to get his attention than Boston U's very own *manwhore*?"

Lily smiled when he threw her words back at her. He sounded much less cranky now. What was he up to?

"Everyone knows you don't date, Nikoli," Lily pointed out.

Nikoli's grin turned wolfish. He knew he had her attention. She wanted Adam, he wanted her, and he'd found a way to get them both what they wanted. Hopefully. It all hinged on her acceptance of his help. He had to be careful here.

"As you pointed out, everyone thinks of me as a manwhore." He couldn't help but cringe at that. He was *not* a whore. Usually. "So, you're going to help me buff up my image."

"And how exactly am I going to do that?"

"By dating me, and making me remain celibate."

Her mouth dropped open. Just the right response. He was slowly reeling her in. Now the tricky part.

"No one is going to believe that," she said after a minute. "Can you even go a day without sex?"

"Of course I can," he snapped. "That's not the

point, anyway. I'm not going to need to go have sex with random women. I'm going to have you."

"Uh, no, you're not," Lily told him hotly. "There is no way I am going to sleep with you just to get Adam's attention."

"Oh, baby, there is so much more to it than that," he said, his voice low and deep. He knew exactly how his voice affected women, and Lily was no different. Her eyes glazed a bit and her cheeks warmed. Despite what she said, he affected her. He hadn't lost his mojo just yet. "You can't just spend time with me. You have to let me touch you."

Her eyes went wide and her nostrils flared. He saw sheer panic in her eyes. "Lily, if you want Adam, you have to be able to let him touch you. I can help you with that. You just need some structure, rules. I promise I won't do anything to scare you, and if I do, I'll stop right away. All you have to do is safe word."

"Safe word?" She frowned and then she glared, getting ready to go all outraged female on him.

Damn those books. Was there a person left on the planet who hadn't read them? "Don't go and get all outraged, Lily Bells, it's not what you think. I don't do pain. I have no urge to inflict pain on you. I'm all about pleasure. The panic in your eyes right now make me believe you'd be more comfortable with a safe word, is all. I don't do BDSM in the sense that you know it."

"What exactly are you proposing then, Nikoli?" she asked softly.

Tricky, tricky. How to do this?

"I'm not going to lie to you, Lily. I want you,

very badly. But I don't stand a chance if I can't touch you. I want you in my bed, and I'm willing to be patient and teach you to trust me, to let me touch you, for a price."

"And what exactly do I get out of this deal of yours?"

"You get Adam," he told her bluntly. "You get to drive him crazy and make him see you for the beautiful, intelligent, and desirable woman you are."

"What's your price?" She sounded belligerent, outraged, and suspicious all at once.

"You, of course, Lily Bells. The chance to seduce you into my bed, to be more exact. I'm not a gentleman, Lily. I *will* get you naked, and then I'll use every trick I have to get you to say yes. That's my price."

She was staring at him like he'd lost his mind. Nikoli needed her to think about this seriously. He could help her, and he'd get to touch that beautiful body whenever he wanted to. Once she felt safe enough with him, he'd be able to seduce her. First he needed to understand where her fear came from, but that was going to be a conversation for another day. He'd shocked her enough for one day.

"Don't give me an answer right now. Go home, think about it, and then if you *are* willing to do what it takes to steal Adam from the blonde, call me. It won't be easy, and you're going to have to be honest with me, but I will help you." He signaled the waitress for their check. "Can I see your phone?"

"Why?"

"So I can put my number in it. You need to know it so you can call," he explained patiently. She was wary, and he expected that. He just needed to be patient and wait her out. Patience, however, was not a virtue he possessed. He was a child of the times. He grew up with the 'I want it now, now, now' generation. It was going to be a test of his own willpower to do this, but he had a feeling she'd be worth it.

She begrudgingly handed her phone to him. He let out a breath he didn't realize he'd been holding. That was new. He'd never been nervous about a girl before, but he'd been afraid she'd just say no and walk away.

First he dialed his own number so he'd have hers and then he stored his number in her phone. "Come on, Lily Bells, let's get you home."

Tonight certainly hadn't gone like he'd planned. He'd taken Lily out with the simple task of seducing her, and instead found a woman who held his attention for more than five minutes, one he actually wanted to get to know. He wanted to help her, to see her succeed. As much as he wanted all that, he was slightly terrified. He didn't do the whole girlfriend scene, and that's exactly the position he'd put himself in.

How the hell had he gotten so far off track?

Chapter Eight

After dropping a shell-shocked Lily off at her dorm, Nikoli drove back to his apartment. The lights were on, so he assumed Luther had already come home. He sighed, gearing up for the ribbing he was in for. He'd gone to dinner expecting to have Lily for dessert, and now he had to face Luther's laughter. Not that he was in the mood to listen to Luther crow. He couldn't really put his finger on how he felt at the moment. Lily had thrown him from the minute he met her, and she continued to keep him off balance with every moment spent with her.

He regretted his offer to help her now, in hindsight. He didn't know if he had the patience to do what needed to be done. The problem was he *wanted* to help her. Those blue eyes of hers haunted him when he remembered the terror and the panic in them. Something bad had happened to her, and it scarred her to the point she couldn't bear to be touched by anyone. Someone as beautiful and innocent as Lily shouldn't be afraid. People loved her, which told him she was special and had a huge heart. His mother would adore her. Which only served to terrify him more.

Manwhore. He shook his head. He'd had no idea that's what people thought of him. Sure, he'd slept with a lot of women, but not nearly as many as everyone thought. He'd heard girls bragging about sleeping with him who he'd never touched and had no plans of ever getting naked with. He'd just never bothered to correct the tall tales and rumors. It only enhanced his reputation. Or so he'd thought. Instead, it made him appear like the male slut of Boston University.

There were reasons he didn't attach himself to anyone. He and Luther worked hard to make sure no one knew they were millionaires. There were several who did know, but they were the ones who read the gaming magazines or the magazines like *People* or *Time* who had interviewed them before. Most of the BU population read the magazines specializing in celebrity lives. Nikoli didn't want a woman clinging to him for his money. When he decided to settle down with one woman, he'd damn well make sure it was for him and not the millions sitting in his bank account. He was paranoid about it, and so refused to go past a single encounter with anyone.

Luther sat glued to the TV playing Call of Duty when Nikoli opened the door. Why Luther loved that game, Nikoli had no idea. He'd played it and won and never had the urge to play again. Currently they were working on a new zombie game, one that would make Resident Evil look like child's play.

They'd employed a graphics team to design the game to look as real as possible. He and Luther were the only ones working on the programming. It was groundbreaking work, and they were keeping it as hush-hush as possible.

"No, no, no, no...dammit!"

Nikoli glanced at the TV to see Luther had been the victim of a sneak attack and was now cussing enough to make even him raise his eyebrows. It wasn't until Nikoli heard him muttering about a grand that he understood the outburst. Luther must have had money riding on the game. Whomever had taken him out must be very good. Nikoli never bet against Luther in gaming.

"Bad luck there, man." Nikoli tossed Luther a beer. "You going for a rematch?"

"No," he snarled. "Little fucker refused. He knows he'll lose."

Nikoli laughed and then joined Luther on the couch. He cracked open his beer and took a long draw from the bottle. Ah, he'd needed that.

"So," Luther drawled. "How did your...*date*...go?"

"We talked."

"Talked?" Luther's eyebrows shot up. "Just...talked?"

"Do people really call me the manwhore of BU?" he asked instead of answering.

Luther laughed. "You hadn't heard that before?"

Nikoli shook his head. "No, it was a little disconcerting. I am not a whore. I don't sleep with every single woman I meet. I enjoy sex, and I won't apologize for that, but I am not near as bad as Lily

67

said."

"Well, you do have a reputation, Nik, that's spread like wildfire through the female population. It's made you into a bit of a celebrity."

"Don't sugarcoat it." Nikoli took another swig of his beer.

"I'm not." Luther shook his head. "You're an icon, man. Every woman on campus wants to mark you off her bucket list."

"Somehow that doesn't make me feel any better," Nikoli muttered.

"So what are we gonna do since you struck out with Lily?" Luther asked, his face deceptively blank. "Wanna head over to T's Pub? I think everyone else is either over at Jillian's or The White Horse."

Nikoli's eyes narrowed. Why was Luther suggesting they stay away from everyone?

"I mean, it's obvious you had an epic failure with Lily," Luther continued. "I'm sure you don't want to listen to every guy we know go on and on and on about it…"

"Not a problem." Nikoli stared pointedly at Luther. "If that were to happen with *any* guy we know, I'd beat him to within an inch of his life."

The grin slid from Luther's face, and he beat a hasty retreat to the fridge for more beers. "At least you're giving up on Lily and…"

"Who said I was giving up on Lily?" Nikoli savored the jaw drop currently on Luther's face.

"But…but…you came home alone!" Luther stammered, slamming the fridge door.

"Yeah, so?"

Luther snapped his mouth shut and glared. "You can't do this, man. She's not a girl you fuck with. She's too nice. I swear to God, you hurt her, me and you, we'll have a problem."

Nikoli's eyebrows shot up. He'd heard Luther talk about Lily before. She'd helped him out in one of his English classes he'd been failing. Nik had no idea Luther was this protective of her, though.

"Calm the fuck down and stop acting like an outraged woman. You look like your sister when you do that." Nikoli chuckled when Luther's glare got hotter. He loved riling him up sometimes. "You got it wrong. Lily and I came to a mutual agreement."

"What kind of agreement?" Luther asked suspiciously.

"She's in love with Boy Wonder," Nik told him, disgusted. "He's marrying the blonde. I promised to help her win over Boy Wonder if she agreed I could try to seduce her."

"And she agreed to that stupidity?" Luther barked.

"Not yet," Nikoli admitted. "I took her home and told her to think about it. If she stands a chance of stealing Boy Wonder, she has to get over her fears, and I can I help her with that. Deep down, she knows she needs help, and she'll agree."

"Fears?" Luther asked, curious.

Nik debated with how much he should tell Luther, but Lily would be spending a lot of time here as well as his other apartment. Luther needed to know her boundaries if she was ever going to be comfortable around him.

69

"Lily has a phobia," he said at last. "I'm only telling you because you need to know so you don't do something to send her running. If she finds out I told you, she'll beat *me* bloody."

"Now I really am curious." Luther tossed Nik a bottle of water as he sat down. "What? We're out of beer. Water won't kill you."

Nikoli grunted. Truth was neither he nor Luther were big drinkers. They could drink with the best of them, but they both agreed after the epic car crash of 2008, they'd keep their drinking to a manageable level. They'd gone out drinking with a buddy, and on the way home, they'd crashed the car. Their friend, who'd been driving, died. After that, both Nikoli and Luther refused to drink and drive.

"She doesn't like to be touched," Nikoli said. "That's where my biggest problem is. If I can't touch her, I stand zero chance of getting her in my bed. If she can't learn to tolerate someone touching her, she stands zero chance of stealing Boy Wonder, who *is* a touchy-feely person."

"Well, damn." Luther whistled, his expression thoughtful. "That explains a lot. So what kind of agreement did you two come to?"

"I'm willing to help her get past her phobia and make Boy Wonder jealous if she agrees to my price."

"And what price is that?" Luther was back to being suspicious.

"I get the chance to seduce her, and she gets Boy Wonder." Nikoli swallowed the rest of his beer and then broke open the water. "It's a win-win."

"Until you break her heart," Luther growled.

"Lily's not…"

"Dammit, Luther, shut the hell up!" Nikoli exploded. "I'm tired of hearing everyone warn me off. She's just a chick!"

Luther's mouth worked furiously, before he snapped it shut. A slow grin spread across his face, and Nikoli's frown deepened.

"I take it back," Luther said. "I think this is the best damn idea you've ever had."

Something was definitely up; Nikoli just wasn't sure what. "Why are you grinning like an idiot?"

"Because you are never going to see it until it's too late," Luther said. "Lily is the best thing that'll ever happen to you, but by the time you figure it out, she'll be gone."

"You don't know what the hell you're talking about," Nikoli denied, even though he knew Luther was probably right. Lily Holmes terrified him.

"We'll see." Luther grinned. "Come on, let's get out of here. The White Horse or T's?"

"T's," Nikoli told him. "I'm not in the mood for trendy. I need a bar tonight."

Luther didn't say a word. He just held the door open and grinned like the idiot Nikoli labeled him. Nik grumbled and headed out. Tonight he needed some stiff whiskey. Lily Holmes wasn't even his yet, and she was already driving him to drink. Just what the hell had he gotten himself into?

***

The phone buzzed again, and Lily sighed. She knew without looking it was Adam. He'd been blowing up her cell since she left the restaurant. He was worried. She got it, but at the same time, he didn't have the right to make her feel like second best to anyone. It may not have been his intention, but that's how she ended up feeling. That's how she always felt around Adam.

It came back to her aversion to being touched. Adam looked out for her, protected her. He saw her as a pseudo little sister. Never once in the entire time they'd known each other had he ever looked at her the way he looked at any of his girlfriends. Even before her aversion started. She was always just Lily to him.

Frustrated, she threw a throw pillow at the wall. Nikoli was right about one thing. Adam *was* a touchy-feely person, and he needed that intimate contact. Her hands started to shake just thinking about letting Adam stroke her hand like he had Sue's, and she cursed herself six ways to Sunday. Why couldn't she get past her stupid phobia?

Someone started pounding on her door, and she closed her eyes in frustration. It was only the first day. What kind of trouble could the girls have gotten themselves into already? Grumbling, she dragged herself to the door, surprised when she saw Adam on the other side. He looked relieved to see her.

"What are you doing here, Adam?" Lily asked, resigned to a potential fight.

"I just need to make sure you were…that you didn't…are you okay?"

Lily quirked a brow. "That I didn't what? Sleep with Nikoli? You know me better than that, Adam."

He let out a breath she didn't realize he'd been holding. Maybe Nikoli wasn't entirely wrong about how Adam felt. Could there be hope? One way to find out.

"Not that it would have been any of your business if I had," she said. "Why do you even care who I sleep with?"

"Can I come in?" he asked, his eyes a little pained. "I don't really want to talk about this standing here where half the hall is listening."

Lily peeked around him and saw that several of the doors had opened and people *were* listening. Damn nosy freshmen. She stepped back and let him in, closing the door. He collapsed on her bed and stared at the ceiling for a minute. She leaned against the door and waited.

He rolled to face her. "I'm sorry."

"For what?" She narrowed her eyes. "For insulting me? For following me to Joe's? For acting like a complete asshole? For embarrassing me in front of Nikoli? For making me feel worthless? What exactly are you sorry for, Adam?"

He had the good grace to wince. "All that," he said. "I didn't mean to make you feel worthless, Lily, or insinuate that you weren't good enough for Nikoli. I swear to God, that's not what I meant."

She continued to glare, and he flushed. "Look, Lily, it's just that Nikoli is more experienced, he's…well, he's…"

"A manwhore?" Lily supplied. "I know that, Adam. No one has to tell me who he is. I know who he is and his opinion of women."

"Then why the hell would you go out with him?"

Adam shouted, his blue eyes starting to burn with his own anger.

"Because I wanted to!" Lily shouted right back.

"You really have lost your damn mind!" Adam growled, sitting up. "He will eat you alive, Lily."

"Again, none of your business!"

"Yes, it *is* my business!" Adam stood and stalked over to stand barely inches from her. "*You're* my business."

"Adam, like I said at Joe's, I'm not your sister, and I'm certainly not your girlfriend. You can't tell me what to do, who to do it with, or where I can do it! If I want to screw the entire football team in the locker room, I can, and it still won't be any of your business!"

His eyes glowed with fury. She could read it in every muscle in his body. His fist landed against the wall beside her head. She'd never seen him this mad. Nikoli was right about one thing. Adam was jealous.

"Lily Isabella Holmes." His eyes softened. "You have been my business since you beat the shit out of Jimmy Carson in fourth grade when he tried to take my lunch. You're my best friend, and I'll be damned if I sit and watch you fall victim to Nikoli Kincaid. You're better than that. You deserve to be treated like something more than a piece of ass."

"Nikoli has been very upfront and honest with me." Panic started to creep in as Adam moved closer, blocking her in. "He never promised me forever, only a good time. If I do anything, I will go into it with my eyes wide open. I'm not stupid, Adam."

74

His hand came up and pushed a stray lock of hair behind her ear. She flinched and whimpered. The small touch made her start to shake. She couldn't bear it, and Adam knew it. He laughed. "I don't think I'll have to worry about that, anyway, Lils."

"Really?" she asked, her fear turning to anger. "Why's that, Adam? Explain it to me."

"You won't let him touch you, Lily." The anger bled out of his eyes. "You and I both know it."

"Bastard," she whispered, tears welling up despite her attempt to keep them back. "Get the hell out!"

His face blanched, realizing what he'd said. "Oh, God, Lily, I'm sorry! I didn't mean it...I'm so sorry..."

"Get. Out."

He moved away from her, and she yanked the door open. "Get *out*!"

"*No!*" he yelled. "I didn't mean it. Please, Lily, I didn't mean it!"

She could hear the doors opening down the hall, and she closed her eyes, mortified. "Adam, I can't talk to you right now. I need you to leave. Please."

"Not until you forgive me." He pulled the door from her and shut it. "I can't leave until you forgive me, Lily, please. I'm sorry. I swear to you, I didn't mean it. I would never try to use that to hurt you."

"Adam, I'm going to ask you one more time to leave, then I'm calling Mikey to come haul you out. I can't, not right now. Please, just leave me the hell alone."

"Lily..."

"No," she cut him off. "I want you to leave. Go

75

find your perfect little girlfriend who can stand for you to touch her."

"Shit, Lily…"

"Shut up!" she shouted. "You have no right, none! *Now. Get. The. Hell. Out!*"

She opened the door. His whole body slumped, defeated. "I'll leave, but this isn't over, Lily. I'm not about to lose my best friend because I can't control my own stupid mouth."

"I already lost you a long time ago, Adam," she said softly. He frowned, confused. "Please, just leave."

Finally, he walked out of her room, and she slammed the door, sliding down until she sat against it. Her whole body shook from the pain of what just happened. How dare he throw that in her face? She felt worse than worthless; Adam had used her phobia to demoralize her. It hurt. Tears burned wet tracks down her cheeks.

Lily was tired of being afraid, tired of feeling like she was worthless, broken, and not worthy of the great Adam Roberts. She was tired of being a self-imposed victim. She deserved better, dammit. Adam was right about that. She'd be damned if she sat here and let her own fear hold her back anymore. She would never let anyone make her feel like this again.

Reaching for her phone, she found Nik's number. He picked it up on the second ring.

"Lily Bells?"

"Okay, Kincaid, you've got a deal."

Chapter Nine

"What's wrong?" Nik sat up in his chair and pushed the blonde off his lap. Lily sounded like she was crying. "What happened?"

"Doesn't matter," she whispered, her voice a little broken. "Do you want the deal or not?"

"Hell, yes, I want the deal," he said. Why was she crying?

"Call me tomorrow and we'll set up the details." Click.

Nik pulled the phone from his ear and stared down at it, shocked. She'd hung up on him. No one ever hung up on him. Why the fuck was she crying? The blonde tried to crawl back in his lap, and he stood up. "Luther!"

Luther emerged from the direction of the pool tables. "Yeah?"

"Find your own way home," he told him. "I need to go take care of something."

Luther nodded and wandered back the way he'd come. Nik waved his waitress over and paid his bill, tipping the girl a fifty. She'd been a good server, actually doing her job instead of flirting. Plus he knew she had three kids at home she was supporting off her tips. He'd overheard her discussing it with one of the other waitresses last year. Since then, he always tried to tip her well when she was his waitress. She appreciated it, and he got great service.

"We're leaving already?" the blonde asked, her eyes lighting up.

"I'm leaving. You can do whatever you want." With that, he grabbed his keys and walked out of the bar, the blonde glaring at his retreating back. He couldn't get Lily's voice out of his head. She'd sounded devastated. He was thrilled she'd agreed, but the thought of this making her cry unsettled him.

It only took him about twenty minutes to get to her dorm. He nodded to Jamie, the security officer, as he strolled in. "Jamie, how's it going?"

"Not too bad," the young guard said with a yawn. "I just got here, so I'll let you know in a few hours."

"I'm supposed to meet Lily Holmes, but I forgot what floor she said she's on," he continued, not missing the look Jamie gave him. "She called earlier and left a voicemail."

"Lily called you?" Jamie asked suspiciously.

Nikoli sighed and pulled out his phone, showing Jamie the last call with Lily's name on it. "What room?"

Jamie's green eyes narrowed further, and his red hair only served to make his face look redder when he glared at Nik. "She's in room 432, but I swear if

78

you upset her, I won't let you back in this dorm for any reason."

Nikoli frowned. He was getting tired of the threats. "Trust me." He forced himself to curb his irritation. "The last thing I want is to hurt her. She's upset, and I just need to check on her." With that, he boarded an elevator and tapped his foot impatiently as he rode up to the fourth floor. When he stepped off the elevator, two freshmen stared at him, but he ignored them as he started searching room numbers.

Lily's door was dead center of the hall, and as he was about to knock, he heard something. Listening, he realized she was crying, and it made his gut wrench. Not letting himself think about why it bothered him, he knocked. He heard shuffling, and then the door opened. Her face was a puffy red mess. "You don't cry well," was the first thing out of his mouth. She tried to slam the door in his face, but he caught it and pushed his way in, closing the door behind him.

"I said we'd meet tomorrow."

"*Milaya,* what happened?" he asked softly. "Why are you crying?"

She just stared at him, tears leaking out of her big blue eyes, and it nearly did him in. It was a feeling he'd never experienced, and it unsettled him. He reached out to touch her, and she shrank away from him, her whole body trembling. He could see the fear in her eyes. This was the first time he'd ever really wanted to comfort someone, to help them, and he couldn't. Her phobia prevented him from even trying to soothe her. Frustration burned inside, both at himself for wanting to comfort her, and his inability to do just that.

"If our arrangement is upsetting you this much, Lily, we won't do it." Nikoli couldn't believe the words escaped his lips, but he wouldn't be the cause of this. People were right in that Lily was special, and maybe that was why he was determined to have her, but he would never deliberately do anything to cause her this much pain.

She shook her head. "No...no, this isn't your fault. Adam..."

When he heard her voice break, he wanted to smash Adam's face. What the hell had the little fucker done? "Adam what?"

She shook her head again and hiccuped. "Doesn't matter."

"It matters to me, *Milaya*." His voice was deceptively calm. When he got his hands on Boy Wonder, he was going to do some damage. "I..." He broke off when someone started pounding on the door. With a growl, he swung around and nearly ripped it off its hinges, hoping Adam would be standing there so he could hurt him as badly as Lily was hurting now. Instead, he saw the same girl he'd seen Lily with earlier tonight.

She stared up at him, surprised. "Where's Lily?"

"She's not seeing anyone right now." Nikoli tried to shut the door, but she slid around him. When she saw Lily in tears and shaking, she turned on him like a rabid dog. "What the hell did you do?"

"Nikoli didn't do anything," Lily defended him. "What are you doing here, Janet?"

"Adam said you were upset and..." Her eyes

widened. "Adam did this? Honey, what happened?"

Lily's gaze shot to Nikoli, and he cursed. Janet did the same.

"Come on, *Milaya*," Nikoli said. "We're getting out of here for a little while."

"I don't know." Lily backed further away. "I…"

"I promise, I'll be on my best behavior," he assured her. "You need to get out of here, away from everyone for a little while."

"I don't know, Lily," Janet frowned at him, which caused him to snarl in return.

"I'm not the one who hurt her," he said, the bite in his own voice shocking him.

"Not yet," Janet said hotly. "She's not a one night stand, and she's not one of your girls who spread their…"

"Enough!" Lily shouted. She'd had it. Everyone needed to shut up. Her head was pounding, and she felt like she'd been dragged over a pit of hot coals. She hurt. Everywhere. She couldn't deal with any of this right now.

"I'm sorry," Janet apologized. "I just…"

"I know, Jan." Lily closed her eyes and let out a long sigh. "You care and you're concerned, but Nikoli isn't anyone's business but mine. Leave it alone."

Janet's eyes went round, but she nodded. "Do you need to come stay at the House tonight?"

Lily shook her head. She couldn't face anyone until after she calmed down. No way in hell did she want Janet pitying her all night either. "No, I'll be fine. Go home, Janet."

"But…"

"No buts," she said firmly. "I'm going out with Nikoli anyway, so no need to stay here. I'll be fine." Lily couldn't believe she'd just agreed to that, but the thought of all those girls in the hall whispering and talking about all the fighting…it was too much. Plus if she stayed here another minute remembering everything that happened with Adam, she'd go a little nuts.

Nikoli held the door open for Janet. Lily expected to see a self-satisfied smirk on his face when he closed it behind her, but instead, he still looked angry. Lily had been surprised to see Nikoli at her door to begin with, but was even more suprised he seemed to be pissed on her behalf. It confused her a bit. She hadn't expected him to rush over here after her phone call.

"Why are you here?" she asked him, more curious than anything.

"I honestly don't know." He grimaced. Lily had the distinct feeling he was as confused by his own actions as she was. Nikoli Kincaid was not a man who checked on women, let alone women he'd just met.

"You didn't need to," Lily told him after a minute. "I'm fine."

He snorted. "You are not fine, *Milaya*. Come on, let's get out of here."

"I just told Janet I was going with you so she'd leave," Lily said. She had no intention of going anywhere with him. She'd changed her mind. "You can leave too."

He studied her, and it made Lily squirm. "Do you really want to stay here by yourself, Lily? As soon as I leave, all those girls are going to start knocking on your door asking questions. Are you up for that?"

Lily frowned. He had a point. She'd seen the number of people staring when Janet left and had no doubt they'd be over here as soon as Nikoli departed. Dammit. She just wanted to curl up and cry in peace and quiet.

"Fine," she said. "But no funny business, deal doesn't start until tomorrow."

He gave her that sly smile she was coming to actually like, despite her better judgement. "Scout's honor."

"You grew up in Russia," she reminded him. "Do they even have Boy Scouts in Russia?"

"No, but I like the American saying. It makes people trust you."

"I trust you about as much as I would a scorpion, Kincaid."

He grinned wider. "Let's go, Lily Bells."

Lily grabbed her keys and followed Nikoli out the door, stopping only to lock it. She stared straight ahead, catching curious faces staring at her out of the corner of her eye. She rubbed her forehead to try and ease the throbbing headache as she walked, knowing she was going to be the talk of the campus after this. So not what she had planned for tonight.

She waved at Jamie, the security guard. He took one look at her and stalked over to them. "What the hell did he do to you?" Then he turned his fury on Nikoli. "I told you if you upset her you'd be banned from this building…"

"Jamie, wait," Lily interrupted him. "Nikoli

didn't upset me. He came to check on me."

"But you've been crying." Jamie frowned.

Lily stared at Nikoli's somewhat pained expression and shook her head, frustrated. "Has this been going on all day?" she asked Nikoli.

He nodded. "Yeah, it's a little hard to get near you without someone trying to get in my face about it."

"Adam." Lily sighed. She should have known he'd pull something like this, which only infuriated her more.

"Oh, no, Lily Bells." Nikoli laughed. "It's not just Adam. I don't think you realize how many people care about you. My phone has been blowing up since lunch."

Her eyes widened. People were warning Nikoli away from her? Why? "Jamie, I'm fine. If you want to blame anyone for making me cry, blame Adam. Nikoli is just being a good friend."

Jamie's eyes widened and he stared at her, nonplussed. Lily headed out, Nikoli right behind her, before Jamie could say anything else. She'd had no idea. Maybe that was another reason Nikoli seemed intent on gaining her as a conquest— because everyone told him he couldn't have her. People needed to mind their own business.

Nikoli didn't try to talk as they drove. Lily was grateful for that. She was afraid she'd burst into tears again. She was angry too. What Adam had said to her…that hurt. He'd used her phobia against her, to make her feel pathetic and worthless. He'd said it deliberately. Adam had never been cruel to her before. How could he do that?

Lily expected Nikoli to take the next turn, but he continued, driving deeper into the heart of the city. This was not the route to his apartment. She'd been with Mikey when they'd dropped Luther off before, so she knew they were not going there. About twenty minutes later, they pulled into the parking deck of a very expensive apartment high-rise.

"Where are we?" she asked when he opened her door for her.

"My place." He motioned her to follow him to the elevator. She frowned when he inserted a key and then punched the button for the top floor.

"But…"

"Luther and I share an apartment close to campus, Lily, but this place is mine. I'll answer all your questions when we get upstairs, okay?"

The ride up the elevator seemed to take forever. Nikoli stared straight ahead, and it made Lily even more nervous than she already was. She shouldn't have come. Why did she let him talk her into this?

When the elevator opened, Nikoli ushered her out into what looked like a foyer or entrance hall. She couldn't see any other apartment doors, so this had to be a penthouse apartment. The floor was black marble and the walls a stark white, with expensive art hanging strategically here and there. Her mouth went a little dry. She knew he and Luther had money, but she hadn't imagined *this*. Lily was a gamer and read the gaming magazines. She knew who Nikoli was, but she hadn't mentioned it because he hadn't. She liked her own privacy, and therefore respected everyone else's.

The inside of the apartment was huge. It had an

open concept look, with the living room flowing into the kitchen and dining room. The furniture was done in earthy shades, with splashes of red to provide a stark contrast to the browns and taupes. It was very masculine. Her mind kept going back to their earlier conversation at the restaraunt. He said she needed a safe word, and her eyes widened at the thoughts of what he did here with other women. She didn't trust him, so why did she let him bring her here? Panic set in, and she glanced back at the door, wondering how fast she could make an escape if need be.

Nikoli kicked off his shoes and walked to the kitchen, where he grabbed two bottles of water out of the fridge before coming back into the main room. He sat down on the couch and motioned for Lily to join him.

Lily stared at him, and Nikoli waited. He had to let her make the decision to come to him. It *had* to be her decision. This was the first step toward her learning to trust him. Without trust, they'd get nowhere fast. The different emotions that ran through her eyes fascinated him. There was fear, hesitation, and curiosity. He was betting on curiosity being the driving factor here.

She'd been quiet on the ride over, and he'd respected that. Whatever Adam had done earlier really messed her up. She was still shaking slightly. Nikoli let out a small sigh of relief when she hesitantly sat down on the opposite end of the couch as far away from him as she could get. He didn't let it bother him. Trust would be learned, and he would learn a little bit of patience in return.

He tossed her a bottle of water. She twisted the cap off and took a sip, her tongue darting out to lick the drops from her lips. His nostrils flared at the sight, but he tamped his own desire down. He had to be careful not to scare her.

"You said you'd explain when we got here?" She looked everywhere but at him.

"This is my escape," he told her. "It's where I come to get away from everyone, where I come to...to share certain experiences with women who enjoy the same things I do."

Her eyes flew up to his face, and he bit back a smile at the anger in her eyes. He knew what she was thinking. She had nothing to fear from him.

"Lily Bells, don't overreact." He tried to keep his voice soothing. "I told you I had certain tendencies, but none of them involve pain. I have never caused a woman physical pain, and I never will."

"You just break their hearts." Her voice was full of her own anger at his behavior. He was relieved. He'd take anger over hurt any day.

"I thought we agreed to disagree," he said mildly. "Now, Lily Bells, what happened tonight? You were fine when I left you."

She pulled her knees up against her chest and wrapped her arms around them. Her eyes took on a haunted look that made him want to hit something. "Adam came over to check..."

"To check what?" he prompted after a minute when she didn't go on.

"You were right," she said, her voice small and anguished. "He was jealous. He came over to check to see if you and I had...if we..."

87

"Had sex?" he offered. He could see how hard this was for her talk about. He needed to know what happened tonight, but more than that, he needed to know why she was afraid of anyone touching her.

She nodded. "I told him it wasn't any of his business, and he got angry."

"Did he hurt you?" Every muscle coiled at the thought of anyone touching her in anger.

"Not like you mean," she whispered. "Adam would never hit me, but he did hurt me." A tear slipped down her cheek, and as much as he wanted to reach over and wipe it away, he kept his hands tightly clenched. "He...he...Adam knows how hard it is for me to..." She closed her eyes briefly, and Nikoli felt his anger burn hotter. He knew what Adam had done. He'd done it deliberately out of anger.

"He used your fear to make you feel inadequate?" Nikoli clenched his fists. She nodded, and his frown deepened. Adam was supposed to be her friend. No matter how jealous the dickhead was, he should never have hurt her like that. "I'm sorry."

She gave a humorless laugh. "He's right, though. I've let it turn me into someone who isn't capable of intimacy. I can't give him what Sue can."

"I told you I'd help you with that," Nikoli reminded her, "but I have to understand why you're so afraid. Did someone hurt you, Lily?"

"I wasn't abused, molested, or raped as a kid if that's what you're thinking." Her fingers twisted the end of the throw cushion she'd picked up. "It's all in my head, according to every therapist and psychologist I've ever been to."

88

Nikoli had expected a story of violence, given how she'd reacted when he'd grabbed her at lunch, so he was very surprised to hear that. "So, it just kind of developed on its own?"

"Do we have to talk about it right now?" Her voice was strained as her eyes fell away from his, but he'd caught the glimmer of shame in them.

"Yes, we have to talk about it right now." he said, his voice firm. "I need to understand this if I am going to help you."

Another hollow laugh erupted from her. "It's not about helping me, and you know it. It's about trying to get me naked."

"That's true." He cracked a grin, despite the seriousness of the situation. "I won't lie about it, but I *do* want to help you, Lily. I don't know exactly why, but I do. And I can help you, more than anyone else, but you have to help me understand why you can't bear for someone to touch you."

She remained quiet for a long time, but Nikoli patiently waited. He couldn't push her, not right now. He would eventually, but for now, she needed to do this, to trust him. It was hard for her. Her face said as much, but when she nodded, he relaxed.

"You know my dad died when I was twelve," she began. "I started to act out after that. Gave my mom some serious trouble. I skipped school, started hanging out with the wrong people, and over the next three years, you name it, I did it. My sister, Laney, decided enough was enough. It was Friday night, and I snuck out of the house. Laney followed me and tried to stop me. She grabbed me, and I pushed her. When she fell, I went running across the street. There was a park across from us that cut straight through to the cemetery where I was meeting up with my friends. She got up to follow me. Our house was on a curve, one you couldn't see around. The driver never saw her. He wasn't even going very fast, but he drove right over her. She died from massive internal bleeding."

"And you blame yourself." Nikoli hadn't expected that. Losing so many people in such a short amount of time had to be hard to begin with, but blaming herself too? It sucked ass. He at least understood her a bit better now and could build from there.

She nodded. "Wouldn't you?"

He could have lied to her, but that wouldn't have done either of them any good. "Yeah, Lily Bells, I probably would have blamed myself too."

She smiled slightly. "After that, it got harder for me to let anyone touch me. I kept seeing her grab my arm and me pushing her away, and then watching as the truck ran her over. Adam tried to help me, he used to grab me in these bear hugs, but I just couldn't…I started to shake, and then I'd start screaming. I couldn't. He gave up after a while. It was an easy diagnosis, but a little harder to cure. It really *is* all in my head."

"You equate someone touching you with death, specifically a death caused by you," Nikoli muttered. This might be harder than he'd expected, but he wasn't going to let her mental hang-ups deter him.

"So how can you fix that?" She laughed bitterly.

"With patience," he said, determined. And some

help from friends in the psych department. A few owed him favors and might be able to shed some light on her phobia for him.

Lily glanced up, surprised. Patience? He seriously thought he could cure her of her worst phobia with patience? Nikoli Kincaid was truly insane if he thought that.

"Adam tried that for over a year, Nikoli. Why would your attempts be any different?"

He studied her, and Lily squirmed. She also blushed when his gaze traveled from her head to her toes and back up, landing on her lips and staying there. She felt hot and took a sip of water. His stare caused all sorts of unfamiliar sensations to assault her. His smile said he knew it too. Here she'd told him her darkest secret, and all that was on his mind was sex! Now she felt really stupid. Why did she believe this could work? Nikoli was the worst kind of womanizer, and she knew it.

"Lily, Boy Wonder is an asshat and an idiot," Nikoli told her. "You needed patience and a firm hand. He couldn't give that to you. It was too hard, and he gave up. I, on the other hand, don't give up, and I love a challenge."

"How are you supposed to help me when all you can think about is getting into my pants?" Lily asked, rubbing her arms.

"It's because I want into your pants that I can help you," he fired back. "I have methods we can use, things that will help you learn to tolerate my touch, enjoy just thinking about what my hands will do to you."

She swallowed, every muscle in her body

tightening at the promise in his voice. Somehow in that moment, looking into his black eyes, she believed him. He might be able to do this for her.

"I'm sorry about your sister," he told her. "I don't know what I'd do if I lost one of my brothers, so I can't begin to imagine what you felt, what you still feel. Hell, all but one of my brothers have graduated and spread out around the country, and I miss them. If I couldn't call one of them or see them…" He closed his eyes, and Lily just stared. She'd never seen this side of him. He sounded like a decent human being for once. "I am sorry, Lily."

"Thank you," she said softly.

"I'm a bastard. I know that, but I'm not a heartless bastard," he said, sliding closer to her. She pushed herself as far into the cushion as she could, but he came closer, until he was sitting only about two inches away from her. Her palms started to sweat. "I want you to understand that simple fact. I'm going to push you, *Milaya*, push you well past your breaking points on many levels, but know that I heard you, heard your pain. I won't let my own needs make me forget how much you're hurting. You will always come first with me. You just need to be willing to try."

His dark eyes burned with an intensity that scared Lily a bit. She'd never had anyone look at her like that. Those eyes held a promise. All she had to do was accept it. Could she do it?

"Will you tell me exactly how you plan on helping me?" She needed to know the specifics.

"We're going to go slowly, Lily. First, you have to be comfortable with me, so you and I are going to spend a lot of time together. You'll be as comfortable with me as you are with Boy Wonder and Mike."

"Hardly." She couldn't repress the giggle that slipped out. She was too nervous. "Neither of them have designs on my virtue."

He smiled, really smiled, and she couldn't help but admire his dimples. Nikoli had a nice smile when he wasn't trying too hard. It was honest. "Once you start to get used to me, we'll move on to something basic."

"Like?"

"Like putting your hand in mine. I won't do anything except let you set your hand in mine. You can snatch it back without fear."

"So you'll let me touch you instead of touching me?" She'd never tried that before. Adam had always forced her to let him hug her.

"It's all about control, Lily," Nikoli explained. "Everyone has been forcing their touch on you, and I won't do that. I may do a few sneak attacks, but I'm going to let you get used to touching me, become familiar with how my skin feels against yours. Once that happens, then I'll touch you. Trust me, *Milaya*, you will learn to love the way I touch you."

"What does that mean? *Milaya*? It's Russian?"

"Yes, it's Russian," he said.

"So?" she prompted. "What does it mean?"

Nikoli wasn't ready to tell her yet what it meant. He wasn't even sure himself why he called her that. It meant sweetheart. He'd never in his life called a woman sweetheart. It slipped out around this one, and it unnerved him a little.

"What it means doesn't matter." He brushed the question aside. "Are you ready for this, Lily? Really ready for it? I want you to be sure."

"I...I don't want to live like this anymore, terrified, unable to show anyone how much I care about them. I can't even hug my mom." She twisted her fingers, her anxiety easy to read. "Even if things don't turn out with Adam, I want to be normal again, Nikoli. I want to have what everyone else has—someone who loves them, a family. I need to be able to touch someone in order to get that. "

Nikoli watched her. So many emotions ran rampant on her face. He couldn't even begin to fathom all the pain this woman had gone through, but here she sat, stronger than most. Yeah, she had a hang-up, but she was trying to get past it. She wasn't taking it lying down anymore. To face your fears took more courage than people ever gave you credit for. He'd faced a few demons himself, so he understood. Lily wasn't just special; she was extraordinary.

"Then you'll have it, Lily. I promise."

"What about you, though?" she asked.

"Me?"

Lily grinned, her inner devil shining through, and Nikoli frowned. What was the minx up to?

"Well, you did say you wanted to improve people's perception of you. If you plan on doing this, it means you can't go out and have sex with whomever. If you want people to believe we're dating, then you are going to have to conform to *my* standards."

So the little minx had a devil in her after all. Two could play this game. He pushed her. He scooted until his thigh was pressed firmly against hers. She sucked in her breath. "As I told you earlier, Lily. I won't need anyone else. I'll have you." Before she had time to respond, he leaned in and softly brushed his lips against hers. It was over and done before she could freak. He stood up and walked over to the row of window overlooking the Boston skyline. He needed to give her a moment and to get his own emotions under control.

Lily's hand shook as she brought her fingers up to touch her lips. She couldn't believe he'd done that! He'd told her he wouldn't touch her this soon, and he'd gone and done it anyway.

"You said…"

"I did say." He turned to face her. "My goal is to help you, Lily, make you comfortable with me, but I also want to touch you, very badly. It's why I'm over here right now. I want to bend you over that couch and fuck you so hard, you'll feel me inside you for a week, but I'm controlling myself."

Lily's mouth formed a silent O. She hadn't expected that. He was honest, if nothing else. "How can I trust you, though, if you can't even keep your word for one day?"

"Lily, I promised we'd take it slow, get you comfortable with me, but part of that includes my sneak attacks. My lips feathered over yours, not even a touch really. I will do it again and again. Get used to it."

She swallowed. He meant that. He was going to do it again. Her insides tightened, but not in fear.

Her hands were shaking, yeah, but there was more than fear there—she felt excitement, anticipation. Why did his touch, even the promise of his touch, do this to her? No one, not even Adam, had ever made her feel like this. Maybe the manwhore really was that good. She laughed, thinking about what Janet would have to say on the matter.

"Something funny?" he asked, his voice low and rough.

Lily looked up and her laughter died. He looked hard, determined. Not the laughing man of before. He looked more like the dominant males she secretly loved to read about, and it made her mouth dry. Dear Lord, what was she getting into? She almost called it off right then and there, but forced the words back. If she didn't take a chance, then she'd never know. This man—not the boy from before, but the man in front of her—could give her back her life. Instinct told her this, and she wasn't going to give up the chance for normalcy.

Not that she'd tell him that, though. "I was just thinking about what everyone's going to say when the manwhore goes straight. Do you think you can handle the ribbing?"

"Connoisseur of women, Lily, connoisseur of women."

"If that gets you through the night," she said, shrugging. "At least you're not hooking on the corner…"

He spewed the water he'd just put into his mouth, and Lily laughed. Oh God, she was going to have to tell Janet about this one for sure.

"You are going to pay for that one, *Milaya*," he

promised. "I may spank you."

"No, you won't," she said, laughing. "You just told me you don't hurt women."

"I never said it'd hurt, did I?" His eyes glittered with intent, and Lily's own widened.

Her own doubts crowded back in, and she pushed them down. This man could be more dangerous to her than anyone else. He struck a chord in her, and it scared her, but she refused to be a coward anymore.

"No touching, remember?"

He grinned, a slow, lazy smile that put her on alert. "Oh, but when I do touch you, *Milaya*…"

Lily took a shaky breath. She needed to get out of here, before they both did something she wasn't ready for. "I think we should probably go back to campus now."

Nikoli chuckled. "Running already. You realize I'm not going to let you escape so easily next time?"

"I'm counting on it," she said and meant it. She needed him to not let her run. Maybe it was what she'd needed all along.

"Come on, Lily Bells, let's get you home."

Chapter Ten

Lily felt like crap, but her growling stomach roused her out of bed. She didn't even bother changing, she just took care of business in the bathroom and washed her face. Lily headed to the cafeteria dressed in her favorite penguin pajama pants and an old AC/DC t-shirt. Stifling a yawn, she grabbed a bowl of fresh fruit and yogurt covered in granola, along with a glass of OJ. She plopped down at the first table she came to and rubbed her eyes. They felt blurry and gritty from her lack of sleep. Her only plans for today were to eat, then go back to bed for a couple more hours, and then *possibly* she'd deal with Nikoli.

Just thinking about last night twisted her stomach into knots. She still couldn't believe Adam had done that, said those awful, hurtful things to her. Never would she have thought him capable of being so cruel. She tried to tell herself it showed he cared enough to be jealous, that she might have a shot at winning him from Sue, but it hurt too much. Lily didn't know how long it would take her to forgive him, but it wasn't going to be soon. It might actually help, too, if Nikoli's plan worked. If she stayed away from Adam, and spent her time with Nikoli, then it might drive him crazy enough to realize she was more than just his best friend.

If Nikoli's plan worked, and that was a *big* if.

Her phone buzzed and she looked down to see Adam's face on the screen. She hit ignore. Too early to even try to deal with that.

"You look like hell, Lily."

Lily let her head fall on the table. Mikey. Of course. Adam probably sent him to feel out how mad she was.

"Well, thank you, Michelangelo," she grumbled. "Make me feel all awesome, why don't you?"

He plopped down across from her, and his plate of steaming eggs and waffles made her grimace. How anyone could eat something that heavy first thing in the morning was beyond her. Just gross.

"Soooo…"

Lily grimaced, and he laughed, but then his face got serious. "Adam got so drunk last night, I thought he might have alcohol poisoning."

"Is he all right?" she asked, alarmed. She might be mad and hurt, but she didn't want him hurt too. Well, not much.

"Sleeping it off, but he told me some stuff," Mike said. "I'm sorry for what he said, Lils, and so is he."

She sighed. "Sorry doesn't cut it this time, Mikey."

"I know, but you realize he only said those things because he was jealous, right?" Mike shoveled eggs in his mouth and swallowed. Man didn't even chew. Lily screwed up her face. "All he could go on about was you and Nikoli. He wants to beat the crap out of him."

"Yeah, well, it's none of his business, especially after what he said to me."

"Janet said you left with Nikoli last night." Mikey put his fork down and stared at her. "Lily, Nikoli…"

"Is none of your business either," she said bluntly.

"I just don't want you to do something stupid out of spite." Mike turned his full attention on her. "You're like a sister to me, Lily, so I have to put my two cents in. Your eyes are bruised and hurt, so I don't know if you're thinking straight. Nikoli is, he's…"

"I know all about him. I'm going to tell you the same thing I told Adam. Stay out of it. I'm a big girl. I know what I'm getting into."

Mike stared at her for a long moment. "Lily…"

"I mean it, Mikey. Leave it alone."

"Leave what alone?"

Lily groaned at the sound of Nikoli's voice. She groaned again when he sat down right beside her. He scooted until only an inch separated them. Her palms started to sweat, but she forced herself to sit still.

"Nothing," she said and sat up. Nikoli was dressed in a pair of faded jeans and a Metallica t-shirt. His hair looked rumpled, and his black eyes twinkled. Those full lips of his were turned up in a half smile.

"*Dushka*..."

"What does that mean?" she asked suspiciously.

He grinned wolfishly. "Wouldn't you like to know?"

"I know what it means in English." Her eyes narrowed.

"But it doesn't mean that in Russian." Nikoli popped a grape in his mouth.

"Why is your English so good?" Mike asked curiously. "Didn't you grow up in Russia?"

Nikoli nodded. "Yes, but my father spoke English. I speak it as well as I do Russian. Now, *dushka*..."

"No," Lily interrupted. "Stop right there. Do *not* call me *dushka*. Ever."

"You don't even know what it means." Nikoli laughed.

"I know what everyone else will *think* it means, and that's more than enough for me. No *dushka*. Promise!"

"No more *dushka*. *Katyonak* instead."

"Note to self, pick up a Russian to English dictionary."

Mike shook his head, barely containing his laughter. Lily shot him an annoyed look, which only caused him to cough to try and hide his choked laugh.

"What's up, guys?"

Lily closed her eyes as no less than three of Adam's football buddies took a seat at their table. They leveled a look that promised pain at Nikoli, which he ignored completely. Instead, he focused on Lily, and she tried to scoot farther away from

101

him. He only followed. She frowned at him and he simply smiled in response. He did warn her he was going to push her, but she thought he'd give her at least a day to come to grips with it. She should have known better.

"Breakfast?" she replied, her tone dripping with sarcasm.

"*Milka*, you are going to fall off the bench if you scoot any farther." Nikoli laughed.

"Maybe you should back off then, Nik." Menace laced every one of Brian Greggory's words.

"No, it's fine." Lily waved her hand dismissively. "Don't worry about it, Brian."

"If he's bothering you…"

Nikoli lazily plopped another grape into his mouth. "I'm not bothering her. The fact is, she and I are going to be spending a lot of time together, so get used to it."

Brian narrowed his eyes, and Lily could see they'd never believe she'd willingly go out with Nikoli. "He's right," she said. "You see, we have a bet." She felt Nikoli go completely still. He had no idea what she was up to, but a plan was forming, and she rubbed her hands together gleefully. This could turn out in her favor after all.

"A bet?" Mikey asked curiously, still shoveling food. She caught a glimpse of waffle and made a face.

"He wants in my pants, and I want his car."

Six pairs of shocked eyes gazed at her.

"Never going to happen, Lily Bells." *His car?* She'd lost her damn mind!

"Never say never, Kincaid." Lily grinned

impishly up at him, and Nikoli almost laughed with her. Almost. His baby was going nowhere. She could get that out of her pretty little head right now.

"You want the 'Cuda." Luther sat down next to Nikoli, rubbing his eyes.

Lily nodded, and Nikoli wanted to throttle her. No way in hell was she getting his car!

"He looks worried," Mikey observed.

"He does," Luther agreed. "I have a hundred bucks that says she gets the car."

Nikoli sent Luther a glare hot enough to singe what little hair was left on his head. They were betting on his car? His baby?

"So what does this bet entail?" Mikey asked.

"I personally don't think our manwhore here can go without sex," Lily said casually. "If he slips up during the next three months, he forfeits his car."

Nikoli focused on the woman next to him. He zoned out all the people around him and looked directly into her laughing blue eyes. She was going to pay for that. "And as I said last night, *Milaya*, I won't need to slip up with you in my bed."

Mike growled something unintelligible, and the other guys got pissed off looks. Nikoli ignored them. "That's the second half of our bet. She has to keep out of my bed for three months, or I win."

"I want the car more than I want you," Lily told him.

"We'll see, Lily Bells." Nikoli grinned. "Speaking of our bet...are you ready to go?"

"Go?" She frowned. "Go where?"

"You'll see." He stood up and waited for her.

"I'm not dressed." Her eyes were wide and

103

slightly fearful when they looked up at him.

"You look fine for what I have planned." He couldn't keep the evil grin off his face. Time for a little payback. "You won't be keeping those clothes on for long anyway."

She narrowed her eyes and shook her head. "I want medical reports. Who knows what you might have."

She did *not*. He narrowed his own eyes. "We discussed this yesterday, *dushka*."

"And I told you not to call me that!" she yelled. The guys sitting across from her were chuckling, and she turned her furious gaze on them. "The next person who laughs will *not* get tutored this year."

That wiped the smirks off their faces.

The girl had more fight in her than she realized. It was what he was banking on. She just needed to keep her fingers off his car. Seriously, where had that come from?

"Ready?" He kept his expression as mild as he could, but from the look of irritation on her face, he knew he'd failed and let the smirk out.

She stood up and grabbed her bowl to dump off at the bins. "I really need to change…"

He shook his head. "Nope, no time. I might even let you drive my car if you get your butt in gear."

Mike snorted milk through his nose at the look of excitement on Lily's face. "What's with you and his car?"

"Ohmygosh…it's a 1970 Plymouth Barracuda!" Her blue eyes lit up like Christmas. "Do you even know how rare that car is?"

"When did you become a car buff?" Mike

frowned.

"She's been a car buff since before she could talk."

Lily's entire body froze and she flinched at the sound of Adam's voice. Nikoli moved closer, and for once, she didn't move away from him. He didn't think she was even aware of how close he was, but Adam noticed. His eyes narrowed.

"Seriously?" Mike asked. "Why did I not know this?"

"Who do you think fixes my car?" Adam set his tray down. "Lily, can we talk?"

"She was just leaving." Nikoli's voice was cold.

"Lily?" Adam stared directly into her eyes, and she flinched again.

"No," she said after a moment. "We're leaving."

"Lily, please…"

"No, Adam, not today." She turned to the other guys sitting at the table. "You guys seem all concerned about Nikoli, but he's not the one you need to worry about. You want to do something for me? Then keep Adam the hell away from me and leave Nikoli alone."

Nikoli smirked at Boy Wonder, who looked pissed beyond belief. Good. He needed to be beaten for the mess he'd left Lily in last night, and from the looks around him, Adam had some explaining to do. He might just get that beating too.

"So, where are we going that I don't have time to change my clothes and put a bra on?"

Nikoli's attention snapped back to Lily, and he zeroed in on her chest. His eyes widened when he realized she wasn't wearing a bra…why had he not noticed this before?

"And stop staring at my boobs." Her laughter bubbled up and spilled out as she started walking toward the door.

"How about I stare at your ass instead?" he called, and she shook her head. He didn't have to look back to know the low growl came from Boy Wonder. "It's a damn fine ass."

Luther caught up to him. "Do you have a death wish?"

"They'll get over it."

"Where are you guys heading?" Luther asked, following them outside.

"To pick up the Mach 1."

"You're taking Lily? In her pajamas?"

Nikoli grinned. "She wants to drive, so I'm letting her drive...just not my baby."

"She's driving the Mach 1 back?" Luther asked, eyes wide. "What if she wrecks? Totals it?"

"Then she does. It's just a car."

"Just a car?" Luther shouted. "It's a Mach 1!"

Nikoli stopped walking, seeing Lily staring at them curiously. He couldn't afford to screw this up. "Lily's not going to total the car. Her dad was Martin Holmes. She probably drives better than either of us."

"That's not the point," Luther argued.

"Look, man. I get that you usually drive them back, but just this once, trust me, okay? You can drive it all day tomorrow. Hell, once the race is over, you can have it for your own baby. Don't think I didn't see the way you were salivating over the online images yesterday."

"Yeah, whatever," Luther grumbled, but Nikoli caught the gleam in his eye. Luther wanted that Mach 1 in a bad, bad way.

"So where are we going?" Lily yawned when Nikoli reached her. She looked cute. Strange that he'd think of this woman as cute, but he did. To him, women were hot or sexy, but never cute. He snorted. It sounded cliché, even to him.

"You up for some driving?"

"You're going to let me drive your car?" Lily asked, her eyes wide and excited.

"No, you're not driving Ellie, but you can drive the Mach 1 we're going to pick up."

"Really?" she asked, squealing like a girl.

"Really. We just need to swing by your dorm and pick up your license."

"I can change my clothes..." She trailed off when he started shaking his head. "Why not?"

"Because I want you comfortable with me, Lily," he told her. "We're going to be spending all day in the car, so I want you relaxed. Those penguin pajama bottoms of yours should do the trick."

She made a face at him, but didn't argue as they piled into his car. Her fingers started gently running over the leather seats the minute she got in. He stared at them, imagining her running them over his skin. Maybe being in the car with her all day wasn't such a good idea.

No, he decided a few minutes later when she hopped out and flew up the front stairs of her dorm, his eyes following her ass. It wasn't such a good idea at all.

Chapter Eleven

"So, what are your brothers' names?" Lily asked curiously. She hadn't been thrilled with the idea of spending all day alone with Nikoli trapped in a car, but the bribe of driving a Mach 1? So worth it.

"Kade is the oldest," he replied, focused on the road. "Dimitri, Viktor, Connor, then me, and Callum is the youngest at twenty."

"Six boys?" she said. "I bet your mama had her hands full."

"You've no idea. If one of us wasn't bleeding all over her floor, then we were all fighting. She has this look that could make us all feel both embarrassed and ashamed in a heartbeat."

"I think all mothers have that look." Her own mother certainly did. She'd used it when Lily announced her plans to move to Boston for college.

"How about you?" Nikoli asked. "Do you have any other brothers or sisters?"

Lily nodded. "Mom remarried when Laney and I were fourteen."

"You were twins?" Nikoli interrupted.

"Yeah. Identical." They couldn't have been more different, though. Laney hated the racetrack, hated cars in general. She'd have rather stayed home and helped Mom with whatever. Lily grew up on the racetrack, Laney grew up shopping and learning to be the future prom queen. No matter how different they were, though, they were also the same. Laney loved Lily more than anything in the world, and Lily felt the same. She still felt empty inside, like a piece of her was missing without her twin. Sometimes it was a physical ache that hurt so bad, she had to lie down until it passed. "So, back to your question. I have a little brother and sister. Twins again. They run in my mom's family. Mia and Mitchell."

"Does your fear apply to them too?" Nikoli asked softly.

Lily sighed. She wished to God she could say no. They were babies and didn't understand why she wouldn't play with them or hold them, or even kiss them. She loved them to death, but she couldn't physically show it.

"I'm guessing that's a yes?" At her nod, he said, "Well, we'll fix that soon enough, Lily Bells."

"Tell me about growing up in Russia." She needed to get off this line of questioning. It was making her nervous. Just talking about her psychosis made her neurotic sometimes. She wanted to enjoy the day, not slump into a depression.

"I'll tell you all about Russia if you do one thing for me." Nikoli's even and calm tone put Lily's defenses on red alert. He was up to something.

"What?" she asked suspiciously.

Nikoli laughed. "Don't look at me like I've just asked you to commit felony murder. It's something simple."

"What?" she asked again, suspecting it was something worse than felony murder.

"I want you to touch me."

She stared at him. He kept his eyes on the road. He wanted her to *touch* him?

"You can poke my arm with your finger if you want," he offered, keeping his tone light.

"Why?"

"Because Lily, you have to be comfortable with me…"

"And you think I'm going to get there by you forcing me to do something I don't want to do?" Her voice sounded shrill even to her, but she couldn't help it. She was already starting to panic just thinking about it.

"I'm not forcing you," he said calmly. "You want to hear about Russia, I want you to touch me. It's a fair trade. If you can't do it, then we'll talk about something else."

Lily took several deep breaths, trying to calm herself. She closed her eyes and counted to twenty like one therapist had taught her to do. This was what she'd asked him to help her with, to help her learn to tolerate someone's touch. Nikoli was even giving her the control, letting her touch him. Could she do it?

Fingertips ran down her arm from shoulder to hand, and she flinched away from them. Her eyes snapped open and she looked at Nikoli, but his eyes were still fixed on the road. "Sneak attack?" she spat. How dare he? He'd said she could touch him, and here he went and took that little bit of control away.

He grinned. "Yup."

Bastard.

"Choice is yours, Lily Bells," Nikoli said. "We can talk about Russia, or you can tell me about growing up on the racetrack."

"Why don't you tell me something else about yourself instead?" she asked. Russia would have to wait. She wasn't ready to touch him yet. It was too soon.

"Nope. You want to know something about me, you know the price."

She gasped. "You...you...you..."

He reached over and hovered a finger in front of her lips, not touching her, but she got the point. "Uh-uh, *Milaya*. If you want to know something about me, it's going to cost you. A simple touch. That's all. If you're not ready, then you're not ready, but that's the price of asking me questions about myself."

Bastard.

"Be pissed all you want, Lily, but those are the rules."

"I thought you said we'd do this with patience." She glared. He said one thing, but did another. What the ever-loving hell?

"I'm being very patient, Lily." His black eyes swung her way, and she stopped breathing for a moment. She could see the blind lust in them. "Your version of patience and mine are two entirely different things. If I did what I wanted, I'd stop the car and take you right here, right now, but I'm not doing that, am I? Instead, I'm giving you options."

"Options?" she nearly choked out. "I don't call those options, more like hostage negotiations."

He laughed. "Hostage negotiations? Well, now, *milka*, I think I can do that if you'd prefer. It's just as easy to tie you up and touch you. I'd like it too."

"I don't even know what to say to that," she squeaked.

His grin was downright evil. "When we do that, *Milaya*, talking will be the last thing on your mind."

"You think I'd let you tie me up?" She gave him an are-you-out-of-your-mind look.

"Yes, Lily," he said, turning his attention back to the road. "You are going to let me do just that. Not yet, but soon enough."

"You're insane if you think I'd ever agree to that."

"We'll see." He smiled. "Are you hungry yet? It's almost noon, and we still have another hour to go before we get to Windham."

She *was* hungry, and her stomach rumbled at the mention of food. Nikoli laughed and pulled into a diner of some sort. She hadn't even realized they were in a town. "Where are we?" she asked as they went in.

"We're in Norwalk. At least that's what the GPS said. Weren't you paying attention to it?"

He could ask her that after his nonsense in the car? She shook her head, but followed the waitress to a booth in the back. It was a charming little place, seaside themed, but then again, they were near the coast. The waitress took their drink orders and left them to look at the menu.

"What are you frowning at?" Nikoli asked. She'd been glaring at the menu for the last few minutes.

"Do you think they have fresh fish or frozen?"

"We're in Massachusetts, Lily, they have fresh fish."

"Ohmygosh, don't you ever watch *Kitchen Nightmares* or *Restaurant Impossible*?"

"Uh, no?"

Her eyes widened. "They're shows that tell you what really goes on behind the scenes in a restaurant. You wouldn't believe the things I've seen…"

"Is that why you asked for no ice?" Nikoli grinned. She looked appalled he'd never seen the shows.

"Yes! Do you know how many places don't clean their ice machines? Have you ever seen what the bacteria looks like that grows when they don't?"

"Nope, not a clue." Nikoli shifted, bringing his right foot up to sit beside her left leg on the seat.

"What are you doing?" she asked, but before she could scoot, he moved his other foot, trapping her. He didn't touch her, but he refused to let her move away from him.

"Stretching my legs," he said. "Three hours of driving and they need it."

"Well, then go take a walk or something, but move your feet."

"No."

"No?" she asked incredulously, and he chuckled. "This is not funny, Nikoli."

"I'd disagree. It's about as funny as you calling me a manwhore in front of everyone this morning."

The poor waitress picked that minute to show up. Julie, as her nametag read, blushed as bright as a cherry and gave him a look he did not appreciate. "Are you…uh…um…ready to…order?"

"Cheeseburger and fries," Nikoli said, scowling at Lily. She was grinning from ear to ear. Damn woman. He was not a whore!

"Is the fish fresh?" Lily asked, smirking at Nikoli.

"Yes, of course. The owner gets it from the docks fresh every morning."

"Chowder then, thank you." Lily smiled at her and handed over the menus. The girl nearly ran from the table. "Don't blame me. That was all you, buster."

"You're supposed to be helping me with my reputation, Lily Bells, not causing it further damage."

"Kinda hard to do when you blurt out things worse than a girl."

Nikoli's mouth fell open, and Lily burst out laughing. He was going to wring her neck yet.

"Are you going to move your feet?" she asked again.

"No." She frowned, and he shifted both feet closer to her. He still wasn't touching any part of her, but she started to fidget. He was hoping she'd get the nerve to push his feet away from her. It would force her to touch him. That first touch was going to be the hardest. He wanted it out of the way quickly. It was like the first time you rode your bike without training wheels. You knew you were going to fall, it was inevitable, but once you did, you got up, got back on, and took off again. That first fall was the hardest, but once you knew what was coming, you were okay with it. She would be okay once she got over that initial contact.

"Why the hell not?" she demanded.

"Because I like you trapped," he purred. "It makes me happy."

"Do I look like I care if *your* perverseness makes you happy or not?" she snapped. "*I'm* not happy, so move your damn feet."

"Nope, you have to make me move." Before she could argue, he interrupted her. "So, about this bet I never agreed to…"

"What about it?" She wasn't even looking at him, she was staring at his foot.

"What in God's name gave you the idea I'd ever put my car up for a wager?"

"Afraid of a little bet, Kincaid?" She looked up and smiled, really smiled, and Nikoli felt his insides twist a bit. She was gorgeous when she smiled. He'd seen her laughing and smiling, but not like this. It was genuine and happy.

"No, I'm not, *dushka*, but you should be." He leaned across the table, invading her personal space. "Do you really think I'd *ever* lose my car in a bet, especially a bet about sex?"

"I told you not to call me that," she whispered, pushing herself back against the seat and as far from him as she could get. Luckily, that was only a few inches.

Her tongue darted out and wet her lips. His eyes

115

followed the movement, and he felt himself growing hard imagining what that tongue would feel like against his skin. "You smell like vanilla, Lily. It reminds me of sugar cookies. Would you taste like warm vanilla sugar cookies, *Milaya*?"

"Uh, Nikoli," she whispered, drawing in a ragged breath. "You're eyes are getting darker."

"Mmm," he said, pushing himself closer to her. "Do you know why, Lily?"

She shook her head, and he smiled the smile guaranteed to get a woman out of her clothes. "It's because I'm imagining all the things I could get you to do with that lovely little tongue of yours."

Lily's eyes widened and her breathing sped up. Nikoli pressed closer, his own mouth a hair's breadth from hers. "Would you like to do that, Lily?"

Someone cleared their throat and Nikoli was forced to look up. Their waitress stood there, holding their plates. He groaned, frustrated, but moved back so she could put the plates down. Her hands were a little shaky when she pulled them back. Lily took one look at her and blinked. He watched all the progress he'd made in the last few minutes slip away as she closed her eyes. When she opened them, they were wary, watchful.

Frustration welled up, but Nikoli refused to show it. Instead, he smiled lazily up at the waitress. "Thank you, Julie."

"You're...ah...welcome." Julie turned and walked away, glancing back several times. Lily made some kind of disgusted noise, but Nikoli ignored her. He picked up a fry and dipped it in ketchup. "So, now back to this bet…"

"The bet stands," Lily said between bites of chowder, "unless, of course, you're afraid you'll lose." Lily worked hard to keep her tone even. Nikoli had gotten to her for a minute there. She'd even *wanted* him to touch her, and that made her nervous. Confused too. She'd gone so long without someone's touch, it made no sense to her that she craved his. She couldn't let him see just how much he affected her.

"We've already established I'm not afraid of losing," Nikoli countered. "Where did that particular little idea come from? It's not something we talked about last night."

"You want people to think we're dating, don't you?"

He nodded.

"Then I had to find a way to make them believe I'd ever date you."

"What's wrong with dating me?" he asked, putting his burger back down. He looked so outraged, Lily couldn't help but giggle. An honest to God giggle. She was not a girl who giggled, but Nikoli brought it out in her. Not even Adam could make her so much as think about giggling.

"You're not exactly dating material," Lily said, laughing as his face became even more outraged.

"Why the hell not?" he demanded. "No one's ever complained before."

"Nikoli, you're gorgeous, sexy, and every girl's fantasy, but no girl would date you."

He growled, his feet inching closer. She glanced down nervously, but her eyes shot back up when a fry hit her in the face. He did not! "You really want to start a food fight when I have clam chowder to throw at you?"

"Explain why no girl would date me." His tone was clipped and hard. Ohh, she'd hit a nerve! Good. The man needed taken down a peg or two.

"You're the bucket list guy," she told him. "You're the guy every girl wants to sleep with just once, but that's it. Oh, you'll get those who think they can change you, but we know deep down, you're a one night stand kind of guy. You've got commitment issues."

"I do not!"

"Really?" she asked. "Tell me when was the last time you had a relationship that lasted more than a night?"

"You."

"I don't count," she said. "Besides, what we're doing isn't really a relationship. The question is why you don't want a healthy relationship with one person."

"I have my reasons," he told her.

She snorted, but continued. "Girls, like guys, don't want someone everyone and *anyone* can have and *has* had at one time or another."

"I have not slept with as many women as you think. Girls tend to let their friends *think* something happened. I just don't correct them."

Like she believed that? Ha! She'd seen him with more women over the last three years than she could count. "You also have *no* respect for women."

"I have respect for them," he said and then paused. "Well, some of them. I respect you and my mother. Doesn't that count for anything?"

"Why don't you respect them?" she asked, curious.

"As you like to point out, I've slept with a lot of women, not as many as you think, but enough. I've seen them cheat on their husbands, boyfriends, and fight with their best friends to sleep with me. I don't say this to sound arrogant or to brag, it's just a fact. Why would I respect people who would throw everything away for sex? If you're not happy, then have enough balls to 'fess up to it. Don't disrespect someone else by cheating."

Lily frowned and shoved a spoon of chowder into her mouth to keep from having to respond right away. She hadn't expected that answer from Nikoli. It's something she would have said. And he had a point, dammit. How could a person respect someone who couldn't respect themselves or others? Well, damn, maybe Nikoli did have some kind of moral code.

"Anyway, back on topic, the bet," she said. She needed a few minutes to process the whole deep side of Nikoli Kincaid. "People know me, they know I'd never go out with you willingly, so I came up with something they'd believe, that *Adam* would believe."

"Boy Wonder does know about your car addiction." Nikoli nodded as if everything made sense. "So it's not a real bet, then? I can do…"

"Oh, it's a real bet," Lily interrupted. "The way I see it, this…proposition of yours is completely one-sided."

"One-sided?" he asked incredulously. "You get

Boy Wonder out of it."

"But what if I don't?" Lily asked. "What if I can't get past my fear of people touching me? Or what if you can help me and I still don't get Adam? What if we're both wrong and he loves Sue too much to leave her? Theoretically, if that happens, you *might* manage to get me to sleep with you. You win in either scenario, and I get jack. This way, I stand a chance of walking away with a car that I want more than almost anything else."

Nikoli watched her through hooded eyes. She hadn't noticed he'd pressed his feet against her thighs. She was so focused on their conversation, she forgot to be afraid. It was definitely progress and proved if he was patient, he'd end up with her in his bed, so why shouldn't he bet his car? Not a chance in hell he'd lose it to begin with. So why not?

"All right, Lily Bells, I'll bite. If you can stay out of my bed for three months, then you can have my car."

Her face lit up and she nearly jumped up and down where she sat. It didn't take a lot to make her happy. He settled back, content to watch for a minute. She still hadn't noticed his feet, and he debated telling her. He didn't want to ruin the moment, but then again, she might be so shocked, she shoved them.

"How old is Kade?" she asked, taking another bite of her chowder.

"He's twenty-seven." Nikoli watched the spoon disappear into her mouth and then slide out between her lips. He rubbed her leg with his foot in response.

"Lives in Virginia and works for the FBI."

"Really?" Lily asked. "He didn't go back to Russia?"

"No, none of my brothers did. We might eventually, but we like America. We have more freedoms here than we do in Russian. Kade and I have been trying to convince our parents to move back to the States for years, but our mother loves Russia."

"Hey, Bob, turn that up!"

Both Nikoli and Lily looked to see the guy behind the counter turn the volume up on the wall mounted TV screen. A reporter stood in a park, a crime scene behind him. The body of the missing girl who had been all over the news had just been found. People started talking all at once, but Nikoli pulled his attention back to Lily. She was frowning and shaking her head.

"Are you worried about that?" he asked.

"Not really worried, just sad. Freaked too. They found that poor girl really close to campus."

"Whoever he is, he doesn't seem to be targeting college campuses, at least," Nikoli offered, hoping to calm her nerves a bit. A lot of the girls on campus were starting to worry about that. Campus security had posted flyers everywhere warning women not to go anywhere alone if they could help it. He might be freaked too if he was a girl.

"Let's hope it stays that way," she said, staring at the TV screen. "Are you about ready to go? I lost my appetite."

"Sure." He signaled the waitress for the check. "One thing, though."

"Hmm?"

"How do you plan on getting out of your seat?"

She gave him a questioning look, and he pointed at his feet, pressed up against her thighs all snug and cozy. She looked down, and her mouth dropped open. Her eyes darted from his face to his feet. He waited patiently for her to get over the shock. Julie set the check down on the table, and he nodded at whatever she said, but didn't break eye contact with Lily.

Lily gasped and nearly had a small heart attack right then and there. Nikoli had managed to press his feet against her and she'd never noticed. How had she not noticed this? She could feel them like a hot iron burning through her pajama bottoms now that she saw them, but God only knew how long he'd been like this. She'd been too distracted to realize he'd pulled another sneak attack on her.

Strange thing was, she wasn't about to hyperventilate. It could be because it was just his shoes and not technically him. There was no skin to skin contact. Did this even qualify as touching? Her brain screamed yes, especially when he rubbed his foot back and forth. She felt it, and it felt...*nice*. It was such a foreign sensation, she reached out and pushed his foot away from her without thinking.

Nikoli let out a low hum of satisfaction. Lily wasted no time in scrambling out of the booth and fleeing the diner. She went straight to his car and stayed there, trying to focus. She did it. She'd touched him. Oh. My. God. She did it! Relief swept through her. She'd been terrified she couldn't do it, scared that she was too broken to fix, but she

122

touched him!

Sure it was only a shoe, but even yesterday, she wouldn't have been able to do that. His sneak attacks were working, making her more comfortable with him. Nikoli could distract her like no one else, and maybe that was the key to learning to touch and be touched. She could do this. For the first time since she was sixteen years old, she had hope. *Hope.*

Nikoli was smart enough not to say a word when he unlocked the car. She climbed in, buckled her seatbelt and smiled. "Tell me about Russia."

Nikoli put the car in gear, and then started them moving again. "What do you want to know?"

"Everything." He laughed and spent the remainder of the car ride telling her about growing up in Russia with his brothers, about their favorite places to play when they were little, and then about their favorite hangouts when they got older. He told her about the castles, the architecture, and the culture. Everything he could fit into an hour, anyway. He did promise to tell her more when they pulled onto the dirt road leading to Jasper Moore's house and his Mach 1.

The house was a bit run-down, the paint peeling, and he could see several shingles on the roof that needed replacing before winter set in. His beautiful car sat in the driveway, prepped and ready to go. When they pulled up, he could see what it cost Lily not to jump out of the car. She was a smart woman, though, and understood you didn't just go wandering around a stranger's property. Nikoli honked the horn, and they both waited for the guy to come out.

Jasper Moore was just as run-down as the house. His clothes were messy. He had a hole in his shirt, and he looked like he hadn't showered in days. Nikoli debated telling Lily to stay in the car, but the way she was eyeballing the Mach 1 said she'd stab him if he tried. Suppressing a smile, he got out, and Lily followed close on his heels.

"You Kincaid?" Jasper had a raspy voice that sounded like he smoked one too many cigarettes. He ran his gaze over Lily from head to toe, eye fucking her as he did. Lily wasn't even paying attention; her focus was all on the car.

Nikoli stepped in front of Lily, cutting off Jasper's access to her ass. He did not like the way his eyes had zeroed in and stayed there. "I am. I've got the check. Keys?"

Jasper pulled them out of his pocket. "You want to start it up first?"

"Always do. Lily?" He tossed her the keys when she turned around. "Pop the hood and start her for me?"

She ghosted her fingers across the top of the car, never touching the paint, before opening the door and sliding in. She popped the hood and then cranked the ignition. It came to life, and relief swept through Nikoli. He'd been afraid the car wouldn't start. It was obvious Jasper had no clue how to take care of it since he didn't understand how much it was worth. "Rev it up for me, will ya, Lily Bells?" Nikoli said as he propped the hood up. The engine roared, and he grinned. This was his four hundred thousand dollar victory car. He might need to tweak it a little, but this one was gonna take it home.

"It still runs like the day my uncle dropped it off here," Jasper said. "He died a couple years back and left me the car."

"How long has it sat idle?" Lily asked. She was already checking the interior for flaws.

"Nearly four years." Jasper moved closer to the car.

"How often did you start it?" she asked.

"I started it up a few days ago before I put it up for sale to make sure it still ran."

Lily gaped at him, and Nikoli chuckled. Jasper here was not a car buff. "Well, that explains why it's almost out of gas," she grouched. "It *might* make it to the station."

Shaking his head at her disgusted tone, Nikoli turned his attention back to Jasper, who was standing much too close to Lily, even if she was safely in the car. There was something about the guy, something off, that rubbed Nikoli the wrong way, and he definitely didn't like the way he stared at Lily. If she was paying attention, she'd be freaking out. For once, Nikoli was glad her car lusting made her oblivious.

"If you'll get the title, I've got the check." He pulled out his wallet and fished out the certified cashier's check.

Jasper turned and disappeared back into the house. Nikoli waited impatiently while watching Lily. She was going over everything, finding imperfections and clucking like a mother hen. The fact that she could lust over a car and not him still blew his mind. It was sexy as hell.

"*Is* there enough gas in that thing to make it to the station?" Nikoli asked to get his mind off things that would drive him insane on the four hour trip back to school.

"I think so, but barely," she said, frowning. "The passenger seat's leather is ripped in two places. There's a crack in the dash, and there's a tiny dent back by the back fender."

"Are you okay driving it back?" he asked. "You said it's been a while since you've driven anything like it..."

"Does that mean I can drive your car?"

"Hell, no!"

"Then, yes, I'm good driving this one back." She looked up at him and winked. "Just try to catch me."

His eyes widened at the challenge, but before he could say anything else, Jasper was back with the title and a bill of sale. Nikoli made sure the title was signed, then handed over the check.

"Good doing business with you." Jasper nodded and went back inside the house.

Nikoli turned his attention back to Lily. He crouched down in front of the driver's window. "Are you sure about this? I can always bring Luther back to..."

"I'm fine, Nikoli," she told him. "I'm more comfortable behind the wheel of a car than I am anywhere else. I'm not going to crash her. I promise."

"Okay, follow me to the station. Let's hope there's enough gas in there to make it. I'd hate to leave it on the side of the road even long enough to go get gas."

Lily nodded and obediently followed him to the station. Once the tank was full, she grinned. The boy had no idea how well she could drive. Her dad may have died, but she loved cars and had spent her teenage years learning all sorts of tricks. This baby had all the bells and whistles she could ever want. Not only was she in the driver's seat of one of the most awesome cars ever created, she'd managed to actually touch Nikoli. That still made her smile from ear to ear. It wasn't major to most people, but it was to her.

Nikoli came out of the store and handed her a cold bottle of water. "You ready?"

"Are you?" She grinned up at him.

"Oh, *Milaya*, I'm always ready." His fingers reached out and traced her cheek. She barely flinched and didn't pull away. She was getting used to the feel of his hands on her. She looked at him, shocked and surprised. Why wasn't she freaking out? It made no sense to her.

He smiled. "I'm going to win."

"You keep thinking that," she said, pulling away from him and starting the car. "See you back on campus!"

With that Lily pulled out, leaving Nikoli running for his own car. She laughed and went from forty to eighty to a hundred. The wind whipped through her hair, and the feel of the car beneath her reminded her how much she loved driving. She'd missed it. There was so much freedom and power in letting a car run flat out. Nikoli was catching up, and Lily smiled an evil smile. The man had no chance. She was in a fully modded racing car. His 'Cuda was amazing, but he would never catch the Mach 1.

Pressing her foot down on the acceleration pedal, she picked up speed and left Nikoli Kincaid in her rear view mirror.

Chapter Twelve

Nikoli cursed six ways to Sunday as he almost ran up the stairs to Lily's dorm. He had never in his life been outdriven by a girl, and it rankled. Granted, he knew the Mach 1 was faster than the 'Cuda, but still, she shouldn't have been able to smoke him. Her driving skills were better than he gave her credit for. He'd lost sight of her fifteen minutes after they'd pulled out of the gas station. Fifteen minutes! The woman could drive. He'd give her that, grudgingly, but she could damn well drive.

Ignoring all the stares, he strode down her hallway and banged on the door. No answer. What the devil was she doing? His car was outside, so she had to be here. He knocked on the door again, and still nothing.

"She's not in there."

Nikoli turned to see a familiar face. The lusty blonde from yesterday. "Where is she?" he demanded, irritated.

"What do you want with Lily?" she asked.

"I want my damn car keys," he muttered. "Look,

Stacey…"

"Stacey?" Lusty Blonde gasped.

"Suzie?" he tried again.

"Stephanie!" she seethed.

"Where's Lily?" He ignored her outrage.

"None of your business," she told him. "She's not stupid enough to fall for your…"

"Steph?" Nikoli let out a small sigh of relief when he heard Lily's soft voice. "Everything okay?"

"Yeah, fine, just telling jerk-weed here to leave you alone."

Lily laughed. "It's okay, Steph. He's here to get his car."

She opened her door and ushered him inside. She stayed to talk to the girl for a minute, and Nikoli used the time to look around her room. He'd been so focused on her last night, he hadn't really seen anything. There were no pink and purple pillows anywhere as he'd half expected. She didn't really scream girly to him, but most women he knew had a deep affection for pink and purple.

Instead, her comforter was a deep red. She had an oversized beige chair in one corner. Her laptop sat on the desk, a simple desktop lamp beside it. A microwave took up residence on an end table, and a TV, PS4, and DVD player sat on top the chest of drawers the school provided every student. The most telling thing about the room were the books Lily had stacked everywhere. They weren't in your face, but if you went to sit anywhere, you'd be hard pressed not to find a book. She loved books. He filed that little fact away. It might come in handy later.

"Done ogling my room?" she asked, closing the door.

"For the minute. Keys?"

She laughed and fished his keys out of her desk drawer. "She runs like a dream." Tossing the keys to him, she smirked. "Stop being a sore loser and pouting."

He caught the keys and shoved them in his pocket. "I don't pout."

"You're mad because I won," she said, laughter shining in her eyes. "You had to know there was no way your 'baby' could have kept up with the Mach 1. Or did you expect me not to know how to handle a racer since my dad died when I was twelve? Did you think I'd granny drive her because I'd be afraid of the horsepower?"

Well, yeah, he *had* thought that, dammit.

"Sorry, Nikoli. Cars are my thing. I've been driving for forever, and I can handle a car better than you. Guaranteed."

"I wouldn't go that far."

"How old were you when you started driving?"

"Fifteen, why?"

"Three," she said smugly. "Trust me when I say I can handle a stick better than you."

She had to be the sexiest woman he'd ever met. "Hmm...you can handle a *stick* better than me, can you, Lily Bells?"

Her eyes widened, and he watched the blush work its way up her neck to bloom onto her cheeks. The blush started under her neckline. He was going to have fun discovering where it started, and soon.

"I didn't mean it that way, and you know it!" she spluttered.

"Oh, *Milaya*, the things you could do to my stick…"

Lily's eyes widened when Nikoli started to prowl closer to her, his body conveying his intent. She backed away slowly, but soon hit the closet door. Nikoli kept coming. He stopped a bare inch away from her. Her pulse sped up, and she glanced everywhere but at his face.

"Eyes up, Lily." His voice sounded firm, hard, a command, and she automatically looked up. His black eyes burned with a deep, lazy fire that stole the air from her lungs. His warm breath feathered over her face. "Are you okay?"

Lily nodded, surprised he'd asked her. More surprising was the fact she *was* okay. The panic was there, but it was manageable. Instead, different sensations assaulted her. Her breath was a little shallow, butterflies fluttered in her stomach, and she felt her own blood begin to burn with something that she didn't recognize. It didn't scare her, exactly. She felt…excited. Her hands moved restlessly, and she started to fidget.

"Stay still," Nikoli barked, his voice stern. "Don't move, *dushka*."

"I said not to…"

Nikoli put a finger to her lips, but it was gone before she could even process it fully. "Hush, *Milaya*. It's hard enough not to touch you. If you start talking, I *will* kiss you."

DEFCON five started flashing in her head, but her body refused to listen to her. It wanted him to touch her, to kiss her. In this moment, she'd never wanted something as badly as she wanted him to touch her.

He must have seen it in her eyes, because his own breathing came out a little more labored. "Do you want me to touch you, *Milaya*?"

"Yes," she whispered, "but I'm afraid."

"I know," he said, his voice soft, "but I'm very proud of you, Lily. You've come a long way in just a day. You truly are magnificent."

Lily took a shaky breath, his praise washing through her. Nikoli's voice was like velvet, wrapping around her, making her feel things in places she shouldn't. How could just his voice make her want to clench her thighs? Dear God, she was starting to understand how so many women abandoned their clothes because of that Russian accent of his. It could make you imagine all sorts of naughty things.

"Lily…"

Nikoli and Lily both turned to see Adam standing in the doorway, staring in shock at the two of them. It only took a moment for his expression to turn to one of fury. "What the hell are you doing here?"

"Came to pick up my keys," Nikoli replied, turning so Lily was behind him. "No one teach you to knock?"

Adam growled, coming into the room. Nikoli rolled his shoulders, preparing for a fight. He'd like nothing better than to shove his fist in Boy Wonder's face after that shit he'd pulled on Lily last night.

Lily sidestepped Nikoli, and he turned baleful eyes upon her. Didn't the woman know when to stay put?

"Adam, what do you want?" she said, resigned.

"I came to talk to you, to apologize, but I see you are busy doing…"

"Don't," Nikoli said softly.

"You need to get the fuck out," Adam snarled. "I came to talk to Lily, not you."

"But I'm not ready to talk to you, Adam." Lily walked over to the door and motioned for Adam to leave. "What you did…I can't just forget it. At least not yet. I need you to leave."

"Lily, please," Adam begged. "We can't leave it like this…"

"You should have thought of that before you decided to be an ass," Nikoli told him. "Now get out."

"Lily, you can't trust him." Adam begged her with his eyes.

"Right now, I trust him more than I do you."

Adam's face paled, but he nodded. "I'm sorry, Lils, for everything. I'll make this right." He started to leave, but stopped in front of her. "I swear to you I will." He gave her a quick hug, looking sad when her entire body flinched.

Nikoli noticed the flinch. She'd been around him all day and hadn't flinched once. His plan was working. The longer she was around him, and the more he forced her to get used to his touch, the less it scared her. Odd that Adam scared her, though. They'd been around each other since they were little kids. She had to know the feel of him better than anyone else. She even admitted that Adam had tried to help her in the beginning. Maybe the key was she hadn't wanted to be helped back then. She wanted help now. Either way, it was a win-win for him.

Lily was pale when she closed the door. Nikoli had wanted to try to push her a little farther, but he knew that was probably out of the question now. "You want to come over for a while? Luther would love to hear all the details of how you kicked my ass today."

She smiled, but shook her head. "No, I have some stuff I need to do, and I promised some of the girls we'd watch a movie later. Besides, I'm not sure I want to go to your place...ever."

"Why the hell not?" he asked indignantly. What was wrong with his place?

"It can't be at all sterile." Lily shuddered at the thought. "I mean, I've heard the stories about your furniture."

Nikoli grinned his lazy grin. "We are going to have some fun on that furniture too."

She shook her head. "You plan on having me sit, yeah?"

"Sit, bend over, lie down," Nikoli purred. "On the couch, the table, the bed...yes, *Milaya*, you are going to become very intimate with my furniture."

"Not in this lifetime," she said, grimacing. "God only knows what kind of fluids are still there. You want me to come over? Get some new furniture, especially the table."

"You want me to get rid of perfectly good furniture just so you'll come over?"

"I want you to get rid of the nasty furniture

covered in countless diseases."

"It's not covered in diseases." He rolled his eyes. The chick was being ridiculous.

"How often do you clean your couch?" she countered. "Do you scrub your table in bleach afterward? Do you realize you could be eating nasty fluids?"

He frowned. "No."

"So gross, Nikoli. I'm not stepping foot in that place till you clean it. There, or your other place, for that matter."

"Lily, you were just there last night."

"I wasn't thinking about it then!" she yelled. "If you think for one second I'm getting into a bed other women have been in, you're insane!"

He laughed. "I'll buy new sheets." He didn't think she even realized what she'd said and where her thoughts were taking her. If she was talking about getting into bed, his chances just got a whole lot better.

"Not gonna happen, buster!" She pointed her finger at him. "It's the principle of the thing! Every time I look at it, I'll think about all the women who've been in it before!"

Nikoli laughed out loud. She looked offended.

"It's not funny!" she fumed.

"Yeah, Lily Bells, it's funny as hell." His grin only made her more furious, but he didn't care.

"Trust me, Kincaid, I'm not stepping foot in there until you buy some new furniture."

"You're serious, aren't you?"

"Dead serious."

"How would you even know if it's new or not?"

he asked.

"I've been to your apartment before," she told him smugly.

"When?"

"Remember when I tutored Luther?"

He groaned. Luther had been embarrassed about failing one of his classes last year, and Lily must have come by the apartment to help him. She knew what the furniture looked like. Dammit. He was going have to spend money.

"Fine, I'll buy some fucking new furniture. Happy?"

Lily smiled. "Yes, very."

"How happy?" he asked, moving closer to her.

Her eyes narrowed. "Not that happy."

He stopped moving and studied her for a moment. She looked nervous, but the fear and panic from last night weren't in her eyes. He wasn't stupid enough to think it couldn't rear back up if he pushed too hard. All the progress he'd made today would be lost if he didn't do this just right.

"Come here, Lily."

"Why?" She took another step backward.

"Come. Here." He put more force into his words, into his voice.

Lily frowned, but shuffled closer. "What do you want?"

"Here." He pointed to the spot right in front of him. "Don't make me ask again."

He fought a smile at her indignant expression. She didn't like being told what to do. At all. She moved to within inches of him, though, despite the anger in her eyes.

"Was that so hard?" he murmured.

"Depends on why you decided to go all alpha male." Her eyes were warier than they had been a minute ago.

"Patience is only a small part of helping you, Lily," he told her solemnly. "The other part is dominance. You need rules and structures to completely heal."

Her eyes narrowed and he held up his hand to stop her before she said anything. "Last night you were a mess, *Milaya*, crying and nearly going into a panic attack at the thought of my hands on you."

"And?"

"And do you feel that way today?" he asked gently. "Do you feel anxious being this close to me? Do you need to run, to hide, or to flinch away from my touch?"

Her eyes widened slightly.

"The answer is no, *Milaya*. I didn't give you choices today. You spent the day with me, dressed exactly as I wanted you dressed. I helped you decide to touch me by trapping you, distracting you so you couldn't panic. I set the rules for our outing today, and you are stronger, more confident now because of those rules."

"I...I'm not sure what you want me to say." Her eyes were full of questions and uncertainty.

"I don't want you to say anything, *Milaya*," he said, his voice firm. "I just want you to stand perfectly still and remain silent. Don't move, and keep your eyes straight ahead."

He studied her profile. She was nervous, but not nearly as nervous as when Adam left. Deciding to take a chance on pushing her, Nikoli walked over to her closet. She had it partially open, and he'd seen several scarves. He selected the thinnest one he could find. He had much more suitable ones at the apartment, but this would have to do for now.

Lily trembled. She could hear Nikoli behind her rummaging through her closet. She'd heard the sliding door squeak as he pushed it out of his way. Why was he in her closet? The urge to look was strong, but she fought it. Honestly, she was almost afraid to look. She closed her eyes and shifted from foot to foot. She wanted to laugh at the absurdity of the situation. The campus manwhore was in her room, giving her crazy orders, and she was obeying. Why? No clue other than she'd never been in a situation like this before and she was curious. Curious enough to tamp down her own fears for a few minutes.

She felt him standing behind her. Heat radiated from his body into hers. If she stepped back half an inch, she'd hit his chest. Her muscles tightened, panic creeping up. She fought hard to stand still, to not give in to her growing unease. Her phobia had the ability to rob her of everything in seconds. She'd been happy, even laughing a few minutes ago, and now she was beginning to feel afraid. She hated herself sometimes.

"Shh, baby," Nikoli whispered, his warm breath blowing on her ear. She shivered in response, an instinctive reaction. "I'm going to put a scarf over your eyes."

"What? No!"

"Be. Still." His voice wasn't harsh, but it held a

definite command that her body obeyed. "Breathe," he told her. "I'm not going to touch you, *Milaya*. Be easy, sweetheart."

Lily's hands started to shake, but she forced herself to remain still as Nikoli's arms rose up on either side of her. She saw one of her favorite wool scarves come up and then gently cover her eyes. He stepped away from her so he could tie the ends together.

"Easy, *katyonak*." Nikoli's voice came out soothing, but there was still a bite of a command to it. "This is about trust. I told you I wouldn't touch you, and I won't."

Could she trust him? He'd given her no reason not to trust him, aside from his sneak attacks, as he called them. They didn't even bother her anymore. She'd stopped flinching about two hours into the drive this morning to pick up the car. It was then she'd realized she was starting to trust him. She shouldn't, had no reason to, but oddly, she did. Maybe she just *needed* to trust him. Needed to have faith she could get better, that he could help her do it.

Believing it was entirely different from trying to convince her body of it.

She felt him move away from her, heard him walking around her room. What the hell was he doing? Her nerves were strung taught and she strained her ears to try and hear him. Where was he? Her mattress squeaked, and she turned in that direction.

"Did I say you could move?" he asked, his voice full of authority and displeasure.

Lily groaned. She wasn't sure if she liked this side of Nikoli or not, but she had to admit her body reacted to it. It clenched up in all sorts of places it shouldn't. Her nostrils flared and she realized her hands had stopped shaking. Other nerves were crowding her right now, ones that had nothing to do with her fear of being touched.

"Did I?" he asked again, an edge of irritation in his voice.

"No," Lily whispered, trying to understand what she was feeling, but failing miserably.

"Back to your position, *Milaya*."

Lily frowned, but turned back to facing the wall opposite her closet. Nikoli stood up, and she heard him walking again. Anticipation flashed through her, and it only served to confuse her further. Her heartbeat sped up when she felt him in front of her. He was close. She could smell his aftershave. It invaded her senses, causing her breath to get a little more labored.

Why was he just standing there?

His breath tickled her ear. "Do you still want me to touch you, *Milaya*?"

DEFCON three exploded in her senses. Her brain said no, her body said yes. What was happening to her? Every nerve was alert, waiting expectantly for him to touch her. She craved it.

"Answer me."

"I don't know," she almost wailed. She didn't understand anything happening to her right now.

"Shhh, *Milaya*," Nikoli soothed. He knew he couldn't push her too far. This whole thing had been about trust. "Your entire body is quivering, *Milaya*.

Not shaking in fear, but quivering in excitement, anticipation, and you're confused. That's perfectly okay. I'm going to remove the scarf now. Hold still for me."

He carefully untied the scarf, letting it fall from her eyes. Her gaze swept up to look at his face, and his lungs refused to expand. The blue was darker, but they were sleepy, filled with desire. He could see the confusion on her face, but he sensed her excitement in the way her body reacted to his nearness. He forced his hands to stay at his sides.

"Better?" he asked softly.

"I…I don't know," she answered honestly. "Why did you do that?"

"Trust," he said simply. "I wanted to show you that I can be trusted. A woman is at her most vulnerable when she cedes control to a man. You needed to understand that I don't take that trust lightly. I promised I wouldn't touch you, and I kept my word, Lily."

She gave him a hesitant smile.

"Do you want to talk about how it made you feel?" he asked. "You weren't expecting to feel anything but fear, were you?"

"I've never done anything like that," she whispered. "I've read books like that. When a woman gives up control and willingly lets a guy hurt her…"

"Did I hurt you, Lily?" he interrupted her, his voice hard and unyielding. He wouldn't let her think this was like those cheesy erotica novels about BDSM. It wasn't. He didn't hurt women for kinks. He liked control, yes, but to do some of the stuff he'd seen in the clubs he frequented? That wasn't him.

"No," she admitted. "It's just when you said you were going to cover my eyes, I thought…" She shook her head. "I'm not that girl, Nikoli, a…a submissive. The one who lets a man take advantage of her, hurt her, use her for his own satisfaction."

"You've got a skewed perception of the lifestyle, Lily," he said. "It's not about hurting a woman or using her. It's about satisfying needs, about trust, and respect."

"But how is it about respect when you take away someone's control?"

"Lily, you obeyed the commands I gave you today. Why?"

He watched a myriad of emotions cross her face as she tried to articulate her answer. More than anything, the part of him that was the dominant alpha male wanted to hold her, to tell her it was okay, he'd take care of everything, but he couldn't do that with her. She needed to come to grips with her own fears first.

"Can I sit?" she asked, her hands worrying each other. Nikoli smiled. She didn't even realize she'd asked permission. He nodded.

She collapsed onto the bed. "At first, I was curious. Then, it was about trying to overcome the paralyzing fear I felt at the thought of what you might do when I couldn't see it coming."

"But it changed, didn't it, *Milaya*?" He sat down beside her, barely an inch separating their bodies. "You found you wanted to obey, to do as I asked. Your body reacted to my voice, and that confused you."

Lily nodded, not looking at him. "It went from fear to...to anticipation."

Nikoli smiled and pride swelled within him. She was being honest, and that, more than anything, was going to cement his authority and her trust, her submission to him. It had to be hard for her, but she didn't hide from it.

"Look at me, Lily."

She looked up, her face hesitant.

"What you felt was natural. You were curious, your body reacted to the desire you felt. It let you know what it wanted, even when you weren't capable of understanding it. Don't be afraid."

"I'm not afraid of you."

He chuckled. "You should be, *Milaya*. You should be terrified of me."

"I know," she told him, her voice breathy, and his own breathing hitched in reaction. He leaned in closer, his shoulder brushing hers. She gasped, her mouth parting as the sound slipped out. His eyes focused on her lips. They were full, lush, and had inspired all sorts of fantasies the last few days. It would be so easy to lean in and brush her lips with his. She tilted her head up, her eyes questioning.

Nikoli leaned in, so close he could smell the strawberry and vanilla scent of her shampoo and body wash. It drove him slightly crazy every time he was in close proximity to her.

"Would you be okay if I kissed you?" He inhaled the sweet scent of her that was sure to drive him mad.

"Maybe." Lily drew in a ragged breath, but

didn't move away. She moved closer to him, and Nikoli groaned. He'd been fantasizing about her lips all day. Just the thought of actually kissing her nearly sent him over the edge right then.

He lowered his head to hers, his nose brushing hers. She didn't flinch. She went completely still, but she didn't flinch. He heard her gasp, the soft intake of breath. His eyes looked into hers. He saw the desire. Saw the fear, but mostly he saw trust. She trusted him not to force her to do anything she couldn't do. She trusted him not to become angry if she couldn't do it.

That, more than anything else, made Lily Holmes the most dangerous creature he'd ever encountered. She could break him, and he didn't care.

His breath feathered across her lips. He waited. She still hadn't moved, but he could see her fingers tearing at each other. She was scared and nervous. He'd go slowly if it killed him. And it just might. "Are you good, *Milaya*?"

"Yes," she whispered. He could smell the peppermint on her breath.

"Good girl," he said and started to move closer, to close the tiny gap between their lips…

"Lily!" The pounding on the door started seconds after the bellow. Nikoli groaned.

"Ignore it," he pleaded, even as Lily started to move away.

"I can't." She sounded just as frustrated as he did, but she got up and answered the door.

Nikoli sighed and let himself fall backward on her bed. So close. So damn close. He wasn't sure if she'd let him try again. She'd been so nervous to begin with, she might have seen the door as the proverbial bell that saved her. Not kissing her might even set them back in their progress, dammit. She'd get all nervous and start having doubts. He had to keep her in the now, not let her past haunt her.

The two girls at Lily's door kept peeking around her to catch a glimpse of him, and an idea started to form. A grin slid across his face. She wasn't going to remember her own fears. Nope, she was going to remember laughter instead. He sat up and pulled his shirt off. The girls' eyes widened, and one of them stammered. Lily turned her head toward him when the girl in question didn't answer for the third time. Lily's own eyes went round. She glanced from him to the girls, her face flaming. Nikoli chuckled. Well, he'd laugh, anyway. She might go to bed screaming in rage.

He watched as she hurried the girls up and then shut her door, before turning to face him. She stayed where she was, but that was okay with him. He loved watching her reactions.

"What do you think you're doing?" she demanded after a minute.

"Doing?" he asked innocently.

"Put your shirt back on!" She did the whisper shout thing, which only caused him to laugh.

"I don't want to," he told her and then grinned. Her eyes widened. She knew his I'm-up-to-no-good grin. He bounced the bed.

Lily's mouth dropped open in a silent O. He bounced it again, the mattress squeaking.

"Stop that!" She ran over to stand in front of

him. "I mean it, Nikoli, stop it right now. You know they're out there listening."

"Make me." He started to bounce the bed again, harder, forcing the old mattress to groan in protest. Lily looked mortified, and when he groaned loudly, using his hand to knock the headboard against the wall, he thought she might faint.

"This isn't funny!" she seethed. "People are *listening*!"

He knew that. He'd heard the footsteps and the whispering too. He chuckled and bounced the bed faster and harder, his hand forcing the headboard to hit the wall repeatedly. He let out another long, deep moan and said, "Lily…"

She grabbed him and hauled him off the bed, falling with him. He turned mid-fall so his back hit the floor, and she landed on top of him. Her leg landed between his, and it took every ounce of control he had not to hiss. He was hard, and the simple touch actually hurt.

Lily stared nonplussed at him, and Nikoli bit back a groan. She moved and rubbed along his length. "Lily, if you move, I won't guarantee you'll walk away unscathed."

"I…" She shifted, trying to push away from him, and her knee pressed in on him. It was too much. He rolled, keeping her safe until the last minute. She hit the floor and he caged her, careful not to touch her. "I told you not to move," he bit out.

She took a shaky breath, and he could see the panic starting to rise up in her eyes. "Am I touching you, Lily Bells?" he asked. She shook her head. "Then don't panic. I'm not going to touch you."

' "Then will you move so I can get up?" she asked, her voice panicked. "Please, Nikoli...I can't...this..." She started to stutter in her panic.

"No," he said. He saw how afraid she was, but she had to trust him. "I like you caged in, trapped. We've already established earlier today how happy it makes me."

"You're perverse," she stammered, a smile tugging at her lips, despite her unease. He let out a small sigh. She was almost to her breaking point. He could see it in her eyes, feel it in the tenseness of her body.

"I just like making you blush," he told her. "I can't wait to see where your blush starts so I can follow it all the way up, tasting every inch of you as I go."

She took a ragged breath, her eyes wide and panicked. He bent his head and let his nose rub alongside hers for a moment before pulling back.

"You always say you're not going to touch me and then you do," she accused.

"But you like it when I do that, don't you, *Milaya*?"

"Yes," she answered honestly, and Nikoli wanted to fist pump at the small victory. Until he looked into her eyes. Weariness tinged them, and Nikoli became concerned. She'd been through a lot the last few days. As badly as he wanted to kiss her, he couldn't push her any more tonight.

He pushed himself up and off her. Lily scrambled back faster than he would have liked, but at least she didn't move more than a foot away from him. Last night she'd have been on the other side of the room. Progress was progress.

"What time is your first class tomorrow?" he asked, picking his shirt up off the floor.

"Nine."

He tugged it over his head. "I'll swing by and pick you up for breakfast then. There's this little dive I know about ten minutes from campus that serves the absolute best breakfast. Even your frou-frou stuff."

"Frou-frou stuff?" she asked, a laugh escaping.

"Don't think I didn't see you giving Mike all those disgusting looks this morning." He winked. "They serve a lighter breakfast for all the health nuts along with my steak and eggs."

Her nose scrunched up, and he found it adorable. He wanted to slap himself for finding it adorable, but there it was.

"Do they have fresh fruit?" She inched closer to him.

"Barney gets a fresh delivery every morning just for his fruit crepes." Nikoli said, keeping still. He wanted to see what she'd do.

"How many restaurant owners do you know?" Lily moved to within a few inches of him.

"Enough to keep you supplied in good food until we graduate."

Nikoli held his breath as Lily stared, her expression terrified, but determined.

"Promise not to move," she whispered.

"Scout's honor," he said.

She smiled and shook her head. "Put your hand out, palm up."

Nikoli did as she asked and simply waited. She

placed her hand on top of his. Barely. He felt her fingertips mostly, but it was something he didn't think she could do, at least not yet.

"Your hand looks massive next to mine," she murmured. She flattened her hand out and let it sit there on his. He felt it sizzle through every nerve ending in his body like a white hot branding iron. He wanted to pull her close, to kiss her, to tell her how proud he was of her, but he did none of those things. He held himself perfectly still until she pulled her hand away.

"You did good, Lily Bells," he told her. "Very good."

"I didn't know if I could," she said, her voice low and soft. "Thank you, Nikoli."

"For what, *Milaya*?"

"For keeping still? For everything?" Her smile was tired, but she looked happy. "For being the manwhore that you are and making me do something I didn't want to do, even if the girls are already texting everyone that we're..."

He grinned. "Means my car stays with me if they all think you've lost already."

"Not a chance, Kincaid." She grinned right back. "That car is mine."

He laughed and opened the door. There were several girls staring straight at him. "Her virtue is still safe, ladies. Little Miss Prude over there didn't appreciate my joke very much."

"I'm not a prude!" she gasped.

"Have sex with me?"

"*No!*"

"Prude."

"Manwhore!"

The girls in the hallway were giggling like a bunch of twelve year olds, and that was fine with him. He'd done what he needed to and made sure they wouldn't be spreading rumors around about Lily. She was fragile right now, and rumors might destroy all the progress they'd made.

"I'll pick you up at seven, Prude," he reminded her.

"Out!" she shouted, pointing her finger at him.

He chuckled and walked on down the hall to the elevator. Lily was coming along nicely. Yes, indeed.

Chapter Thirteen

Lily stood gazing out the window onto the street below. Traffic crawled by. Downtown Boston was almost as bad as New York City during rush hour. There was a good portion of the city that took the bus or walked. The bus was out of the question for her. She'd gotten Mike to bring her to her shrink's office. After the last few days, she needed to talk. Badly.

The office door opened, and a middle aged man scurried out, looking emotionally battered. She recognized the look, having worn it herself more times than she could count after an office visit with Rebekha.

Dr. Rebekha Purdue popped her head out and smiled at Lily. She was in her mid to late forties, about the age of Lily's mom, with chestnut brown hair and warm brown eyes. She reminded Lily a lot of her mother. Maybe that was why she had connected with her after seeing three other psychiatrists in the greater Boston area when she'd moved here.

"Lily, come in, come in." Rebekha stepped back so Lily could enter. The office was warm and cozy, done in soothing shades of blue and gray, with a random yellow throw pillow nestled on one of the couches.

"Thank you so much for fitting me in." Lily dropped down on the couch nearest the door and grabbed the throw pillow.

"Of course." Rebekha took her seat in the armchair across from Lily. "It's not often you call and ask for an emergency meeting. The last one was a year ago, I believe. Is everything okay?"

She'd been seeing Rebekha twice a week when she'd first started therapy sessions three years ago. Now she was down to a visit twice a month as needed. The last emergency session had been when Brian tried to hug her and she'd flipped out. Hiding her phobia from everyone after that had been impossible. All the guys she'd tutored had become extremely protective of her after Adam explained it to them. That was part of the reason they rode Nikoli so hard over her. Sometimes she thought they'd all adopted her as an honorary little sister.

"I met someone." Lily stared at her fingers twisting the end of the pillow. Rebekha waited for her to go on. She'd learned from the beginning to let Lily talk at her own pace, something Lily truly appreciated. Talking about her feelings and her phobia was hard for her. "He says he can help me learn to deal with my phobia."

"Help you?" Rebekha shifted in her seat and gave her a questioning stare.

Lily spent the next twenty minutes going over

the last few days and told her about Nikoli and his crazy proposition, about all the crazy emotions she'd been feeling, and how Nikoli made her feel.

"That's crazy, right?" Lily finally looked up. "I don't understand why my panic level doesn't skyrocket around him, or why he can touch me when Adam can't."

"It's not crazy at all," Rebekah assured her. "Lily, your phobia is not extreme or as severe as some of the other patients I treat. I have patients who can't even leave their apartment because they are so petrified of physical contact. You are a functioning member of society. You have limits, yes, like cutting your own hair instead of going to a salon, but your fear is a controlled one. You don't let it stop you. Let's look at what we know about your phobia. Your fear is centered more around your family than the general public. You are afraid that showing them love or any emotion through physical contact can somehow cause them harm or even death. You think of Adam as family, don't you?"

"Of course."

"Adam became part of your fear, but Nikoli is new, he's not someone you consider family."

"Still, I shouldn't want him to touch me. I've known most of the football team for years, and I can't even give Mikey a hug. I don't understand what is going on with me. Why is he different?"

Rebehka smiled, and Lily fidgeted. "Maybe he's different because you are attracted to him?"

Lily swept her eyes back down, but she couldn't hide the blush that bloomed on her cheeks. "Only a blind woman wouldn't be attracted to him."

"Lily, this isn't a bad thing. It means you are finally ready to start to forgive yourself. You *want* to get better. It's what we've been talking about for months. This isn't all of a sudden. It's been a long time coming. Your mind needed a way to let you express yourself, to let you touch someone who isn't family, and somewhere in the last few days, you've decided that someone is Nikoli."

Lily groaned and let herself fall back against the cushion. The need to be normal had been driving her nuts for months, especially now that she was graduating college and starting her life. All she wanted was to be normal. Was that where this willingness to let Nikoli touch her came from?

"Tell me about Nikoli," Rebekha encouraged. "You said he's different than Adam. What's so different?"

"He doesn't treat me like I'm his little sister who's going to break apart at the first gust of wind." Lily opened her eyes and looked at the abstract art lining the walls. "There's something else."

"Hmm?"

"Adam...well, Adam and I are not talking right now. He acted like an ass when he found out I was going on a date with Nikoli, and then he...he used my phobia against me to make me feel worthless."

"Why would he do that?" Rebekha kept her face neutral, but concerned.

"Nikoli says he's jealous, and part of me hopes he is. All I've ever wanted is for him to see me."

"His wedding is soon, isn't it?"

"Christmas." Lily stood and paced the room.

"I've wondered if maybe my willingness to let Nikoli touch me is part of that."

"Is it?"

"I don't know." Lily sank back down on the couch. "I just don't know. All I know is I'm confused. Nikoli makes me feel things, want things, things I've never felt or needed from Adam. I love Adam, but what if I'm not *in love* with him? What if I just latched onto the one person who made me feel safe, the person who's always there for me?"

"Maybe this little experiment of yours with Nikoli will help you answer those questions, Lily."

Maybe. Lily had been thinking about this for days. Nikoli sparked a response in her that she'd never felt in Adam's presence. It was probably just lust, but it also said to her that her feelings for Adam may have been morphed into something bigger in her own head. Adam was her constant.

"Do you think we can go back to two sessions a week for a little while?" she asked abruptly. "I feel so out of control right now. All these emotions and sensations are new to me, and I feel overwhelmed."

"Of course, Lily, if you feel you need it." Rebekha smiled at her in such a motherly fashion it made her miss her mother in that instant. Her mama would help her hash this out, but she was miles and miles away in Florida.

"For a little while," she said absently. "Nikoli pushes me, he won't let me hide, but he never pushes me too far, or at least he hasn't yet. I need to talk about it, though. I can't talk to Adam about this, especially not right now."

"Now, tell me how you are feeling in regards to

your argument with Adam." Rebekha moved the conversation back to Adam.

Lily's shoulders sagged. "Adam has always been there, never unkind, always supportive, until I started dating Nikoli. I never knew he could be so cruel. He hurt me more than I can express. He's sorry, but I can't get past what he said to me, how he made me feel."

"Sometimes those we love hurt us more than anyone else, Lily."

Lily fiddled with the cushion again. "I'm trying to forgive him. I need him in my life, even if from a distance. He is the one stable person in my life, the one person who never made me feel guilty about Laney. Sometimes my mom looks at me, and I can still see the pain in her eyes and just a little bit of blame. I don't know if I imagine it or not, but I see it." Lily rubbed her neck, trying to loosen the tension knot. "I've been talking about Laney with Nikoli."

Rebekha's eyebrows went up just a bit. Lily refused to willingly talk about her sister with anyone, but with Nikoli, she found she could talk about her. She wasn't sure why.

"Maybe it's because Nikoli didn't know the two of you, and you feel safe from the doubt and the blame? This is good, Lily. It's progress, a massive step forward in forgiving yourself for her death."

Lily wouldn't go that far, but it was nice to talk to someone about her without any blame or guilt, imagined or real, aimed at her. It helped.

"Time's up, Lily." Rebekha stood. "Stop at the desk and make your next appointment for Friday with Sharon. If you need me, you have my office number and my cell number. I want you to call if you start to feel too out of control. We don't want another repeat of your last incident, but I think you'll be fine. You're stronger than you think."

Lily gave her a small smile and thanked her. She stepped out and waited behind a woman to make her next appointment.

Maybe this really would work. Maybe she could be normal again. There wasn't anything she wanted more than that.

***

Nikoli paced the small apartment like a caged animal. He was sexually frustrated and there wasn't a damn thing he could do about it. Except get surly, which he'd been for the last week. Lily, damn her, grinned when she saw him. She was betting he couldn't last without sex, but he was just as stubborn as she was.

Luther started a betting pool on it. Most people gave him two weeks, tops. Luther gave him a week and three days. He threw a glare at the top of Luther's head over that one.

"You know, if you wear a hole in the carpet, we lose our deposit," Luther said casually, his gaze focused on the game he was playing.

"And?" Nikoli growled.

"Just saying, bro." Luther paused the game and turned to face him. "It's only been a little over a week and you're ready to explode. You need to de-stress."

"You're not winning the pool, Luther," he said, his glare hot enough to singe what little hair was on his friend's head.

"Hey, man, I'm just saying you need to de-stress. Why don't you go out and have a few? I'll even come keep you company."

"No," Nikoli snapped. "If I do that, I'll end up fucking someone."

"Then go pace in your own fucking room," Luther snapped back. "It's getting on my nerves."

Nikoli flipped Luther off and stalked to his room, slamming the door. Damn, but he was in a foul mood. Who the hell knew going without sex could cause this much irritability? Porn wasn't even helping. Well, not much. He sat down at his desk and stared at the computer screen. He should be programming, but he was too wired.

He trolled his Facebook page for a few minutes before giving up and dragging out his phone. Lily's face appeared when he pulled up her contact information. He just stared and felt himself get even harder. Damn, this girl was messing with him in more ways than should be possible. He missed her. It was odd. He'd never missed anyone before, except his family, but certainly not a girl.

His Skype pinged and he glanced over to see his brother Viktor had sent him a photo of him and his new girl. Vik was the only one of his brothers who'd had a relationship with a girl for longer than a week. The rest of the brothers thought he was weird, willing to tie himself down to one girl.

Lily made him wonder what it would be like to be tied down to one girl, and even though it set off alarm bells, he found himself thinking of it more and more. She was unlike any girl he'd ever met. She knew cars maybe even better than he did. Sexy as hell *and* she could keep him interested in an actual conversation for more than five minutes.

He glanced from his phone to his open Skype and back to his phone. Why didn't he have her on Skype? He grinned. Maybe seeing her on cam would alleviate some of his irritability. Hell, just seeing her get riled and irritated as much as he was might help. He enjoyed getting her all worked up and spitting fire at him.

First he searched her name, and there were too many hits to even sort through. He tried her email with no results. Frowning, he sent her a text.

Nikoli: What's ur Skype name?

Lily: What makes u think I have Skype?

Nikoli: FFS, who doesn't have Skype?

Lily: Me?

Nikoli: LILY!

Lily: Fine. Arabella.

Nikoli: Arabella?

Lily: Game account.

A game account? She was a gamer? He'd never

seen the name. She probably played those girly Facebook games. Farmer Lily. He chuckled at the thought as he searched Arabella. Six popped up.

Nikoli: Which 1?

Lily: Girl with the finger to her lips.

Her Skype had a provocative picture? So many things about her didn't make sense to him. She had a severe issue with being touched, but her Skype profile picture oozed sex? He shook his head and sent her a contact request.

And waited.

And waited.

Nikoli: FFS, Lily, accept the damn request.

Lily: My Skype isn't on.

He rolled his eyes in frustration and let out a long-suffering sigh.

Nikoli: Then open the fucking program!

Lily: Hold your damn horses.

Nikoli: I'm about 2 come over there.

Lily: Sheesh!

His eyes roamed back to the screen to see she accepted, but her status was set to away. His eyes narrowed. Such a liar. Her Skype had been on the whole time; she'd been messing with him.

He hit video call and waited and waited and waited until it hung up. Damn that woman. He opened the Skype chat box.

Nikoli: Answer the damn call!

Lily: Busy.

Nikoli: I'm getting in my car and coming over there right now.

He hit the video call button again, and she answered before the first ring finished. Her irritated face greeted him, and he laughed. She looked pissed.

"What the hell do you want, Nikoli?" she asked. "I'm trying to study."

"I just wanted to see your smiling face," he said, the laughter in his voice apparent. She sounded so grumpy.

"There, you've seen it, I need to…"

"Now, now, my little prude," he interrupted. "It's either talk with me here, or I come pick you up. Your choice."

The glare she gave him rivaled the one he'd just leveled at Luther.

"Fine," she huffed. "What do you want to talk about?"

"You."

"Me? Why?"

"You're a fascinating girl, Lily." That was an

understatement. "Stand up."

"Why?"

He sighed. "Lily, don't argue, just do as you're told."

Lily stood up and his mouth went a little dry. She had on an old *Metallica* tee shirt and a scrap of white lace panties. Damn. He shouldn't have asked that, but he was curious to see what she wore to bed.

"Well, at least you're not wearing granny panties like I assumed," he said. "You're a lace girl, huh?"

She sat back down and nodded. "Yeah. I don't like to feel anything else against my skin. Why would you think I wore granny panties?"

He laughed. "Because you are a prude, Lily."

"Says the manwhore," she quipped and tossed her heavy hair over one shoulder. "I bet Luther's pissed."

Of course she knew about the pool going around. "He tried to get me to go drinking tonight."

"Mikey thinks you'll last three weeks. He's being generous."

"And what about you, Lily Bells? How long do you think I'll last?"

She smiled, and it lit up her face. "I think you'll go the distance."

"Why's that?"

"You want to keep your car as much as I want it."

Hell yes, he was keeping his baby. He kicked off his shoes and stretched. While the bulge in his pants wasn't going anywhere, the sound of her voice calmed him. It took the edge off. That irritated him, but he wasn't going to complain.

A knock at Lily's door interrupted them, and he watched as she got up and opened it. He couldn't see around her, but he did hear several girls. They sounded agitated. Lily was shaking her head, and he chuckled at the sound of the girls' raised voices. Being a floor advisor had to be an adventure in and of itself.

"What was that about?" he asked when she sat back down.

"Nothing," she said, pulling a book in her lap. "Just teenage girls being teenage girls."

"How long have you been a floor advisor?"

"Since sophomore year." She flipped several pages and wrote something down on her notepad.

"Why?"

"Because it pays for my room and board," she told him, looking up. "After my dad died, it was hard financially, and then when Laney died, it got worse. After Mom married Dave, it got better, but she couldn't afford to send me to college. I had to pay for it with grants, loans, and scholarships."

Here was a girl who understood hard work and paying your own way. Another first for him. Most of the girls he knew wanted people to do everything for them. His respect for Lily went up a notch.

"Why do you call me Lily Bells?"

"I don't know." He shrugged. "It just popped in my head that first day. Besides, it suits you."

"My name is Lily Isabella Holmes. I wasn't sure if you knew that or not, and if you did, how you found out."

"Nope, sorry, I didn't know that."

She shoved her glasses on, and he burst out laughing. She had these old fifties-style black rimmed glasses that screamed nerd. She wound her hair up in a loose knot and settled back, getting comfortable.

"Appreciate the nerdy bookworm," she told him.

"Oh, I am. She's sexy as hell." It was true. Even with those awful glasses on, she was still gorgeous and sexy sitting there in her t-shirt and lace underwear. It made him want to take the scrap of material in his teeth and strip it off her slowly.

"Tell me about Laney." He needed to distract himself from that thought or he'd never get to sleep.

"What...why?" she asked, her eyes wide.

"Because, *Milaya*, part of your problems stem from what happened to your sister. You feel guilty. Talking about her will help."

• "What do you want to know?" she asked cautiously.

"Whatever you want to tell me."

Lily stared at Nikoli's face and frowned. Talking about her sister wasn't going to help. It might make it worse. Anytime she thought of her twin, she always got depressed and lonely. She missed her more than anything and wished she could take back that awful day. Talking about Laney hurt.

What if he was right, though? What if not talking about her was part of the problem? Rebekah seemed to think talking about Laney was helping her to forgive herself, and it was easier to talk to him than anyone else about her sister.

"You remember I told you Laney and I were twins?"

165

He nodded and waited for her to continue.

She smiled. He was as patient with her as her psychiatrist was. Her fingers caught the hem of her t-shirt and started twisting. "When we were little, we did everything together, even finished each other's sentences. Very twinish. She was a mama's girl, though, and I was strictly a daddy's girl. Our personalities were so different, it didn't matter that we were identical. Anyone could tell us apart." A grin lit up her face. "Unless we didn't want them to."

"You two were devils, weren't you?" Nikoli asked. His laugh filled the room.

"Terrors," she agreed, smiling. "My grandpa used to swear in frustration every time he watched us. We always talked him into doing things our parents said no to."

"How was she different from you?"

"I was the quiet one with her nose either in a book or buried under the hood of a car. Not Laney. She had this bigger than life personality that drew all kinds of people to her. Everyone loved her. She was kind and sweet, but loud and boisterous too. Always the center of attention. The epitome of what a girl was—she loved shopping, purple was her favorite color, she loved cooking, fashion, you name it. If it was girly, Laney adored it."

Lily paused and closed her eyes, flashes of her sister's smiling face assaulting her. A tear leaked out at the pain that hit her in the gut. God, she missed Laney. So much. Missed the long talks they used to have, the sound of her laugh. Pain ripped through her and she almost doubled over from the force of it.

"*Milaya*, it's okay to hurt, to grieve," Nikoli said softly. "It's how we deal with loss and move on. If you don't let yourself grieve for your sister, you'll never get better."

"I miss her," Lily told him, her eyes closed. "Every day. It feels like there is this big hole where she was. We were twins, two halves of the same whole. I always knew what she was thinking, what she was feeling. Now that's gone. I'm empty inside, Nikoli. So empty. And every damn bit of it is my fault. If only I hadn't been such a stupid…"

"Lily," he interrupted her. "Your sister loved you, didn't she?"

"Yes."

"Then do you think she'd want you to keep blaming yourself? How would it make her feel knowing you were putting yourself through so much pain, when what happened to her was an accident?"

"No."

"Then start to forgive yourself. From everything you've said, I know your sister would have forgiven you a long time ago. Neither of you had any idea that car was around the corner. Had you known, you'd have done everything to get to her, to save her. She knows that, and I guarantee she wouldn't hold you responsible for what happened. It was an accident, *Milaya*, a tragic accident, and not your fault."

Lily wiped her tears. Laney wouldn't want her to be in this shape, but it was going to take more than a pep talk from Nikoli to make Lily forget what she'd done to her sister. She was starting to heal, even she realized that. Maybe it was just time, or maybe it was because of Nikoli. Either way, she was getting better. Talking with Rebekha had helped her come to that conclusion.

"Tell you what," Nikoli said. "Every day, starting tomorrow, I want you to tell me something new about Laney. Tell me about some adventure you two went on, the pranks you pulled, anything you want to tell me about the happy memories you had with Laney. Can you do that?"

She nodded. She could do that.

"What are you doing Saturday?" he asked.

"Studying?"

"Nope." He shook his head. "We're going shopping."

"Shopping?"

"You did tell me you weren't stepping foot in either of my apartments until I switched the furniture."

Lily shuddered thinking about all the gross fluids that had to be in his apartment.

"We're going furniture shopping. Then you are going to help me and Luther move it all in."

"You're really going to get brand new furniture?"

"Just think of all the new memories we can make...you bent over the couch, laying on the kitchen table, your legs wrapped around me, tied to my bed while I kiss every inch of your skin."

Lily felt the blush start to heat her cheeks, and she watched Nikoli's eyes sweep her face and then follow the blush down to her shirt.

"Take off the shirt for me?" he asked.

"No!"

"I just want to see where the blush starts, *Milaya*." His grin turned evil. "I'm in my apartment and you're in your dorm room. You're perfectly safe."

"*No*," she said adamantly. "I am not giving you a boob show."

Nikoli laughed at her outraged tone. He loved getting her riled up, like a virgin who's never even thought of a naked man before. He loved her outrage. It was refreshing.

"Lily, I'm not asking for Skype sex, I'm just asking for you to take off your shirt. Here, watch me take off mine." He reached down and pulled his own shirt over his head and tossed it to the side. "See how easy that is?"

"I'm still not taking my shirt off." She laughed, her eyes tracing his tattoos.

"Such a prude," he said.

"Yup," she agreed. "No boob show for you, Kincaid."

"What do you want for breakfast?" he asked, changing the subject. If he teased her much more, he might really go over there, as hard as he was right now.

"Um, I hadn't thought about it?"

"There's this new place that opened a few blocks away from the Italian place you love. It's only open for breakfast. I thought we might go check it out."

"Sure," she agreed, "but if they only serve heavy breakfast food, you're stopping somewhere so I can get a yogurt or something."

"Yogurt is boring, Lily Bells. Why not try something else, like biscuits and gravy?"

"I'm from the south," she reminded him. "Biscuits and gravy is a staple where I'm from. If I didn't eat it growing up, I'm not eating it now."

"That's too bad," he said. "I would have loved to pour the gravy over your belly and lick it clean."

Her gasp was loud, and he chuckled. He'd shocked her again.

"You think about sex too much," she said after a minute, her voice just a little breathy.

"You can never think about sex too much," he countered. "You, my prude, don't think about it enough."

"You're an ass."

"I'm your ass, though." He grinned wickedly.

She shook her head. "I'm hanging up now. I really do have to study. I have a test in the morning."

"Fine, Lily Bells, I'll let you escape back to your studying, but I'll swing by at six to pick you up. I have class at eight, so we need to go early."

"That means I have to get up even earlier to take a shower, dammit."

"Deal with it. Good night, *Milaya*."

"Good night, asshat." She disconnected the call, and he laughed. God, that girl was something else.

***

"I hate you, Lily."

Lily grinned at Luther and flipped him off as she carried in the table lamp.

‡ "Man up, Luther," Janet said. "You're the only one complaining."

"Easy for you to say," he grumbled. "We're doing all the heavy lifting."

Mike shot him a warning look. Lily only laughed. She'd love to see Janet go all Terminator on his ass. Luther needed a good kick in the rear anyway. He really had been complaining all day.

"I wouldn't," Adam whispered. Lily was close enough to hear him. "If you get her started, she'll never shut up."

Luther gave him a horrified look and ran back out the door to see what else needed to come up the three flights of stairs.

Lily had been surprised Adam volunteered to come help them move furniture. When he'd shown up with Mike and Janet, she'd almost told him to leave. Except they needed the help. Nikoli meant it when he said he was getting new furniture.

Goodwill had come by this morning and picked up every piece of furniture they owned, except for what was in Luther's bedroom. Nikoli had dragged them both to several furniture stores after renting a U-Haul. He'd made Luther follow them in his car so she wouldn't have to freak out over having to sit between them. She couldn't handle that, and she knew it. Apparently, so did Nikoli.

Adam and Mike sat down the sectional in front of the TV. The fabric was a soft, dark beige and went well with the pale walls. Lily had picked it out not based on the color, but on sleep worthiness. She'd stretched out on several in the store and rolled around, testing comfort. This one was the softest, but had just a little resistance so you could nap with ease.

Nikoli tossed the red throw pillows at her and shouted, "Drinks in the fridge, guys. Grab a cold one before we go after the next load."

Janet took a long swig of water and then whispered to Lily, "Why did he buy new furniture?"

"I refused to set foot in the place until his disease-covered filth was gone," she said, not bothering to lower her voice.

Nikoli just smiled wanly and chugged his beer.

"Why do you think I don't sit when I go over to Mike and Adam's frat house?" Lily said, her expression scrunching up in disgust. "Just think about all the bodily fluids in *that* place."

"Ewwww." Janet looked disgusted. "I never thought about that."

"We clean," Mike defended.

"With bleach?" Lily asked. "And on every surface?"

"Well, no…"

"Not clean!" Janet did her grossed out dance. "I'm not going back there ever again."

Mike shot Lily a what-have-you-done look, and she smiled. "Deal with it, Michealangelo."

Luther let out a groan, and they all turned to see him sitting on the couch, a look of utter joy on his face. "Oh. My. God. I could live here."

"Off the couch!" Lily demanded.

"What? Why?"

"Because it's brand new and you're dirty, sweaty, and you stink," Lily told him.

"It's my damn couch," he grouched, but moved

172

when he saw the look of promised pain Lily aimed at him. Instead, he rambled over to the fridge, which Nikoli had replaced the day before. The fact he'd replaced it made Lily shudder at the thought of what might have happened there.

Nikoli grabbed the drink out of Luther's hand. "Nope, man, not yours. These are Lily's." He walked over and handed her the can of cherry Dr. Pepper.

"I like those too!" Luther protested.

"Don't touch 'em," Nikoli warned, his voice hard.

"How did you know these are my favorites?" Lily asked, perplexed. She'd never told him.

"Every time we go out to eat, it's the first thing you ask for." Nikoli shrugged like it wasn't a big deal. "Not hard to figure out."

"Thank you, Nikoli," she said softly.

He nodded and went back to the fridge to get a beer. He'd started to regret the arrangement he'd made with her. Not because he didn't want to help her, but because he could feel himself changing, and it bothered him. He found himself doing little things for her, like making sure his fridge was stocked with her favorite drink, or walking her to every class even when it made him late for his own.

Lily appreciated the smaller gestures as opposed to the grand ones. It was something he'd figured out about her over the last two weeks. The smile she'd given him over the can of pop was enough to make his stomach do a little flip of its own. It disturbed him that she had this kind of effect on him, but at the same time, it was a new feeling, and one he liked. He snorted at his own indecision. The girl was really starting to get to him.

Adam pulled out a chair for Lily at the table, and Nikoli's eyes narrowed. His first instinct had been to beat the shit out of Boy Wonder and send him packing, but Lily hadn't told him to get lost, so Nikoli held his tongue. Adam had been useful at least, lugging more than his fair share up the stairs.

Janet wandered over and turned on the radio. Maroon 5's "Sugar" blared out of the speakers. "Ohhh, I *love* this song!"

"Make the karaoke champ sing," Mike said, his eyes vengeful.

"No." Lily shook her head.

"Karaoke champ?" Nikoli asked, brow arched questioningly.

"Girl can sing," Adam confirmed. "She sings good too."

"This I have to hear."

"Uh, no," Lily refused. "Not gonna happen."

"Aww, come on, Lils," Adam cajoled. "Sing for us."

"You first," she said, a wicked smile spreading across her face. "Only fair the runner up goes first."

Adam opened his mouth and started to sing along to the lyrics. Nikoli stared, open-mouthed. Boy Wonder had a decent voice. Lily laughed at Adam's antics as he danced around the living room. He tossed her the remote control, and she started to sing with him, belting out the song. Their voices blended well, and it was obvious to anyone they'd sung together a lot.

His mouth went a little dry when Lily stood up

and started to dance with him. The next song that came on was "Worth It" by Fifth Harmony. Her dance turned from fun and flirty to sensual and just a little dirty. Oh damn. His eyes followed her hips as they swayed and grinded.

Fuck. She said she loved to dance, but…fuck. His mouth watered when she went down and her hips did a little circle on the way back up. He barely suppressed a groan when she did some kind of wicked shimmy. Where did the woman learn to dance? If she kept this up, he was throwing them all out, and Lily was going to get her next lesson in controlling her fear. Fuck, he was hard. Glancing up, he caught Luther staring and punched him in the arm. "Eyes up," he growled.

Nikoli swung his own eyes back to Lily and noticed Adam had gotten closer to her, dancing, his hips insinuating, grinding against hers, and a stab of jealousy struck him. What the hell? As much as he tried to deny it, the closer Adam got to her ass, the more he wanted to beat the little shit. Lily hadn't noticed how close Adam was to her. She was having fun, and Nikoli moved closer, ready to intervene if necessary.

Lily laughed to herself when she caught Nikoli almost drooling. He'd tortured her for two weeks, and now it was her turn for a little payback. His eyes followed her hips, watched her ass bounce to the rhythm of the song, and she smiled, turning and moving with the grace of a cat.

Someone moved against her and she stilled, the song dying. Adam. She knew it because Nikoli looked furious. Her muscles tensed and she worked to control the tremors that started in her hands. Panic started in the pit of her stomach, and when Adam shifted his body, coming fully against her, his arms encircling her waist, she couldn't stop her reaction. She jumped away from him and backed up until she hit the kitchen island. Eyes wide, she stared at him and fought to gain control.

He looked hurt, but dammit, he knew not to touch her. Her breathing sped up and she sank down to the floor as the panic attack took hold. She tucked her head between her legs and tried to breathe, tried to remember no one could hurt her.

"What the fuck do you think you're doing?" Nikoli roared, and she winced. She couldn't breathe. Oh, God, she couldn't breathe. She felt more than saw Janet hovering. Janet saw her have one of her attacks last year when Brian tried to hug her after she'd helped him pass his English class. He'd been so sorry, when he'd done nothing wrong.

"I thought she was getting better," Adam said quietly.

"She was." The anger in Nikoli's voice was deafening. "If you've set that back, I swear…"

"Nikoli," she whispered and hoped he could hear her.

He was there in an instant, kneeling. "*Milaya*, be easy. You're safe."

His voice sounded calm and soothing, but when his fingers grazed over the top of her head, she couldn't stop the whimper. "Don't, please." She couldn't. His touch right now only set off panic. "Don't touch me…I can't…I…"

"Shh, *katonyac*, I'm not going to touch you."

176

Lily saw him stand and stalk over to Adam. He grabbed him by the front of his shirt and hauled him close, his fist rearing back to strike.

"Don't," she whispered, tears pooling in her eyes. "Please don't, Nikoli."

She lifted her head enough to see his arm pulled back, the muscles so tight, they looked ready to snap. Instead, he threw Adam like he was a rag that you tossed in the kitchen sink.

"Get out, all of you."

She heard Janet protesting, but it was useless. He emptied the room and walked over to the radio to turn it down. He didn't cut it off, just lowered the volume. Then he grabbed a bottle of water from the fridge and sat down in front of her, a good foot between them. He set the bottle of water down where she could reach it.

"Easy, *dushka*," he murmured. "You're safe."

Her lungs felt like they were closing in on her, and her vision got blurry. "I…I can't breathe," she gasped.

"Close your eyes," he told her, his voice calm. "Listen to the sound of the music and don't think about anything but the words to the song. Sing them in your head, *dushka*. Just listen to the music and relax."

Lily closed her eyes and listened to the song that was playing on the radio. John Legend's "All of Me" drifted through the room. She let the soft melody invade her mind and began to hum along. Her breathing slowed down as she hummed along to the lyrics. The song itself was soothing, and she started to relax.

Her eyes popped open and she looked at Nikoli in surprise. The panic was still there, but she could breathe. How had he known to do that?

"Do you remember I told you my dad was in the army?" he asked and continued when she nodded. "He has PTSD, post-traumatic stress disorder. He used to have panic attacks all the time after he came home from his last assignment. It was right before he sent me and Callum to live with our uncle. My mom used to calm him down with music. I thought it might help you too. *Is* it helping?"

She nodded. It was helping. Her body was still stiff as a board, but her breathing was almost normal. She felt embarrassed too. She'd thought she was getting better, but all it took to send her scurrying away like a coward was a simple touch from Adam. He'd tried to wrap his arms around her, and that was it. Full blown panic mode kicked in, and she'd run.

"Hey, hey, no crying now, *Milaya*," Nikoli soothed when he saw the tears falling from her eyes. She wiped them away, but couldn't stop the tide.

"I'm sorry." She hiccupped.

"Sorry? What do you have to be sorry for?"

"You've been working so hard to help me, and it's not working. I'm sorry you're wasting your time."

"Hey, now, *dushka*, getting you better isn't something that is going to be accomplished in a week or two, or even in a month. We can take this as slow as you need to. I'm not upset that you had a bad moment. Boy Wonder shouldn't have just up and grabbed at you. You weren't expecting it, and that's why you got scared. That's going to happen, Lily, but you *are* getting better. Don't doubt that."

"What does *dushka* mean?" she asked. She always forgot to look it up.

"Nope, Lily Bells, I'm not telling."

She shook her head and sat up, reaching for the water bottle. She took a cautious sip. Last time this happened, she'd thrown up. She had no desire to puke all over Nikoli's new furniture, especially after scolding Luther.

"You are not what I expected," she murmured after a minute.

"What do you mean?"

"Well, you are, but you're different too." She thought about how to word what she wanted to say. "You're brash and you have this fuck off attitude, but you're also kind and patient. I didn't expect that from you."

Nikoli watched the confusion consume Lily's expression and had to admit he was just as confused as she was. Normally, he did have a fuck off attitude and would go on, but not with Lily. Sure, he wanted her in a bad way, but he also had this inane urge to help her, to give her back everything she'd lost. He couldn't explain it, but Lily mattered to him. In just two weeks, she'd gone from a fuck bet to someone he cared about.

"Don't say that out loud." He laughed to cover his own emotions. "I have a reputation to uphold. Now, what do you want for dinner? I'm starving. I'm going to feed you and then take you home."

"What about the furniture?"

"Don't worry about it. Luther and I will get the

179

rest of it up later tonight. Now, what do you want to eat?"

"Cuban?" she asked, her voice hesitant.

"Sure. Joe's always happy to see you come in. You go on and get cleaned up. I'll deal with everyone outside, okay?"

She nodded and stood up. He watched her until she closed the bathroom door and then headed out to talk to everyone. Damn Adam. Boy Wonder had to always go and fuck everything up. No more.

They all waited outside, grouped around the U-Haul. He went straight for Adam, but Mike blocked his access.

"Take it easy, man. You do him any damage and Lily might not forgive you. She loves the idiot."

"I'm not going to hit him," Nikoli promised. Mike didn't budge. Smart man.

Adam glared at him from angry and belligerent eyes. The man was so jealous he couldn't see straight. It was a feeling Nikoli himself was becoming accustomed to. "You fucking go near her again, and you won't walk away from it."

"She's my best friend." The anger rolled off Adam in waves.

"Then why *the fuck* would you do that?" Nikoli exploded. "You know how she is."

"I've seen you touch her," Adam said through clenched teeth. "I thought she was okay, that she was better…"

"She's not better!" Nikoli interrupted. "She only lets me touch her because she *trusts* me."

"And she doesn't trust me?" Adam shouted.

"Obviously not," Nikoli yelled over Mike's

shoulder.

"Calm the fuck down!" Luther intervened before Adam could say anything. "It was a mistake. Let's all just calm down and move on."

Nikoli snapped his mouth shut, his fist needing to hit something, Boy Wonder's face his first choice. Luther was right, though. As angry as Lily was with Adam, she did love him. He'd been her best friend since she was a little girl. For that reason, he wouldn't screw his face up.

"Stay the fuck away from her," he warned, his voice hard. "She needs to heal, and she can't do that with you acting like a jealous fool."

"I'm not jealous of you," Adam denied hotly.

"You're acting like a jealous ass, Adam," Mike piped in.

Adam shot him a glare, but kept his mouth shut.

"I'm taking Lily to eat to try and calm her down," he said and turned to go back inside. "Mike, keep him the hell away from me and from Lily, or I won't be held responsible for what happens to him."

He left them with that and went to check on Lily.

***

Joe's was packed as always, but he managed to squeeze them into a booth near the back. It was a little more private than some of the tables where they'd been seated when they came here, and Lily was grateful. She wasn't up to having everyone stare at her. The lighting back here was dimmer, so it was a little harder for people to see her splotched face.

181

She looked around and settled into the booth. The warmth of the place always relaxed her. The warm tones of the wood and the subtle touches of the Cuban culture gave the place a relaxed, fun feel. Joe's booming voice as he greeted people made her smile. He'd taken one look at her and leveled a baleful expression at Nikoli, who just shook his head and demanded a table.

"Tell me about Joe," she said softly, watching him move around the restaurant.

"What about him?"

"How do you know him?"

"I eat here," he said, his eyes not meeting hers.

She gave him a "duh" look. "Yes, but *how* do you know him?"

He didn't want to get into this, at least not tonight. It might scare her. Not that he was hardcore into the lifestyle or anything, but she'd had enough of a scare already. "Does it matter?"

"Yes," she told him. "I remember the first time we were here, the two of you seemed so…territorial almost. It made me curious."

"Joe took me under his wing when I first came to Boston," he said after a minute. Lily was going to keep asking, might as well tell her. "He and I share the same kind of needs in the bedroom."

"Oh my God, you're bisexual!" She clapped a hand over her mouth, her expression so shocked it would have been funny if she hadn't been staring at him, a little horrified.

"No. I. Am. Not!" Nikoli spewed the words.

She just stared at him, eyes wide. "It's fine if you are, Nikoli."

182

"Of course it would be fine," he said, his voice low. "There's nothing wrong with it, but I'm not into guys."

"Hmmm…"

"Look, I'm serious, Lily. If anyone wants to make that life choice, that's their call. My brother Connor is bisexual, so trust me, I'm *fine* with anyone who makes that choice. It's just not one I'd make."

Wow. Lily hadn't expected that. Or that he'd be so Zen about it either. "That's cool your family supports his choice."

"I didn't say that," he said, a wry smile decorating his face. "My brothers and I are close, and while all of us may not agree with his choices, we do support it. My parents and my grandparents? They were all raised Catholic, and if they knew about Conner's choice of partners, they wouldn't be so happy."

"I know you said you supported him, but how do you feel about it?" She was curious. He'd sounded so outraged when she'd accused him of being bisexual.

"He's my brother," he said after a minute. "I want him to be happy, and it doesn't matter to me who he's with, as long as he's happy. Right now he's in a relationship with a girl, but who knows, a couple months from now he might be banging some dude. What do I care, as long as my brother is happy?"

Here was another facet to the manwhore she never suspected might exist buried under that fuck you attitude. He just kept surprising her.

The smile that broke across Lily's face made him stop breathing. Her entire face lit up like an angel shining her grace upon him.

"So back to Joe," she said, her smile still in place. "Where did you two meet? Here at the restaurant?"

"No, I met him at Bastian's," he continued. "It's a sex club."

She didn't looked shocked at that, which irritated him.

"Joe saw that I needed control in sexual situations, but back then, I wasn't so good at it. I fumbled a lot. Joe took me under his wing and taught me how to have that control and still make sure the woman came out as satisfied as I was."

"So, what he and you…" She trailed off and wiggled her eyebrows at him.

"No!" he hissed. "I'm not into men. I already told you that. They don't do a thing for me."

"So then what did he do exactly?"

"He and I shared women," Nikoli told her. "He showed me how to control the situation, how to be the person I am in the bedroom today. He showed me how to be dominant and gain submission. Some of the things we've seen at Bastian's…" He shook his head, disgusted. "Neither Joe or I are into pain. I mean some people are, and that's fine if that is what they need, but I would never hurt a woman. It gives me no pleasure. It's why Joe decided to help me. He saw that I was struggling with how to be dominant without hurting someone. We've been friends since that first night, but we've been like brothers for a long time."

184

"Ah, here is my beautiful girl," Joe's voice interrupted them. "Now, tell me, what has Nikoli done to cause my girl to cry?"

Lily looked up to see the concern and the anger in Joe's face. She wondered what was going through his head. He seemed so upset she'd been crying. She and Nikoli had been in together several times over the last few weeks, and Joe had taken to calling her his girl. It always rankled Nikoli, and now she was beginning to see why. They'd shared women before. What did that say about his feelings for her? Did he even have any?

"Nikoli didn't do anything," she said. "I was upset about something, and he made it better."

"A soul as beautiful as yours should never have cause to cry," Joe told her, smiling. A low growl emanated from Nikoli, which he ignored. "Anyone who would hurt you will answer to me."

"That's my job, Joe." Nikoli's voice came out low, hard, and cold.

"And did whomever did this answer for it?" Joe turned his attention to Nikoli.

"Yes."

That one simple word satisfied Joe, and his smile returned. "*Bueno*. Now, I have a special today, something that isn't on the menu normally. Would you like to try it?"

"What is it?" Nikoli asked suspiciously, which caused Joe to burst out laughing.

"The last time I convinced him to try something, it burnt his mouth so badly, he drank three gallons of water," Joe explained when he saw Lily staring at them curiously. "He doesn't trust me now."

185

"So what are you wanting us to try?" she asked, smiling at Nikoli's disgruntled expression.

"*Es estofado de carne.*"

"Beef stew?" she asked.

"Well, it's more complicated than a simple beef stew." Joe winked. "Think beef stew, but Cuban style."

"Bring it on." She laughed. "I'm willing to try it."

"*Excelente.*" Joe grinned. "I'll bring you both a bowl of it."

Nikoli muttered something Lily didn't quite catch, but it made her laugh, which earned her a glare. She smiled all the more at his exasperated expression. She was feeling more like herself now. Her muscles had relaxed, and she wasn't ready to run screaming for the door. Nikoli had kept his word too. He hadn't attempted to touch her in any way. He never lied to her. Maybe that was part of why she trusted him, part of why she never had a panic attack when he touched her. It was weird, and she didn't really understand it, but as Adam always said, it was what it was.

"So, Luther said you guys were gonna work on the Mach 1 this week. Your race is coming up soon, isn't it?"

"Yeah, it's about a month away. It doesn't need much work, but we want to modify the engine just a little more than it is."

"Do you want some help?"

Nikoli's eyes snapped up and he saw her smiling at him. Was she serious?

"You really want to get all dirty and greasy?" he

186

asked.

She laughed. "I'm more comfortable under the hood of a car than anywhere else. My dad taught me, and I just kept learning even after he died. Adam has had enough junkers over the years to keep me on my game."

Nikoli grinned at the image of Lily under the hood of his car, her ass sticking out for him to admire. He started to get ideas about lessons he could teach her involving his car.

"Love to have you help," he said with a grin that had her narrowing her eyes. Before she could say anything, Joe brought their food. He set it down with a wink. "I also brought a carafe of cold milk just in case it's too hot for Niki boy there."

Lily snickered, and Nikoli gave her a menacing look. His mouth was not meant to be scorched so bad all his taste buds were burned off. "Go ahead. Take a bite, *dushka*."

"How many times do I need to tell you not to call me that?" she asked, irritated.

He only nodded toward the bowl of soup. It smelled delicious, but he knew better. He could see the chilis floating in it.

She scooped up a bite and shoved it in her mouth. He watched her for the first signs of the hot chilis assaulting her tongue, but she only closed her eyes as a look of intense pleasure came over her. His eyes widened when she took another spoonful into her mouth, "Mmmmm...this is delicious, Joe."

Nikoli frowned and took a bite of the rich stew himself. It was delicious, but no sooner had he swallowed than the fire ripped through his mouth. He glanced at Lily and saw her taking another bite. She hadn't touched her drink or her milk. He turned a suspicious look on Joe. Had the man added more chilies to his bowl than he had Lily's?

"Something wrong, Nikoli?" Lily looked up and watched him curiously.

He shook his head, refusing to admit he couldn't handle the stew when Lily was scooping the shit up like it was ice cream. His brothers would never let him live it down if they found out about this. Damn Joe and his spicy Cuban food.

Once Joe left, Nikoli took a small sip of the cold milk. Lily picked up her glass of cherry Dr. Pepper. Nikoli had asked Joe to stock it for her, and the man had complied readily. Lily ate here a lot, more than even Nikoli did.

"So now, my little prude," Nikoli said, deciding to rankle her, "where did you learn to dance like that?"

She wrinkled her nose at him. She hated the word prude as much as she did *dushka*. If she only knew it meant sweetheart. He suppressed a grin.

"Watching music videos," she told him. "I spent hours in my room growing up, and I danced and sang along to my favorite bands and singers."

He could just imagine her dancing around in her room with a hairbrush while she belted out whatever song she listened to. It was definitely something she'd do.

"You're really good."

She shrugged. "I'm all right. You're not eating your food."

188

"I'm not really hungry. I wanted to feed you. Food relaxes you."

"It does not."

He laughed. "Yes, Lily Bells, it does. Don't look so horrified. I love watching you eat." He held up his hand before she could spew whatever was forming on her lips. "It's not what you think. No fat jokes. You savor food like you do life. It makes you happy, and anyone around you can see it. Here, you can have the rest of mine. You ate every drop of yours."

She frowned, but didn't refuse. He figured the girl had a hell of a metabolism. She didn't eat a lot, she just ate at odd times. She took a bite of his food and her eyes widened. He watched sweat break out across her forehead, and she reached blindly for something to drink. He handed her the milk, and she gulped the entire glass down at once.

"What the hell is in that?" she gasped once she could talk.

"I knew it," Nikoli growled. "The bastard. He filled mine with extra chilis."

"Is he trying to kill you?"

"His idea of a joke." He knew something was off. Joe was nowhere to be seen either. Bastard. "Are you ready to go?"

She nodded and reached over to grab Nikoli's milk while he got the check. Her mouth was on fire and tears burned her eyes. She'd never eaten anything so hot in her life. When Nikoli stood up, she followed him to his car and tried to think if she had anything to drink in the dorm. She needn't have worried, though. He stopped at a convenience store and got them both a gallon of milk, saying it took an entire gallon to calm his mouth down the last time Joe pulled that stunt.

When he pulled up to her dorm, he didn't try to kiss her or even touch her. He'd kept his word all night and had been a true gentleman. Maybe she was more than attracted to Nikoli. Rebekha had made her think about him and her relationship with Adam in an entirely new light. What was she going to do about this man and the things she was starting to feel for him?

She still had no answer three hours later when she finally fell asleep.

Chapter Fourteen

The next two weeks flew by for Lily. Her classes this year were harder, and she found herself struggling to find time for much of anything outside of studying. When she wasn't in class or tutoring, she was with Nikoli. Which still felt a little odd, only because she found she liked spending time with him. The manwhore was interesting, funny, and she found herself becoming as comfortable with him as she was with Adam and Mike. Nikoli said she would, and she was getting there. He never pushed her too far, gave her breathing room when she panicked, and they talked shop for hours. Cars were her thing, and he was the first guy who got how much she adored them. Nikoli was as big a car junkie as she was.

Not that she'd ever admit anything to Nikoli. Give him an inch and he'd take a hundred miles. No need to inflate his already oversized ego. He wasn't nearly as bad as she'd pegged him for, though. He had a very sweet and caring side he didn't show to everyone else. Said it was bad for his reputation.

Lily was constantly reevaluating her opinion of him. It irked her too. She preferred him the slutty manwhore who only cared about himself. Nikoli wasn't as selfish as she'd thought. He was almost a great guy when he wasn't around other people. Almost. His ego kept getting in the way.

She was just glad she had some time to hang out with her friends. Mike had asked her to come help him and Adam with a bit of a situation online. They were all huge gamers, Halo being a specialty of theirs. It seemed that a team of guys had been destroying Mike and Adam when they played online, especially in the tournaments. Lily was a better shot than either of them, and Mike had begged her to come play today so they could get some payback. Luther was there too. He'd been a victim of the bullies as well. Seriously, a group of eleven guys teaming up against one or two people was not all fair.

The guys had moved the coffee table out of the way and set up shop in the main room. She and Mike had sat down in front of the couch, on a blanket she'd brought, while Luther sat on Lily's left. Adam sat in the chair that flanked the couch next to Mike. Lily was still barely talking to him, but Adam had learned if he kept his mouth shut, she wouldn't leave. He'd kept trying to explain himself, and Lily didn't want to hear it. He'd hurt her a lot, and he knew it. She needed time, and he'd finally realized that. The episode at Nikoli's apartment had shown him that more than anything.

They'd spent the first hour running around like lunatics so she could get a feel for how the other team played. They went out and just killed. Sheer brute force in numbers. Lily smiled as she watched from her hidey hole. The first one was coming into her line of fire. She let him pass, though. She wanted to see how many traveled in the smaller packs. Three more brought up his flank. She'd been tracking their movements for the last twenty minutes. She was in her favorite spot, completely hidden. Before they even realized what hit them, she'd have half of them taken out.

Nikoli grabbed a beer out of the fridge and went looking for everyone. Luther had texted him earlier to say he was at Boy Wonder's frat house with Lily. They were doing some kind of online tournament. He'd known she was a gamer, but had no idea she was a tournament player. He should know by now not to be shocked by anything when it came to Lily Bells. She constantly surprised him. It was refreshing, and it scared the hell out of him. She mattered to him without even trying. He couldn't let this go on for much longer or he was going to be a situation that would cause them both a lot of pain. The thought of losing her, though, it made his stomach hurt. What the hell was he going to do?

He couldn't stop the smile from flashing across his face when he spotted her sitting on the floor, eyes on the screen, barking orders at Mike and Luther. She was so focused on the game, she wasn't paying attention to anything else, and it gave him a minute to watch her. He found he loved watching her. Her face was one of the most expressive he'd ever seen. She never hid anything. It wasn't who she was. What you saw with Lily was what you got.

She didn't pretend, and she didn't play games with people. Again, something Nikoli wasn't used to, and he found it fascinating.

She leaned forward and narrowed her eyes, and Nikoli glanced at the TV screen. Three guys were going past where she was hiding, and he watched as she took them out one by one with single shots. His eyebrows shot up when three more came running, and she took them down as soon as they appeared. He laughed. She was a sneaky little thing. Luther and Mikey cheered, which earned them each a glare, and they both quieted back down and started hunting.

Chuckling at their obvious scolding, Nikoli looked around for a seat. Lily and Mike were sprawled in front of the couch. Luther sat on Lily's right and Boy Wonder was across from Mike. No place to sit...an idea began to form. Oh, Lily Bells was gonna hurt him later, but it would be worth it. She'd gotten so much better at letting him touch her. She didn't flinch anymore and had gotten in the habit of touching him as well. Granted, she wasn't anywhere near where he wanted her, but he was thrilled with her progress.

He kicked off his shoes and then climbed over the back of the couch, his legs coming to rest on either side of Lily. She was so focused on her game, she didn't even notice. Slowly, he brought his legs in so they were resting against her, and to his delight, she leaned back against the couch, resting against him as she took two more opponents down. Mike and Adam stared, shocked. He simply stared back. After a minute, Mike nodded to him and turned back to the game, but Adam's stare turned into something like hate. Nikoli grinned at Boy Wonder, which only pissed Adam off more. Small pleasures in life.

"How many are left?" Mike asked, his shot missing his target. He had to dive for cover, and Luther backed him up, taking the guy out. "Thanks, man."

"Four," Lily answered absently as she inched along a covered ravine. "Don't bunch up. You're giving them two for the price of one."

Mike obediently split from Luther. Lily crouched and waited. "Mikey, pull them this way. I have a shot from here."

"What? Why me?"

"It's your turn to be bait," Adam said, his voice low and rough, causing Lily to glance up at him. His glare was hot enough to melt icebergs. Frowning, she started to turn to look toward Nikoli.

Nikoli was aware the moment she realized she was trapped between his legs. She went completely still. He didn't let her retreat. Instead, he pressed his legs against her arms and leaned down to place a kiss on the top of her head. Softly, so only she could hear, he said, "Easy, *Milaya*, you're fine."

Lily let out a long breath and he could feel her entire body relax. It took her a moment, but she did it, and he couldn't have been more proud of her. "Good girl," he whispered and nuzzled his nose in her hair. She always smelled so good, like strawberries and vanilla.

"Mike, you've got one coming up on your six," she said, her voice a little breathy. "If you don't

195

move, you're gonna get shot, and then I'll have to beat you."

Nikoli laughed and settled back to watch the game. Lily was good, more than good. She impressed the hell out of him as she took down two more from angles she shouldn't have been able to make. He might let her play their current zombie project. He needed a beta tester for the weapons. His thought process froze. Did he actually just consider telling her about his gaming business? He'd never told any woman about his business. It invited trouble. He'd learned that lesson a long time ago.

"Man, your girlfriend is a badass," Luther said, watching Lily. It was only a second before he realized what he'd said and turned wide eyes to Nikoli. Luther looked horrified and regretful all at once. Nik knew Luther adored Lily and was afraid Nik would say something to hurt her. Nor had he meant to put Nikoli on the spot.

Lily wasn't paying attention. Her sole focus was on the game, but everyone else in the room, including the other guys who had come in to watch, were all staring at him. Everyone knew Nikoli wasn't a girlfriend kind of guy, and while he and Lily had spent the last several weeks together, he'd never specifically called her his girlfriend. He glanced down at the top of her head and found he couldn't say she wasn't. It was odd, really. He tried to say the words, but they just wouldn't roll off his tongue. Dammit. He was in so much fucking trouble.

"She is," he agreed and leaned back against the

196

couch. He heard the shock of their indrawn breaths and saw it on the faces around him. The horror on Boy Wonder's face made him smirk. Adam didn't like Lily being with him one bit. Too damn bad. Boy Wonder didn't deserve Lily. No one did. She was too good for all these assholes, including him. His own thoughts stopped his thought process. Shocked didn't even begin to describe what he felt right now. He wanted to frown at his own self, but he kept his face neutral and amused. He liked calling her his girlfriend, liked that she belonged to him. Something inside of him cracked open and pleasure leaked out. He didn't like it, not one bit.

He lifted his eyes and saw his buddy Craig in the corner not paying attention to anything but the girl all up in his business. Cute blonde, big boobs, and Craig's hands were full of her ass. Just the sight made him start to get hard. He let out a slow breath and looked down at Lily nestled between his legs, her head only inches from his cock. He got harder thinking about her mouth wrapped around him, her nails digging into his ass as he pushed deeper into her mouth, making her take all of him. Fuck, he needed to get laid.

But he couldn't. Dammit. It had been weeks since he'd had sex, all because of the woman sitting in front of him. He needed to alleviate the pressure. He wrapped her hair around his hand and marveled at how soft it was. Slowly, so as not to startle her, he pulled the heavy mass of black hair back and started to braid it, an idea forming in his head. They would go back to the penthouse in the city when she was done here and he would push her, push her the way he'd wanted to for weeks. He was going to touch her, kiss her, to show her that his touch brought only warmth and desire. Plans began to form, and his smile was slow and full of the promise of naughty thoughts.

So caught up in his thoughts, he hadn't noticed the last two opponents taken out and the group around them disperse. All that was left were Mike and Adam. Even Luther had gotten up and headed somewhere. Lily sat peacefully, letting him braid her hair. He'd done it several times over the last three weeks, so she was used to it. Adam and Mike were just staring, their faces masks of shock and disbelief. He sighed. Why had none of them ever pushed her? They were supposed to care about her, yet they had let this go on. In two months he'd made more progress than either of them had in years.

"Lils?"

"Hmm?" she answered Mike, leaning her head against Nikoli's knee, thoroughly relaxed. She loved when he braided her hair. Her mom used to do it when she was little, but it never felt like this. Nikoli made each movement feel like a caress, like a gentle touch she felt everywhere, even though he only held her hair.

"You got gems for sale?"

She perked up at the mention of the form of money used for their online social game. Mikey had been hinting for a week or so he might be doing some big spending. He always bought from her because she always had a lot of gems. She bought and sold gems at a discounted rate. It had made her a small fortune in the game and kept her bank account healthy.

"How many you need?" she asked, sitting up a little straighter.

"Five thousand at least, maybe more later in the week."

"What the hell do you need five thousand gems for?" she asked, trying to calculate how much it would cost.

"Gems?" Nikoli asked, his voice a little sharp.

Lily ignored him and focused on Mike. "Well?"

"I bought Janet a ring," he confessed sheepishly as he pulled a tiny black velvet box out of his pocket.

Lily squealed and jumped up, ignoring Nikoli's grunt when he was forced to let her hair go. "Let me see," she demanded and held out her hand. Mike laughed and put the box in her outstretched palm. Lily opened it and gasped with delight. Inside lay a simple diamond engagement ring. It wasn't huge, but it was elegant, and so very Janet. She would adore this.

"It's beautiful, Mikey," she told him and handed it back to him. "You did good."

"I hope Jan likes it." He shoved the box back into his pocket. He sounded so nervous, and Lily couldn't help but smile.

"She'll love it," Adam assured him. "Don't worry so much, bro. It's not about the ring anyway."

"Adam's right," Lily agreed. "She loves *you,* so she'll love the ring."

"I guess."

Lily and Adam both laughed at Mike's nervousness. They knew how anxious he could get over things he really cared about.

"Now, why do you need so many gems?" she asked.

"Well, I thought I'd do a surprise wedding for her," Mike said. "I want to plan it for the day after I propose to her. I thought it would be special for us to get married in-game to celebrate."

"That is *so* sweet." Lily smiled.

"Wait, hold up a sec," Nikoli interrupted. "You're talking about VSL? Virtual Social Life?"

"They are." Adam laughed at Nikoli's shocked expression.

"You play a *sex* game?" Nikoli demanded, and Lily cackled like a crone. He sounded outraged.

"It's a little more than just a sex game," Lily told him. "It's an online world."

"Essentially, Lily Bells, it's a game to meet and fuck," Nikoli disagreed.

"Maybe for you," she said. "I have fun there going to clubs, exploring new places, and hanging out with my friends."

"Do I know you there?"

"I don't know," she teased. "Do you?" Her grin only widened when his eyes narrowed. She was enjoying watching him struggle with this more than she should.

"What's your username in-world?"

"Uh-uh." She shook her head. "Not telling."

"*Dushka*..."

"I asked you not to call me that."

"Tell me your name, and I won't ever call you

dushka again."

"Nope," Lily said. She watched his expression harden and felt the first flutter of nerves. It wasn't apprehension, it was more of anticipation nerves, thinking of how he was going to react. She loved the feeling, loved that it could push her fear away and let her just *feel*. Nikoli was accomplishing what everyone else hadn't been able to. He was healing her. The thought brought a smile to her face until she saw his black eyes narrow further. Oh, this couldn't be at all good.

Nikoli worked to get his expression under control. He hadn't been able to suppress his surprise upon learning his sweet, innocent little Lily played a sex game. It was true, there were a lot of other things to do in VSL, but he had yet to meet a single player who didn't have virtual sex. They did other things, sure, but sex was a big part of it too.

Why wouldn't she tell him her name?

"Are we friends there?" he asked, his voice calm and even. Lily only smiled, not answering the question. He knew Mike played, and they'd hung out a few times, but Lily? Mind. Blown.

"Mikey?" Lily tilted her head to look at Mike, the question plain on her face.

He laughed. "Don't worry, Lils, my friend list is hidden."

"You know I am going to figure this out," Nikoli promised, his smile feral. Lily's eyes grew wider and even Mike looked a little alarmed. As well he should. Nikoli could make his life hell in that game, and Mike knew it.

"Don't worry about the gems. I'll take care of

the wedding," Lily said, sliding farther away from Nikoli. He snorted. As if that was going to save her.

"Weddings in VSL are expensive," Mike protested.

"Couple people owe me some favors," she said, waving his protest away. "Remember when Jan and I helped with the Sabotages' wedding? Jan showed me exactly what she wants for her own wedding, right down to the dress and the cake design. I got it handled, Mikey."

"What about the theme?" Adam piped in. "You can't reserve the venue till you get the theme down."

While the three of them discussed various in-world venues, Nikoli made up his mind. He'd been using kid gloves with Lily up until now, but he was going to push her today. They were going to the penthouse and she was going to get her first lesson in feeling his hands against her naked flesh. He felt his entire body tighten just thinking about running his hands over her.

"Lily Bells, you almost ready to go?" he asked, interrupting their conversation. He needed to get her moving. "I made a reservation at Mason's, and you and I both still need to get cleaned up if we are going to make it."

"I don't know if I have anything to wear there!" Lily gasped.

"Don't worry, I bought you something," Nikoli assured her, "but we need to get going soon."

Lily frowned and Nikoli ignored it. One thing he had discovered was Lily was very uncomfortable accepting gifts from him. She didn't want him to spend money on her, another first for him. He'd only spent money on one other girl before, and only because she'd demanded it. The experience had soured him. Lily was different, though. She made him want to get her things, just to make her happy. It was cute when she'd frown and say he shouldn't have. Another sign he was getting in too deep, but he wasn't sure what to do about it.

"How did you swing reservations at Mason's?" Mike gawked at him.

Nikoli shrugged. Mason's was one of Boston's most exclusive restaurants, and it usually took months to get a reservation, but Nikoli knew the owner. Mason's teenage sons were fans of Nik's games. They always got pre-release copies, and Nikoli got reservations when he needed them, no questions asked. An idea popped into his head, and he grinned a Cheshire cat grin.

"What are you up to?" Lily demanded.

Nikoli laughed. "Tell you what, Mike. You give me Lily Bell's in-game name, and I'll make sure you get a reservation at Mason's for the night you pop the question. I'll even pay the bill. You order whatever you want. It's on me."

Mike's mouth dropped open, then slowly closed. He got all bug-eyed and he started to sweat. Nikoli wasn't playing fair, and he knew it. Mike would want the very best for Janet on the night he proposed. Nikoli was betting his need to make the night special for her would win out against a simple name.

"Don't do it, Mikey," Lily said. "Stay strong."

"It's Mason's, Lils," he pleaded. "Do you know

how much that would mean to Janet?"

"I'll even make sure they do something special for her, a desert or something no one else can order," Nikoli threw in.

"Not fair," Lily snarled, and Nikoli laughed. She'd gone from smug, to worried, to outright pissed off.

"Mike," Adam interrupted them. "Think it through. Do you honestly think he can follow through on that promise? Seriously, unless he's Mr. Money Bags, there's no way he can do it."

"If Nikoli says he can do it, then he can," Lily defended. "He never makes promises he can't keep."

A burst of pleasure shot through Nikoli at her quick defense of him, but it also alarmed him. She was starting to mean more to him than she should. He had no clue how to stop it, aside from walking away here and now, but he couldn't do that. He'd tried several times, but the thought always made him nauseated.

"Cassia," Mike blurted out. "Her name is Cassia." He shot Lily an apologetic look. "You can put him on iggy, Lils, but this is Mason's we're talking about. I had to."

Cassia? Nikoli thought about everyone he knew in-game, and the name brought up a blank. He didn't remember ever meeting a Cassia. "Do you have me on iggy?" he asked suspiciously. If she had him on ignore, she'd damn well take him off the list.

"No," she said, her eyes shooting daggers at Mike. "We just don't hang out with the same people."

"Well, Miss Holmes, we are going to hang out together in-game," he promised. "No running, no hiding, and no iggying me."

"You're a bigger manwhore in-game than you are in the real world. Why would I want to hang out with you there?"

His eyes narrowed and he started forward, his intent clear. Lily let out a small squeal and ran, laughing as she went. He caught her around the waist and swung her around, coming to a stop when her back rested against the wall. His hands braced on either side of her, palms flat against the wall. There was only an inch of space between them. He watched her pupils dilate, but not in fear. In anticipation. He stayed perfectly still so she could adjust to the situation.

"Care to call me that again?" he asked, his expression hard.

"You mean manwhore?" she whispered.

"Yes, *dushka*, I mean that."

"Aren't you a manwhore?" she asked, her expression innocent.

"No. I. Am. Not." He closed the space between them, his body pressing against hers. He felt her tense, but he refused to move away. She needed to get used to the feel of his body against hers.

Adam growled behind them, but he paid Boy Wonder no mind. He knew Mike wouldn't let him do anything stupid. Nikoli focused his attention on the woman in front of him.

"Nikoli," she said softly, "I…"

"Shhh, *Milaya*." He leaned in, touching her nose

205

with his. "Relax, baby."

Her breathing hitched up a notch and Nikoli let his own out, mingling with hers. She shuddered, and he closed his eyes, feeling it go through him. God, what he would do to bend her over something right now. He couldn't, though. He took several deep breaths and pulled his head away from hers. Lily's eyes were glazed and flared with lust. The almost sleepy look she gave him made him hard instantly. Fuck. He needed to get this under control, but hell, he didn't want to.

He leaned in, letting his lips rest softly against her cheek, letting her feel the warmth against her skin. She whimpered, and he pressed his body harder against hers, his lips trailing butterfly kisses from her cheek over her jawline and up to her earlobe. His tongue swiped the soft flesh, and then he pulled it into his mouth, sucking on it gently. Lily let out a low moan, and he smiled. Yes, she was ready to be touched. He bit down softly, and a full body shudder went through her.

"Time to go, *Milaya*," he told her and stepped away from her. He took her arm and pulled her against him, his arm wrapping around her. It was as much to keep her from falling as it was to show Boy Wonder over there who she belonged to. Mostly for Boy Wonder's benefit, he admitted.

Lily didn't say a word, just let him lead her out and into his car. The fact that she hadn't flinched away from him in terror hadn't been lost on either Mike or Adam. Mike had looked grateful, but Adam had been pissed off. Boy Wonder was starting to see what he had lost out on. It was what Lily wanted, but Nikoli found the thought of her with Adam made him want to punch something.

Yes, he had to get control of this, even if he didn't want to.

Fast.

Chapter Fifteen

Lily picked at the sheer black lace of the dress. It was so short it barely covered her bottom. A black choker encircled her neck, and strappy black heels made up the rest of her ensemble. Never in her life had she worn something this revealing. It made her uncomfortable, but more than that, looking at herself in the mirror before they'd left, she'd felt sexy for the first time in her life. And all that was due to the man sitting across from her, thanking the waiter for their food. She murmured her own thanks when he set her tilapia down in front of her.

"You okay, Lily?" Nikoli asked, and she looked up to see a hint of concern in his eyes.

"If you don't count the fact I'm practically naked, then yes, I'm fine," she said, cutting her fish.

"Don't be a prude," he laughed. "You look beautiful."

"You're not the one showing off your naked ass, are you?"

"Want me to?" he countered, grinning. "I'll be more than happy to drop my pants in here so everyone can get a good look at my naked ass."

He stood up, and Lily hissed, "Don't you dare!" She shook her head when he sat back down. He delighted in upsetting her. "Are you and Luther ready for the race next weekend?" They'd been gearing up for the race in Miami since she'd started dating him.

"Yes," he said. "Luther still wants to add a few things, but I don't want any electronics on that car. That is where we got caught with our pants down last time."

"No, just let her run," Lily agreed. The Mach 1 didn't need electronics. They'd equipped it with a nitro system, but other than that, she was good. Let everyone else get taken out because of their electronics. If someone was going to beat Nikoli, they'd have to do it the old fashioned way—by racing.

"Want to come?" Nikoli asked softly, and Lily's eyes shot up to his face. Had he just asked her to go to Miami with him?

"I…"

"I remember you told me your dad never let you go to this kind of race, and you've put as much time into getting the Mach 1 ready for this race as Luther and me. I thought maybe you'd like to be there to see her run."

She stared. He was inviting her to go away for the weekend. Sure, Luther would be there, but she was betting Nikoli wasn't going to be sharing a room with him. Could she do that? Could she go away with him and not give in to what she wanted to do more than anything else?

"You don't have to answer now." He smiled his snake-charmer's smile. "You can tell me tomorrow."

She smiled hesitantly in return. This was the Nikoli everyone else didn't see. The guy who was sweet and kind and charming. Oh, he could be charming in the manwhore way, but this charm she'd only seen him use on her. The kindness in him was her downfall, and she knew it.

"So, tell me about VSL and how you ended up on that type of game." It wasn't a request, and Lily heard the command in his voice. She started to automatically answer, but stopped herself. She'd gotten in the habit of following orders, and she didn't like it. The fact that she trusted him enough to do as he asked irritated her and overwhelmed her at the same time. It was very confusing. She and Rebekha had had several conversations about this very subject. It worried Lily that she was turning into one of the women she read about in books. Rebekha had assured her she wasn't, had in fact pointed out how much stronger she'd gotten over the last month. She wondered what Janet would say…Janet would tell her to run screaming. She wasn't into being a submissive any more than Lily was. Although, Lily admitted to herself, she found herself wondering what it would feel like to do just that with Nikoli. She'd mentioned to Rebekha that she'd been thinking of this, and Rebekha had neither encouraged her nor discouraged her. She'd told Lily to trust herself. Lot of help her shrink was.

"Why are you on there?" she countered.

"My brother introduced me to it," he answered.

210

"I was visiting him and saw it up on his laptop. Asked him what it was, and when he explained it, I was a goner. Perfect game for me."

"It's about more than just sex," she told him. And it was. It wasn't why she was there, not really. She loved the friends she'd made, and her business thrived because she treated her customers like family and helped them out when they needed helping. Lots of other gem merchants didn't do credit. She did.

"Yes, Lily, it is," Nikoli agreed. "Now, tell me how you found it?"

He made it a question, and she smiled. He always knew when to switch tactics on her. She was well aware of when he did it, but she didn't mind. She'd rather answer questions than commands any day of the week.

"Well, Mike was the first one to find it. I never asked *how* he found it, mind you. He got Adam into playing it, and they both decided it might be good for me."

"Good for you?"

Lily took another bite of her fish while she thought about the best way to answer him. It all had to do with her fears and those two trying to find ways of helping her. She loved them for it, and in truth, she'd discovered a place where she could be herself without fear of anyone or her own fears taking over. She felt safe there, to be herself. As safe as she felt with Nikoli.

"Mike and Adam thought it would help me," she said finally. "Adam thought if I could get used to being intimate with someone online in a virtual

211

setting where I couldn't get scared, it might help me be able to deal with my fears in the real world. I was so embarrassed." She laughed, remembering that conversation. "It wasn't something I wanted to discuss with him. Virtual sex." She shook her head, grinning.

"Did it help at all?" Nikoli asked, curiously.

She thought for a minute before answering. "Yeah, it did. Not with the physical aspect of my phobia, but with my own bashfulness and self-esteem. It was a place where I could be myself, be the person I hide from everyone else. No one cares in there how messed up I am in the real world, they only care about the little pixel person in front of them. It helped me learn to be myself in the real world."

Nikoli stared at the woman staring at him and took a deep breath. Her honesty always shocked him. It was something he valued, though. Most women, while not dishonest, tended to stretch or avoid the truth. It was one of the reasons he never bothered to get to know many of them. Oh, he had a few friends who were girls, but only a few, and he never talked to them for hours like he did Lily Bells.

"So, did you ever have virtual sex?" he asked, the devil in him wanting to make her blush.

"That's really none of your business," she replied, picking at her food, the blush blooming on her cheeks.

"Come on, *Milaya*," he wheedled. "You can tell me. It *is* VSL after all." He watched her duck her head, and he smiled in response. She was nervous.

The one thing she didn't need to be with him.

"Really, Mr. Kincaid, it's *none* of your business."

"Oh, but I beg to differ, Miss Holmes," he said, his voice soft. "You are my business, and now that I know you're on VSL, you'll be my business there too."

"Well, no, I don't think so," she replied, finally looking up, and his breath caught at the devilment in her blue eyes. They were shining with laughter. "I may already be someone else's business on there."

Anger and jealousy swelled up within him. The thought of her being with anyone else, even some virtual boyfriend she'd never meet, had him seeing red. She was his. In the real world or in the virtual world.

"Do you have a boyfriend on there, *Milaya*?" His voice came out whisper soft, but the steel in it was impossible to mistake, and Lily's eyes flared in response. When she didn't answer, he let out a low growl. "Answer the damn question, Lily."

"No," she said. "I haven't had a boyfriend on there for months. The guys on that game are bloody cheating bastards."

Relief swept through him at those words. She would have broken up with the guy if she'd had one. "Well, it is a sex game, *Milaya*. They are there for one reason, and one reason only. If you aren't giving them what they want, they move on."

"I don't do voice or video," she said. "I think that is part of it."

He nodded. He'd never thought of that, but then

213

again, his same rule applied online as much as it did in real life. He never dated girls online either. He had lots of friends on there, but the girls he had sex with in-game stayed off his friends list.

"You shouldn't," he said. "They aren't just cheaters, Lily. Some of them are downright stalkers."

"Creepers." She smiled. "That's what I call them. The ones who creep me out."

He shook his head. Leave it to Lily to come up with a cute name for the weirdos who liked to stalk girls online. "Now, next question. I'm assuming you've had virtual sex on there?"

"Yes." The one word sounded low and almost torn from her. She was so embarrassed, and it was adorable.

"How long have you been a member?" he asked.

"Since our sophomore year."

He sat back and stared. Two years on a sex game. She wasn't as innocent as he'd thought at first. Then again, virtual sex wasn't the same. "Do you touch yourself, Lily? When you're in the moment, do you touch yourself for them?"

"No." She shook her head. "I've never felt the need to do that with anyone. I just lie and say I do."

Again her honesty shocked him. So she'd been playing this game for two years and never so much as stroked herself? He shook his head this time. Time for his girl to understand the beauty of being touched. She'd been depriving herself for far too long.

"Well, Lily Bells, that is all about to change," he said, the grin on his face causing her eyes to widen.

She knew him well. She knew he was up to something. "I have something planned for you."

"Look, you have a reputation to uphold on VSL." Nerves made her voice crack just a bit. "Won't chasing me there ruin that rep?"

"Have I ever cared what anyone thought of me, Lily? Why would it be any different there than here? Besides, you don't need to worry about that right now. I have other plans for you tonight."

She let out a low strangled sound, like that of a trapped animal, and his grin widened. The waiter came, and he said no, they'd be skipping dessert. He asked for the check and just watched her.

Lily fidgeted in her seat. What was he up to? What plans? The look in his eyes made her want to run and never look back, but at the same time, she wanted to lean forward and demand to know what he was going to do to her. She waited while he paid the bill, then collected her purse and let him usher her out to the car.

He never said a word while he drove, didn't even look at her, and it made Lily that much more nervous. What was he going to do? He'd been watching her for days, his eyes broody and heavy. She knew he wanted her badly. The truth was she wanted him just as much, but she wasn't going to give in. She wanted that car. Then again, it might be moot. If he touched her like that, she might end up screaming her head off, her body's instinctive learned fear taking over. She hoped to God she wouldn't, but she simply didn't know.

They drove to the apartment complex she'd only been to once before. The penthouse. Her breath came out in a low, ragged sound when she realized where they were. There was no one to interrupt them here. No Luther or Mike or Adam. No residents knocking on her door. No one. She would be all alone with Nikoli Kincaid.

Oh, damn.

He parked and then got out to open her door. She took his hand and let him help her from the car before following him to the elevator that led to the penthouse apartment. The ride up was quiet, and when the bell chimed their arrival, she jumped. Nikoli only smiled and led her out of the elevator and into the apartment. Her eyebrows shot up. New furniture decorated the main room, and she saw he'd even gotten a new kitchen table. He'd kept his word. A small smile flirted with her lips.

"Do the furnishings meet your approval?" he asked, his voice almost formal.

She nodded, not trusting her voice yet. The furniture was modern and done in softer tones than he'd had before. It was as if he'd shopped with her in mind, which was ridiculous. He wouldn't decorate this place just for her.

"Have a seat, and I'll get us something to drink." He motioned toward the couch, much as he had the first time he'd brought her here. She didn't see another option, so she took a seat, tugging her dress as far down as it would go, which wasn't saying much. She felt exposed, naked in this skimpy little black dress.

"Take your shoes off," he said, his voice casual, and Lily glanced up to see him surveying the contents of the fridge. She frowned, but unbuckled

216

the strappy heels. Her feet were killing her. It'd been a while since she'd worn six inch heels.

Nikoli came over and dropped down on the other end, handing her a bottle of water. Lily took it and massaged her aching feet with the other hand. Nikoli brushed her hand away and pulled her feet into his lap. His fingers began to massage the bottom of first one foot and then the other, working out the tense muscles. He didn't say anything while he did this, and Lily watched him. He hummed to himself, and she grinned. She didn't think he even realized he was humming. He did it sometimes when he was very relaxed. Lily loved to watch him at times like these, when he was peaceful and carefree.

His smile was soft, and his black eyes glowed with contentment. His humming calmed her rising panic, and she slumped back against the couch cushion, a low moan of pleasure slipping out of her lips. This was nice, and she loved it when he was sweet like this. She was starting to love a lot of things about him, and it worried her. Nikoli didn't do girlfriends. Sure, for the sake of the bet, he'd called her his girlfriend earlier, but she knew he didn't really think like that. He may be helping her, but he had his own reasons for it. She had to remind herself of that. Daily. Hourly, really.

The problem was, that little reminder stopped working weeks ago, and she wasn't sure how to stop herself from falling for the manwhore. She admitted she may have already fallen for him and was just too stubborn to admit it. Either way, she was in deep trouble. Her heart was bound to suffer an epic heartbreak by the end of all this. Of that, she was certain.

Nikoli watched her from underneath his lashes. Her face was pensive. He wasn't sure what she was thinking about, but her body was completely relaxed. It was exactly what he needed her to be. His fingers worked their way around to the top of her feet and up her ankles, slowly massaging the muscles. She was so relaxed she wasn't even paying attention to his wandering fingers, and he smiled as he moved higher to her calves. He kneaded the muscles and chuckled at her little sigh of pleasure.

He made it all the way to her knees before she realized what was going on. She bolted upright and stared at him, her eyes a little wild. He simply stared back for a moment, and then continued his gentle massage around the back side of her knees and then up to her thighs. He slowed his pace, but increased the pressure of his fingers, soothing and kneading away the tension. She let out a little moan, but still he didn't look up.

Her hand grabbed his when he got to her upper thighs, right below her hemline of her dress. She tugged, and he refused to stop. When he looked up, her eyes were overflowing with several emotions. He could see fear and panic, but there was also curiosity and lust. He needed her to focus on the latter two.

"Lily, I am going to take your dress off."

"No."

He did look up then, his eyes stern. "Yes, *Milaya*. You need to learn to feel my hands on your bare flesh. It's time to push you just a bit further.

You know I'm not going to hurt you."

"I...I...Nikoli..."

"Shh, *Milaya*," he crooned. "You are fine. You can do this. I know you can. Do you trust me?" He reached his hand out to her and waited. She looked at it like it was the hand of the devil, but he didn't grow impatient. He simply waited for her to decide she was going to trust him.

It took her a good five minutes, but she finally whispered, "Yes."

She put her hand in his and he sat up, pulling her toward him. She landed in his lap, her legs straddling his own. Her blue eyes were so dark they were almost black. He saw her fear and forced himself to stay calm, to go slowly with her.

"Easy," he murmured, placing his hands on her thighs, where the bottom of her dress had bunched up higher. She gasped and put her hands on top of his to stop him, and he let her, knowing she needed to feel more in control.

She looked into his eyes and took a deep, steadying breath. "I don't know if I can do this, Nikoli. I don't know if I'm ready."

"How can you know, though, if you don't try, Lily?"

Her gaze swept down to where her hands lay on top of his. He could feel the tremor in them. He understood she was scared, maybe even terrified, but that was the point of all this. She needed to stop being afraid, and that wouldn't happen if she refused to push herself.

It took every ounce of strength she had for Lily not to jump up, run into the other room, and huddle in the corner, screaming. Her panic was so severe, she felt her throat closing up on her and she started to shake. Just the thought of what Nikoli was going to do terrified her. Right now panic was all she felt.

"Look at me, Lily."

Lily pulled her head up and met Nikoli's gaze. His face was only a few inches from hers. His black eyes were calm, warm. She gave him a hesitant smile, doing her best to make herself relax.

"Have I ever hurt you?" he asked softly.

"No."

"Do you think I ever would?"

"No."

"Then stop thinking so hard," he said, a small laugh escaping. "Just look at me and breathe, *Milaya*, just breathe."

Lily did what he asked her to do. She thought about the last two months, about all the time she'd spent with him. She thought about the way he made her feel when he kissed her, when he made her laugh, when he held her, and how safe she felt. The more she thought about him, the more her body relaxed and the more her mind began to panic. Looking into his patient, dark eyes, Lily realized a hard truth she'd been hiding from.

She loved him.

Not just loved him. She was *in love* with him.

"What's wrong?" he asked, his voice concerned. "You just tensed back up, *Milaya*. Tell me what's wrong."

Wrong? Everything was wrong. Her panic shifted from his touching her legs to touching her heart. She felt like her entire world had just bottomed out. How had this happened? When had this happened? She couldn't be in love with Nikoli Kincaid.

"Easy, baby, everything is okay. Just take slow, deep breaths and calm down."

Calm down? How was she supposed to calm down when she was in love with the manwhore? Dear God, how did she let herself fall for him? She knew better. Sure, he might have called her his girlfriend for the sake of the bet, but he didn't want one. He was helping her get over her fears, yes, but he had an ulterior motive. He wanted in her panties. Simple as that. He didn't love her. She couldn't ever let him know how she felt.

"Lily?"

"Give me a minute," she told him, her voice a little sharper than she'd meant for it to be.

"I got all night, Lily Bells. You take as much time as you need."

Damn him. Why couldn't he still be the manwhore to her? Why did he have to be sweet, and kind, and considerate?

He started rubbing his fingers back and forth over her thighs, and she closed her eyes. The panic tried to come back, but her fear of his breaking her heart drowned that out enough for the sensations of his fingers to break through, and it felt...*good*. Oh hell, it felt *really* good. She was in so much trouble.

"Do you have to do that?" she asked, trying once again to pull his hands up.

"Yes, I do," he said, the laughter evident in his tone. "Besides, you like this."

His hands slid higher, slipping under the hemline

of her skirt and pushing it farther up, his fingers continuing to massage the flesh he exposed. Holy hell. It was all she could do to stop a moan from slipping past her lips. She wanted to squeeze her thighs together to relieve the pressure that was starting to build.

"Easy, baby," he murmured. "I got you. It's okay. You're safe with me."

Lily did moan when his wandering fingers traveled up, her dress inching up her hips. Her hands fell away as he caressed her hips, moved around to cup her ass, and squeezed gently. She felt every caress travel from his fingers in a little path of lightning all the way to her core. She did squeeze her legs together then, and he let out another low chuckle that sent a shiver through her.

His hand drifted up her back to where the zipper rested. She felt him tug on it, heard it as he slowly pulled it down, felt the cool air against her back as it was exposed. He laid his hand flat against her back and looked up, his eyes meeting hers.

"We need to set a safe word for you, Lily, something you'll be able to remember no matter what happens here. Think, baby, what word will you remember?"

The first word that came to mind was Laney, but that didn't seem appropriate. They had both loved one thing, and it was something she was sure she could remember.

"Butterfly."

Nikolas regarded her curiously. "That is the first girly thing I've ever really heard you mention."

"I am a girl." The sarcasm wasn't lost on him.

She shifted and he hissed. Her eyes widened when she felt him through the sheer lace of her panties. Flutters started in her stomach, but that sense of everything closing in on her came back. She closed her eyes and breathed slowly in and out.

"Are you good?" he asked.

"I...I don't know," she answered honestly.

"If it gets to be too much, *Milaya*, just say your safe word and I'll stop. Promise."

She nodded. Nikoli had never lied to her. He would stop if she asked him to. The real question was, *would* she ask him to?

"Good girl." He smiled and moved his other hand to small of her back. Then he moved both hands up and around her shoulders. Lily's fear was fast receding, replaced by a completely new fear. The fear she wouldn't say stop. His fingers felt like a trail of fire as they danced their way up her neck, to bury themselves in her hair. He pulled her toward him, his lips settling over hers. Nikoli wasn't gentle with his kiss. It was hard and demanding. Lily shuddered, her arms coming up to cradle his neck, her fingers tugging at his hair. She felt his groan go through her, causing another full body shudder.

His lips moved from hers, his kisses going across her cheek, then her jawbone, along her throat. He stopped to nibble at the pulse point, and she moaned softly, her fingernails digging into his hair. He continued his lip torture while his hands came to rest on her shoulders, pulling the lacy concoction that couldn't really even be called a dress aside, letting it slide down her arms, over her breasts, to settle around her waist.

223

Nikoli pulled back and looked at her through heavily-lidded eyes. "Beautiful." He'd been thinking of this all night, and now that it was here, he wasn't going to rush it. She sat on his lap in her black lacy underwear, her dress bunched around her waist, her arms trapped within the sleeves. Magnificent was more the word he should have used. She was truly magnificent.

He let his fingers roam over every silky inch of flesh he'd revealed. She shivered, a whimper escaping from her, and his nostrils flared. He'd never wanted anything more in his life than to flip her over and thrust into all that wet heat. He pushed those thoughts aside. He'd be inside of her soon enough. Right now was about getting her used to the feel of his skin against hers.

Slowly unbuttoning his shirt, Nikoli watched her. She was nervous, but her eyes were locked on his chest as he revealed his bare skin with each button he undid. He pulled the shirt off, tossing it aside. He gave her a moment before he leaned back and then tugged her forward until she landed against his chest, her breasts pressed tight against him. He could feel her pebbled nipples and closed his eyes. God, this felt so good. Too good. His arms wrapped around her and she relaxed, her head tucked under his chin. Lily's warm breath ghosted over his naked flesh, and he suppressed the groan that was building.

She fit him perfectly. Her little purr of contentment made him smile. She trusted him. It was a truth Nikoli was proud of. She knew he would never hurt her. He wanted to see just how far that trust went.

"Lily?"

"Hmm?"

"Time to go to bed."

He felt her entire body tense up, and he laughed. "Shush, now, *Milaya*. I don't mean what you think I mean. I just want to touch you. That's all."

"That's all?"

"I promise."

"Okay."

A smile spread across his face, and a feeling of sheer happiness overwhelmed him. He didn't let it bother him. Instead, he sat back up, helping Lily to swing around. He stood up, Lily in his arms, and walked the short distance to his bedroom.

The brand new king sized bed dominated the room. Her gaze shot to the bed, and he squeezed her hand, reassuring her. "It's okay, *Milaya*, you're safe with me. You know that."

He left the door open so her panic level would stay down. Kicking off his own shoes, he set her on her feet by the bed.

The dress fell and pooled around her feet. "Stay still."

He went to his closet and found the scarves he was looking for. They were thick, soft, and very sturdy. He took them back out and leaned in close to her ear. "I'm going to blindfold you, *Milaya*. You enjoy that, don't you?"

"Yes," she whispered, a shudder going through her.

He smiled and covered her eyes, tying the scarf tightly so it wouldn't slip. Now that she couldn't see the open lust on his face, she was calmer. "On the bed, *Milaya*." Gently, he pushed her backward until her knees hit the mattress. She fell back and lay there, her breathing a little erratic. Nikoli picked her legs up and said, "Go, on, lay back on the bed, baby." She scooted and twisted, pulling her legs free from his hands.

The rigid way she held her body made him laugh softly, and he watched her mouth turn down in a frown. "It's not nice to laugh when I'm scared."

"There's no reason to be afraid, Lily," he said. "I'm only going to touch you. Nothing more, nothing less."

"That's all?" she questioned, nervous.

"That's all. Now give me your hands."

"Why?" she asked suspiciously.

"Do you trust me, Lily Bells?"

"Yes."

"Then give me your hands."

Lily lay frozen, her mind whirling with a hundred different thoughts. He was going to tie her hands up. She knew it. She didn't want him to, but she did. Why did he want to tie her hands? *So she couldn't run from him*, her mind whispered to her. She thought about getting up and running now, but her skin felt like it was on fire, and all she wanted was to feel his hands on her. Since he'd told her he was going to touch her, her mind seemed to fixate on the image, her skin already craving the touch of his hands.

Could she do this? Could she let him tie her up, give up all the control she had to him? Did she trust him, he'd asked her. Her reply had been instant.

Yes, she did. She trusted him. As much as she did Adam, maybe more. He'd never hurt her, he'd never pushed her too far. He'd been gentle and kind. And she loved him. She could do this. She could. Maybe.

She lifted her hands, and he crooned something nonsensical to her. She felt a soft material wrap around her wrists until they were bound. Nikoli tugged on the knots to make sure they were secure, and then lifted her hands up and fastened them to the headboard. He tugged once more, and she pulled at the bonds as well. They were tight. She wasn't getting out of them anytime soon.

Nikoli moved away from the bed, and Lily lay there, her anxiety growing with every second. What was wrong with her? Why had she let him do this? She couldn't handle this, and she started to twist her hands, tugging hard, needing to be free. The panic rose fast and fierce, and she started yanking harder. She needed out, she needed free. She couldn't do this.

"Shhh, *Milaya*." Nikoli's hand covered both of hers. "You're safe. I'm not going to hurt you. You know this. Just *breathe*, sweetheart. Breathe and relax." His fingers started rubbing slow circles over her hands, and oddly, her body did start to calm down. Not her mind, but her body began to unwind, to melt into his touch like it always did.

"Relax, baby," he whispered, and she felt the bed give where he sat down, his hand giving hers a gentle squeeze before moving away. "It's okay, baby. We're going to take this slow. Just relax."

The sounds of Blue Foundation's *"Eyes on Fire"*

filled the room, and Lily focused on it and the thud of her own erratic heartbeat. She took deep breaths and just listened the sultry sounds of the hypnotic song. His touch began to chase away her panic, and she sighed. His fingers ghosted up the length of her arm and back down again, like a flame trailing sparks behind it. He ran his fingers down her other arm and then back up. When he came down again, she felt him. His fingertips were against her skin, and she shivered where they touched her.

He trailed his hand down her side, ghosted over her ribs, over her hips, and she jerked, not expecting the flare of desire that sparked inside. He continued his slow exploration down her leg and then back up along the inside of her thigh. Her breath caught when his fingers glided up over the lace of her underwear, pressing down slightly right where her clitoris was, and she whimpered. His fingers ran up to her abdomen where he splayed his hand flat against the muscles of her belly. His hand traced over her stomach, up and down, across and down again. His touch sent hot shivers running through every inch of her body, and she cried out when his hand cupped her breast, squeezing gently.

"Shh, sweetheart," he whispered against her fevered skin. "Just relax, baby, just relax and feel."

His mouth closed over one nipple, and Lily nearly came off the bed. If it hadn't been for the bonds holding her to it, she would have. His mouth suckled at the tortured nipple through the lace, the material growing damp. Fire flashed through Lily and she cried out again. The sensation made a blazing hot trail straight to her clitoris. The little nub of bundled nerves began to ache and throb. The harder Nikoli sucked on her nipple, the more she ached. He didn't even have to touch her there for the fire to build. She moved restlessly, squeezing her legs together tightly, trying to alleviate some of the pressure.

Nikoli let her nipple slip from his mouth, and she cried out, not in relief, but in something like pain. Her body throbbed, and she shifted. He stood up and she heard a rustling sound, but it didn't register. Her entire being was focused on the sensations in her body and the sound of the music.

"Lily, I'm going to cover your body, baby. You're going to feel my skin against yours." Nikoli's voice was almost hoarse, but she paid it no heed. She felt the bed dip again, felt his hand spread her legs, and she whimpered, trying to close them, but he wouldn't let her. He wouldn't let her hide from him. He pushed her thighs wide and settled himself between them. She felt his skin touching hers, the heat seeping into her flesh, her bones. His body swallowed hers, he was so much bigger. "There's my girl," he said, his voice a purr. "Are you good?"

Lily's entire body tensed up at the unfamiliarity of him. He stayed perfectly still, giving her time to adjust to the feel of him. She took deep, steadying breaths, the panic there, but not as severe as before. She forced herself to relax, to let the heat seeping off of him soothe her frazzled nerves. The sound of his voice whispering in her ear helped as well. Her body began to relax, to become loose and boneless at just the feel of him. She sighed, a low sigh not of fear, but of…something, something she didn't have a name for.

"Good girl," he murmured against her ear, and she whimpered when she felt his tongue trace her earlobe before sucking it into his mouth. That same fire from earlier began to snake its way down her body, settling at the junction between her thighs. She moaned when his teeth bit into the soft flesh ever so slightly. His lips left her ear alone and worked their way down her throat, nuzzling, his tongue swirling over the sensitive skin. She let out a sound even she didn't recognize when his teeth scraped against the pulse point on her neck.

"I thought you said you were only going to touch." She gasped when he started to lick his way back up her neck, over her jawline, and across her bottom lip.

"I never said exactly what I'd touch you with, now did I, *Milaya*?" His voice was soft and dark, like a deep, rich chocolate you indulged in late at night. You knew it was bad for you, but you wanted it anyway. That was how she felt about Nikoli. "I'm touching you with my hands, my mouth, my tongue, my teeth."

His lips settled over hers, and she couldn't stop the sigh of relief. She'd gotten used to him kissing her over the last few months. She loved the feel of his lips, the way they slid across hers, sucking at her bottom lip. This time was different, though. She felt his kiss like a caress that wrapped around her entire body. Blindfolded, tied, and unable to move, the sounds of the rich, hypnotic song seemed to enhance each touch, each stroke, and each small movement of his skin against hers. She'd never felt anything like it, and despite being terrified of the strange sensations, she refused to give in to her fear. She wasn't the same girl she'd been two months ago.

His tongue invaded her mouth and she moaned, her tongue curving around his, dueling as he deepened his kiss, shifting so he fit more snugly against her. Lily could feel the hard length of him pressed tightly against her, and she instinctively arched her hips upward. Nikoli let out a low, ragged moan and tore his lips from hers. He buried his face in the crook of her neck, breathing heavily. His tongue swiped against the soft skin, and she groaned.

Nikoli forced himself to stop, to calm down. She trusted him enough to let him tie her up and to blindfold her. Trusted him to take care of her and not frighten her. He wouldn't take advantage of that trust. At least not tonight. He'd go to bed with blue balls again, tonight and every night. Miami...well, that might be an entirely different scenario.

He pushed himself up until he was sitting on his knees between her spread legs and simply stared at her, not making a sound. He could hear her breathing, knew she was wondering what he was doing or what he was *going* to do. A small smile spread across his face as he thought about that. She had to be so nervous, and yet she lay there, waiting. Waiting for his touch, his taste. Simply his.

His.

She was his, and there was no denying that anymore. No matter what happened in the next while, for right now, she was his. He wasn't going to make it another three weeks, the end of their three month bet. His body couldn't handle it. He was going to seduce her soon. Truthfully, if he pushed, he could take her now, but he wouldn't. He wanted her to be completely and utterly lost to his touch, no thoughts but the feelings running through her body.

She moved restlessly, and he refocused on her instead of his thoughts. He laid his hands flat against the insides of her thighs and rubbed them up and down the silkiness of her skin. She always felt so damn soft, like a balm to his callused hands. She let out a low whine, and he increased the pressure, the gentle massage becoming a deeper one. Each time he went up, he got closer and closer to the apex of her thighs, and she shivered every time.

He let one hand slide up her hip and then trace the top of the bit of lace that had been driving him crazy since he'd seen it on her. His hand worked its way down, his index finger pushing down, forcing the fabric between her folds. He loved the sound of her voice as she cried out, loved the wet material that told him how ready she was. He pressed down and rubbed hard circles around her clit.

"Do you like that, baby?" he asked, his voice hoarse. God, he needed relief soon or he was going to hurt all night.

"Yesss," she gasped, her hips pushing up.

Nikoli smiled. The look of desire and lust on her face was enough to almost push him over the edge. He pushed the lace aside and slipped his fingers into her folds. God, she was wet, so wet. Her soft cries when he touched her swollen clit had him putting his own hand down his underwear, and he stroked himself as he stroked the girl bound to the bed, writhing under his touch, spread wide across his thighs.

His thumb switched places with his index finger and he slid a single finger inside her, and a low guttural sound was ripped from her. Fuck, she was so tight. He closed his eyes and thought of sliding inside all that tight heat, her walls surrounding him, holding him in their velvety depths. He groaned and let out a cry of his own.

Her hips were thrusting up, and he made himself focus. If she was a virgin, he would hurt her. It would be so easy to get carried away and push his finger in too deep. She was close. Her thighs were tense, trembling. She was thrashing, moaning.

"Nikoli...I...what..."

"Shhh, sweetheart," he soothed, pushing two fingers inside of her. "Don't fight this. Just relax and let it happen. Easy, baby, just let go."

He gripped his cock and stroked hard and fast, his fingers stroking Lily in time to the hand on his cock. He was close himself. God, it felt good, and he wasn't even inside her. His fingers pressed harder against her clit, he scraped the inside of her walls, and he felt her tense, felt the climax swell inside her, and then he felt it give way, the rush of fluid coating his fingers as Lily screamed and bucked beneath his hand. Nikoli groaned and felt his own climax hit him hard. He cried out her name and fell forward, landing on top of her. It took him a moment to get his breathing under control, but even then he didn't move. He let her take his weight and reveled in the knowledge he'd made her scream his name. Not Boy Wonder's, but *his* name.

Lily could barely catch her breath at the rush of sensations that had just torn through her. Never in her life had she felt anything like that. She still ached a little, but his fingers were still buried inside her. She'd heard him yell out her name, and she loved it. Despite the fact he was too heavy and made breathing difficult, she refused to ask him to move. This felt good, it felt right, and she didn't want to lose this feeling yet. Didn't want to lose Nikoli, even though she knew she was going to lose him soon enough.

When Nikoli finally shifted and lifted himself up, Lily dreaded what was coming. He pulled his hand free of her panties, and she whimpered a little. The flesh was still swollen and sensitive. He untied the scarf that served as a blindfold, but she kept her eyes closed. She didn't want to see what was in his eyes. If it was gloating, she couldn't bear it.

"Open your eyes, Lily."

She groaned, but did as he asked. His black eyes were hooded and sleepy, but there was no sign of gloating.

"Are you okay, *Milaya*?" he asked, reaching up to untie her hands. He took them in his and rubbed her wrists gently, first one and then the other.

She nodded, not trusting her voice. He was being so gentle, so kind. How could she not love this man? Not the manwhore everyone else knew, but Nikoli, the man no one else ever really saw. How was she going to survive it when he left?

He pulled her up into a sitting position so she faced him. He cupped her face and leaned in to give her the softest, gentlest kiss he'd ever given her. Lily melted into the kiss. It was so sweet. He had never kissed her like this before, and she savored the feel of it.

"There's my girl," he whispered against her lips. He ran his tongue over her lower lip, and she let out a tiny sigh, which caused him to chuckle. "Was that so bad?"

Lily felt her face flame up and she ducked her head, her mass of heavy, dark curls swinging in her face. Her hair had become unbound somewhere in between all that, but she couldn't for the life of her remember when.

"Hey now, my little prude, no hiding," he chided, lifting her face up. "There's nothing to be embarrassed about."

"It's just that I...I've never...I..."

Nikoli laughed and pulled her into his arms, before falling backward so she landed on his chest. "Lily, don't worry, your virtue is still intact."

"So I didn't lose the bet?" She lifted her head and looked at him, her eyes twinkling. Truthfully, she didn't care. That would have been worth losing a bet for.

Nikoli burst out laughing, and she found herself laughing too. His entire chest vibrated with laughter. "No, Lily Bells, you didn't lose the damn bet. Technically, we both orgasmed, so you could say we had sex, but I don't count it until I'm buried so deep inside you that you can't tell where you end and I begin."

The visual that assaulted her pulled a gasp from her, and Nikoli chuckled softly. He started stroking her hair as he pulled her tighter against him. She snuggled in and let herself relax. For once, there was no fear, no tensing up, nothing but a boneless feeling of contentment. She didn't question it, she just enjoyed it.

"Nikoli?"

"Yes?" he said, his voice as lazy and relaxed as hers.

"If I go with you to Miami, do you think you could take me to my mom's? I haven't seen her or the twins in over a year."

"Of course," he said. "You shouldn't go so long without seeing them, though, Lily. Family is important."

She heard the reprimand in his voice and winced. His family was spread out all over, but she knew for a fact he talked to them all the time on Skype. He may have loose morals when it came to sex, but he had strong family values.

"I know, but before...well, we always ended up feeling awkward, and my mom blames herself for my phobia, I think, even though it's not her fault. It's no one's fault but my own. I'm getting better, thanks to you. I think maybe...maybe I can hug her without panicking. I'd like to try."

"I have faith in you, Lily Bells," he said. "You can do it. I'll book you a ticket tonight."

"No, I'll pay for my own ticket," she told him.

"Lily, I can afford..."

She leaned back and put a finger to his lips. "I don't care if you can afford it. Thank you for offering, but I'll pay my own way, thank you very much."

"You are the most stubborn woman I've ever met and the first who didn't jump at me buying her things."

She smiled at him. Lily knew exactly who Nikoli Kincaid was. She read the gaming magazines. "Nikoli, all I want is you, not what you can give me."

"You mean that, don't you?" he asked, surprise in his voice and on his face.

It was her turn to laugh. She pushed herself up and sat on the edge of the bed, looking for her dress. If she let this conversation go further, it might cause her to say things she'd rather die than confess.

"It's late, Nikoli, and I need to get back before security locks the door at the dorm."

"We can stay here tonight if you want."

Lily glanced over her should her at him. He looked satisfied, yet hopeful, like a little boy asking for a new toy. "I wish I could, but I have to be there for the girls. I can't stay out unless I make arrangements ahead of time for someone to cover my floor."

"That's too bad." He ran a finger up her spine and she gasped, her skin still sensitive.

She felt the bed shift as Nikoli stood up. She spotted her dress sticking out from under the bed and grabbed it, slipping her legs in and then sliding it up her body. Nikoli came to stand behind her. He pushed her hair over her shoulder, and then zipped the dress up. He bent and placed a soft kiss on her collarbone.

"I want to show you something," he said. He was wearing his pants, but no shoes or shirt. Taking her hand, he led her out of the bedroom and down a hall. The last door on the right opened into an office.

It was full of dark mahogany wood furniture, and bookshelves lined three of four walls. A wall of windows overlooked downtown Boston. Lily skipped the scenery and went straight to the books. It was a jumbled up mess of computer programming books, fiction, classics, and general science. The man did not know how to organize his library.

"Leave it to you to beeline to the books," he said with a laugh. "Come over here, please."

Lily looked up to see him sitting behind the desk, turning on the computer monitor. He typed a few keystrokes and then hummed as he waited for it to log him in. She walked over to stand beside him. He wrapped an arm around her waist while he logged into a program.

"Lily, you're a pretty decent gamer."

She laughed. "I guess."

"Well, would you want to test a beta game?" He looked up into her eyes, and she frowned. Was he asking her to beta test one of his games?

"It would depend on what kind of game it was," she said at last.

"It's a first person shooter," he said. "Zombie game."

"Sure, if you want me to. I'm a big fan of horror games, and first person shooters are my favorite."

"I thought as much," he said. "You kicked ass today in that tournament."

"It had been a while since I'd played," she said, playing it down. "It was a team effort, really."

"Bullshit." He shook his head. "You took out almost that entire opposing team by yourself. That requires a lot of skill."

"It's no big deal." She shrugged it off.

"Lily, when I said before I could afford to buy you a ticket, I meant it. I own a gaming company."

"And when I said before I didn't care, I meant that too. I know who you are, Nikoli."

"You know?" His mouth fell open, and she laughed. For once, she'd one-upped him.

"I'm a gamer, Nikoli. Of course I know who you are. I just didn't say anything because I thought you wanted to keep that part of your life private, and it wasn't any of my business."

"You knew who I was all this time, and you never asked me for anything…"

"Because I didn't want anything from you," she said. "Well, I do want your car, but that's beside the point."

"You're not getting my baby," he told her, his eyes still wide with shock.

"That remains to be seen, Kincaid."

"I think you and I both know you're not getting that car." His grin turned wolfish.

"We don't know any such thing," she said, her own smile turning slightly wolfish. "I can say no."

"We shall see, my little prude."

"So we shall," she agreed, praying she could say no to him.

He gave her a gentle squeeze and focused on the monitor.

"Is this something you're working on?" she asked.

"Yes," he answered. "Luther and I are working on it, and we need beta testers to analyze the weapons, how they handle, glitches, things like that. Could you do that for me?"

"Sure," she said, jumping up and down inside. She'd heard rumors of this game on the 'net, but their company was being so closed-mouthed about it, no one could get details.

He popped a blank CD into the computer and started the burn process. "Lily, I'm trusting you with this. You can't show this to anyone."

"I won't. Not even Mikey."

A few minutes later, he popped the CD out. He rummaged around for a sleeve and handed it to her. "Come on, *Milaya*, let's get you home."

She cast one last look at the couch, her face flaming before she followed him out of the apartment. She truly hoped she could say no.

But somehow she didn't think she was going to.

Chapter Sixteen

The next morning, Lily woke up to someone pounding on her door. She groaned and cracked an eye. 5:30 a.m. Who in God's name was pounding on her door this early? Sighing, she threw back the covers and sat up, rubbing the sleep out of her eyes. She'd gone to sleep less than an hour ago. Nikoli's damn game kept her up till all hours, engrossed in it.

Another round of loud knocking earned the poor door a glare. "I'm coming! Give me a minute!" She grumbled, standing up. She dragged herself to the door and nearly ripped it off the hinges. Adam stood there, his eyes bloodshot, and he smelled like a brewery.

"Hey, Lils." He grinned down at her. "Can I come in?"

A door cracked down the hall and Lily stepped back, not wanting any of the very gossipy girls on this floor to see him. "Hurry up," she said as he took his sweet time stumbling inside. How did he even get in here? Guys weren't allowed in the girls'

241

dorms past eleven at night.

"You're drunk, Adam," she said, a glare that would torch even Satan himself on her face.

"Just a little," he agreed, his eyes drooping.

"What are you doing here?" She frowned when he tried to sit on her bed and missed, his butt landing on the floor with a loud thump.

"I don't know," he said, the confusion in his voice as puzzling to him as it was to her. Or it could have been the slight slur when he talked. "I just started walking and ended up here. I'm sleepy."

Lily sighed. She couldn't boot him out when he was drunk. She locked her door, and then threw him one of her pillows and grabbed a blanket out of the closet. "Here. You can sleep on the floor."

He gave her a crooked grin and lay down, pulling the blanket close. He was always a blanket hog, even when they were kids. She climbed back in her bed and tried to ignore his shuffling. She needed sleep too.

Just as her eyes were closing, she heard, "Lily?"

"Yeah?" *Go to sleep dammit.*

"I'm sorry."

He sounded pitiful and lonely.

"I need you to forgive me, Lils…I miss you. What I did, it was unforgivable, but I need my best friend back. Please."

There was that heartbroken little boy she'd loved so much. The same one who'd stuck by her through everything. She missed Adam too. He'd hurt her deeply, yes, but he'd suffered enough. She'd forgiven him a while ago; she'd just been teaching him a lesson.

"Okay."

"Thank God," he whispered. "You remember that summer we went to Myrtle Beach, and I ignored you because I was flirting with what's-her-name?"

Lily laughed. Yes, she remembered it. It was the summer she realized he didn't love her like she wanted him to. It wasn't until he'd started liking other girls she'd understood he didn't feel that way about her. It used to hurt a lot, but not so much anymore.

"You were so mad at me 'cause I left you out of everything. I didn't understand why you were so mad until now, until you stopped talking to me. Now I know what it feels like to have your best friend ignore you. I'm so sorry, Lils."

He must really be drunk to be going down memory lane.

"It's okay, Adam. Let's go to sleep, okay? I'm tired."

"Okay."

Lily breathed a sigh of relief when he stopped talking. She was damn tired and needed sleep.

"Why are you dating Kincaid?"

"You know why," she said, groaning. Why? Why tonight? Why did he have to start talking about this when he was drunk and she was dead tired?

"No, not that bullshit reason you told everyone. Why him, Lily?"

"Why not?" she asked.

"Because he is…"

"None of your business," Lily interrupted before

he could start in on Nikoli's character. Yeah, he might be a manwhore, but he was also a decent person at heart. And she loved him. She still couldn't figure out how she'd let it happen, but there was the cold truth of it. Scared, she should be scared, but she wasn't. Even if he broke her heart, and he would, she didn't regret it. She thought she might once she started to really think about it, but she didn't. Nikoli had given her more in a few months than anyone else had in her entire life.

"He's gonna hurt you, Lils," Adam told her, the slur back in his voice.

"I know," I whispered.

"Then why?" Adam asked, confused.

"Because I love him," she replied softly.

"Damn," Adam cursed. "You're not serious? He will eat you up and spit you out, Lily."

"Why do you care, Adam?" she asked, irritated. "Who I do or don't love isn't your business."

Adam sat up and looked at her. His eyes were serious. "I care because I love you, Lily. I've always loved you."

"I love you too, Adam, but this big brother complex has to stop. I can make my own choices, my own mistakes. You don't have to protect me. I need to live my own life instead of hiding behind you and letting you protect me from anything that can hurt me."

"No, Lils, you don't understand. I *love* you."

"And I love you too," she laughed.

"No, dammit," he growled. "I love *you*, Lily, not Susan. You."

Lily's mouth fell open. Did he just say what she

thought he said? He loved her? Like loved loved her? No way. And why did he say it when he was drunk?

"Adam, you're drunk and not thinking straight," she said at last. "It's the booze talking. Go to sleep and you'll forget all this in the morning."

"I'm drunk, Lily, but not nearly that drunk," he said softly. "I know what I'm saying."

"Adam, you love Sue," she said, trying desperately to remind him. Why now? Was it just a response to her telling him she was in love with Nikoli?

"Yeah, I do love Sue," he agreed. "I loved her enough to ask her to marry me."

"Then why are you saying you love me and not her?" Lily searched his eyes, and she saw a truth there she would have jumped up and down for a few months ago, but not now.

"Because I'm a blind fool," he said bitterly. "My mom said something to me over the summer when I told her about the engagement. She said I was foolish for not seeing what was right in front of me. I didn't understand what she meant, but I do now. When I thought I lost you, I went a little nuts. I kept thinking of how much I hurt you and the look on your face when you told me to get out. The thought of losing you, it broke me. I can't imagine my world without you, Lily."

Her heart stuttered at the shattered sound of his voice, and a single tear slipped down her cheek. Why couldn't he have said this even a few weeks ago? She loved him, but she loved Nikoli more.

"You're the one I want, Lily, the one I want to

marry, to have kids with, the one I want to grow old with. Just you."

"Adam…"

"Please, Lily, tell me you love me, that you'll marry me, please."

Her heart broke. She saw the truth of what he was saying in his face, heard it in his voice. Drunk he might be, but he was being honest with her, maybe *because* he was drunk. It might have given him the courage he needed to tell her all this. Liquid courage, Mike called it. He'd heard the expression in some old western his dad had made him watch. It fit.

"I…"

"Don't say anything now," he interrupted her. "Just think about it, okay?"

"You might wake up and regret all this in the morning," she told him.

"No, Lily, I only regret it took an ass like Kincaid to make me realize how much I love you and how badly I hurt you. Just promise to think about it, please? Just think about you and me and everything we've shared, about all we could share in the future? That's all I'm asking, to just think about it."

"Okay," she whispered, and he lay back down. When he didn't say anything else, Lily turned over and stared at the wall. Her mind felt fuzzy. She was so tired, and now it was full of thoughts and questions about how she felt, about everything.

Why the hell had Adam decided to spring this on her tonight?

And what was she going to do when they both

woke up?

***

Nikoli whistled as he walked down the hallway to Lily's dorm room. It was nine, and he figured she'd had enough time to sleep. He told himself he was here because he wanted to hear her thoughts on the game, but honestly, he just wanted to see Lily. He knocked on her door and shouted, "Wake up, Lily Bells!"

The next thing he heard was a loud thump and Lily cursing worse than a sailor. He laughed, just thinking of her face. She must have fallen out of bed. When she wrenched her door open, his smile faded. Adam was passed out on the floor.

"Shhh," she whispered and pulled him inside. "He's still asleep."

"What's he doing here?" Nikoli demanded, the caveman inside yelling *mine*.

"He showed up drunk early this morning, and I let him sleep on the floor," she said, her voice weary. "What are you doing here?"

"I came to take you to breakfast," he said, looking at her face. She looked tired, like she hadn't slept at all last night. "Did you sleep?"

"Some," she said, yawning. "I was playing your game all night, and then this one woke me up less than an hour after I went to sleep."

"Come on," he said, "let me take you to breakfast, and then you can go sleep at the apartment."

She yawned again and then glanced at Adam

before nodding. "He'll sleep most of the day. He sleeps like the dead when he's drunk. Let me go to the bathroom, and then we'll leave."

Lily grabbed her toothbrush and toothpaste before leaving. Once she was gone, Nikoli studied Adam. He couldn't figure out what Lily saw in Boy Wonder. He was average, generic. He also had bad taste in women. Sue was an empty-headed shrew with a care for no one but herself. Nikoli had had the chance to fuck her in his sophomore year, but even he had standards. Sue was a real piece of work, and he'd nipped her in the bud before she could get past hello.

Adam, unfortunately, was beginning to understand his feelings for Lily. Nikoli wouldn't be surprised if he dumped the Barbie for Lily. Just the thought of Adam and Lily together set his teeth to grinding. Adam and Lily would be good together, though. They'd get married and have the traditional two kids and a dog, the white picket fence. Lily would have everything she ever wanted. She'd be happy. She deserved to be happy.

She deserved better than him.

Not that she wanted him. Oh, she wanted him sexually, but she didn't want *him*. He knew what she thought of him. Granted, her opinion may have changed a little over the last months, but she still thought of him as the manwhore of Boston University. She would never see him as anything else. And that was okay. He didn't want her to see him as anything other than that. He needed her to think of him that way so it would be easier when they broke up. For both of them.

"Hey," Lily interrupted his thoughts. He turned and saw her smiling. How had he not heard her come in?

"Hey, my little stealthy ninja," he said and pulled her to him. "You smell all minty fresh."

She laughed, and he couldn't resist leaning down to sweep her lips with his. He felt the sigh go through her and pulled her closer in response, increasing the pressure of his kiss. Every time he kissed her, he lost more of his desire to let her go. This was getting to the point of no return. He needed to end it soon. After Miami. He'd end it when they got back from Miami.

He pulled back and stared down into her blue eyes, sparkling with laughter and warmth. Miami. Well, fuck, now he was dreading Miami. The dread slammed into him with all the force of a sledgehammer.

"You okay?" she asked, her eyes becoming concerned. "You look like you're gonna puke."

"I'm fine," he said. "Ready to go?"

"Sure." Her eyes remained worried, but she grabbed her purse and followed him out the door.

The ride to his latest hole-in-the-wall discovery was quiet. He kept glancing at her, and she kept staring out the window. She had something on her mind, something that wasn't good. Nikoli couldn't explain how he knew this, but it was like an itch right at the base of his neck. It wouldn't go away.

Once they were seated in the dinky diner with their orders placed, he asked, "What's wrong, Lily Bells? Something's bothering you."

She turned confused and frustrated eyes to him,

and he sucked in a breath. "Adam said some stuff this morning."

"Did he hurt you again? I swear I *will* beat him this time."

"No, no." She shook her head. "Nothing like that. He was drunk, and I don't think he meant what he said, or maybe he did because he was drunk. I don't know."

A sick feeling settled in Nikoli's stomach. He knew what was coming. "Then what, Lily?"

Lily sighed and looked into Nikoli's eyes. They were darker, almost angry. If she didn't know him better, she'd say he was jealous, but the manwhore never got jealous. He didn't love her. She reminded herself of that forcefully. He might want to have sex with her, but he would never want *her*.

"He told me he was in love with me, and that he wanted to marry me and not Sue."

"I see," Nikoli murmured, and Lily shot him a glance. His eyes were blank and his face closed off. "That is what you wanted, wasn't it, Lily?"

"Yes," Lily agreed quietly. "It was what I wanted."

"Then why don't you look happy, *Milaya*?"

"Why now, Nikoli? Why now that I'm getting better? Why now that I'm with you? I don't know if Adam really means it, or if he's just reacting to something he's never experienced before. I was always there for him before, and now I'm not. What if he misses that and is confused about how he feels because of it?"

"*Milaya*, Boy Wonder *is* in love with you. Is this recent, or has he always felt that way? I don't know, but I do know how jealous he's been. He can't stand the thought of me and you together. It drives him crazy."

"Maybe," she muttered.

"Well, if you decide to take Boy Wonder up on his offer, you renege on this imaginary bet, and Ellie stays with me."

His car? That was his first thought? His car? It only solidified Lily's opinion that Nikoli didn't love her, that he didn't want her. He just wanted his damn car. She felt her face heat up, but this time in anger. Why should she care or be shocked? He was Boston University's very own manwhore, after all.

Nikoli watched Lily's cheeks fill with color and her blue eyes flash with fury, and he frowned. Why was she mad? Boy Wonder was what she wanted. She should be happy. Nikoli should be happy for her, but he couldn't be. He wanted to hit something. To beat someone bloody. Anger fought with jealousy inside of him, and he hated it. He didn't get attached, ever, but this woman had gotten under his skin. She would leave him. He'd known that from the beginning.

"Hey, May, turn that up," someone shouted, and he and Lily both turned to see another crime scene pictured on the flat screen in the corner of one wall. Another girl had been found, and it appeared to be the same guy who'd been killing all summer. Boston was officially in the grips of a serial killer, and everyone was on edge.

"That's two blocks away from the university." Lily's eyes widened. "Oh my gosh, he's been getting closer and closer to the college since he started."

"Don't worry, *Milaya*, they'll catch him."

"Yes, we will."

Nikoli's head snapped up and he saw his brother, Kade, grinning down at him. The mess of curly black hair and sleepy black eyes made Nikoli laugh. Kade looked like he hadn't slept in a week and had a serious case of bedhead. He shook his head and stood up, wrapping his brother in a bear hug.

"Good to see you, Nik," Kade said when they let go. "One would think you were hiding from your brothers the way you never call."

"Just busy, bro," Nikoli said. "Lily, this is my brother, Kade."

"Hello," Lily said, smiling. "It's very nice to meet you."

Kade's eyebrows hit his hairline. Not that Nikoli blamed him. He and his brothers were all alike. They didn't take girls to breakfast. They had sex, and they moved on.

"You're the oldest brother, right?" Lily asked.

"Uh, yeah," Kade murmured and gave Nikoli a look that said 'what-the-fuck, dude?'

"Kade, have a seat, man. We just ordered breakfast, and the food here is stellar." Nikoli scooted over so his brother could sit. Kade slid in, but his eyes stayed on Lily. "How did you find me?"

"FBI, remember? It's easy to track you down."

"Pretty sure that's a violation of my right to privacy." Nikoli snorted at his brother's pious look.

"Brothers don't have an expectation of privacy." Kade laughed. "So, Lily, how long have you known my brother?"

"I've known the manwhore for a couple months," she said, her voice completely innocent, causing Nikoli to spew the mouthful of coffee he'd just taken.

Kade's laugh boomed through the diner. "Manwhore?"

"Well, he does have a bit of a reputation," Lily said, "but he has been behaving the last few months."

"Has he?" Kade asked, glancing at Nikoli, who shot him a fuck-off look. "That doesn't sound like him. My brother doesn't know how to behave."

Lily just smiled. "Then you don't know him as well as you think you do. Nikoli is a decent guy…for a manwhore."

"I thought we agreed you would stop calling me that," Nikoli seethed. He hated that nickname. Truly hated it, especially when Lily used it.

"Did we?" she asked, her voice all sweet, and his eyes widened. She was still pissed at him. But why? He hadn't understood it to begin with. Why was she mad at him because her dreams were coming true? The woman made no sense.

"Yes, *dushka*, we did." He leaned closer, eyes narrowed.

"Don't call me *dushka*!" Lily's own eyes narrowed.

"Oh, I'll do more than call you *dushka*," Nikoli said, his eyes a clear threat.

"You can try, Kincaid."

Nikoli's grin grew at the sly tone in Lily's voice.

Kade interrupted before Nikoli could respond.

"Um, big brother here…do I need to leave so you two can get a room?"

"No." Nikoli sat back when the waitress came to set down their food. He waited for her to take Kade's massive order that had Lily scrunching her nose in disgust before asking, "So what are you doing here, Kade?"

"Your serial killer." Kade's usual carefree face was serious for once. "The Boston PD called, and we were sent to do what we can to help catch the guy."

"Called?" Lily asked.

"I'm Special Agent Kade Kincaid," he said. "I'm a member of the BAU…"

"The Behavioral Analysis Unit," Lily finished for him, and Nikoli sighed. Lily was a true fan of the show *Criminal Minds*. She could watch that show for hours when the reruns came on. Truthfully, it had grown on Nikoli too. He found himself watching it even when Lily wasn't around.

Kade gave Lily his best 'come here and let me hit that' grin. Nikoli turned so he could look his brother dead in the eyes. "No."

Kade's eyebrows shot up again. Nikoli knew how territorial he was being and how unusual it was for him, but he'd be damned if he sat here and watched his brother flirt with his girlfriend.

He saw Lily shake her head out of the corner of his eye, and he shot her a glare. "I mean it, Kade. Hands off my girlfriend."

"Your *what*?" Kade spewed his coffee across the table and right onto Lily, who let out a dismayed gasp. Coffee stains covered her t-shirt.

"Girlfriend." Nikoli leaned over to wipe the coffee off Lily with a napkin. She looked so shocked at his use of the dirty word, *girlfriend*. She was his until he broke up with her after Miami. Or until she said yes to Boy Wonder, whichever came first. A brick settled in Nikoli's stomach at the thought. Damn, he wanted to hit something.

"You don't do girlfriends," Kade sputtered.

"I do now," Nikoli growled. "Apologize to Lily Bells."

Kade stared at her with his mouth open, and Lily suppressed the urge to laugh. The man looked like he'd been kicked in the teeth at the thought of his little brother having an honest to goodness girlfriend. So funny.

"Sorry," he muttered at last, confused and frowning. It was all she could do to keep from smiling at his so Nikoli-ish look. She'd seen it on Nikoli's face a lot the last month or so. If he hadn't been so blasé about Adam this morning, she might have actually thought he cared. Nikoli confused her. He acted like he didn't want her, and then he went and told his brother she was his girlfriend.

It was seriously pissing her off, to be honest. She loved the idiot, and he couldn't seem to make up his mind about what she was to him. Lily knew deep down Nikoli would never be hers, but moments like this gave her hope that maybe she was wrong, maybe he did feel something for her. God, she wanted him to feel something for her. Needed it more than she needed anything else. And it scared her because she was going to be so broken when this ended.

"So, Lily, are you a senior or…?" Kade left the question hanging and brought Lily out of her dire thoughts.

"Senior." She smiled. "I graduate at the end of this semester."

"Same as Nik," Kade said. "What's your major?"

"English," she told him. "I'm going to be working at a literary agency in New York when I graduate. They've already offered me the job."

"So you'll be working with authors? Not an author yourself?"

"Oh, I am an author," she said, smiling. "My novel is almost done. When I finish and revise it, I'm going to try to get published."

"You're writing a book?" Nikoli asked. "You didn't tell me."

"No, I didn't," she agreed. "I don't tell you everything, Kincaid."

"Apparently," he growled, and Lily laughed. He was in full testosterone mode this morning. "What's it about?"

"None of your business," she said, laughter brimming in her eyes. She knew it would drive him nuts until he found out. If he only knew…she shook her head. He'd read it eventually and understand what she wanted to say to him. It was their story. She'd write the ending once they'd ended things. That was all that was missing from their story.

"Why don't you want to tell me?"

Kade said, "Writers don't normally share their work until it's published. Something about needing their privacy."

"And how would you know that?" Nikoli asked.

"I dated a writer for about a week." Kade popped a piece of sausage into his mouth. "She got all pissy when I peeked at what she was writing."

"That sounds about right," Lily agreed. "Come near mine and you'll get hurt."

"Come on now, Lily Bells," Nikoli wheedled. "Let me read it."

"No."

"Just the first chapter?"

"No."

"Leave it be, Nikoli," Kade said. "She'll hurt you. Don't you see that gleam in her eye that says she's ready to stab you with her fork?"

"Lily wouldn't hurt me," Nikoli scoffed.

"Wanna bet?" Lily asked, remembering his blasé attitude earlier.

This time it was Nikoli's turn for his eyebrows to shoot up. Ah, he was finally getting the message of how pissed she was. He probably had no clue why, but he didn't need to know why, only that she was.

"So, Kade, you are working on the serial killer case?" she asked so she wouldn't have to deal with Nikoli. "Do you guys have any leads?"

"I really can't discuss an ongoing case, Lily," he said. "I will tell you that we just got here last night and are catching up on everything. We'll get him. Soon."

"I hope it's sooner rather than later." She shivered. "That last one was too close to campus."

"Yes," Kade murmured. "We are asking for the college to allow a police presence there, just in case. Make sure you never go anywhere on your own, always bring someone, walk back to your dorm with a friend. Never alone."

"I'll make sure of it," Nikoli promised.

Kade's food came, and Lily turned her eyes back to the TV. The news was still talking about the latest victim. If the FBI was here, then the situation was serious. She'd been nervous about the whole situation since she'd seen the first news broadcast over the summer.

She hoped they caught him soon.

***

When Lily returned to her dorm room, she expected to find it empty, but Adam was sitting on her bed, his face troubled. She closed the door and leaned against it. When his eyes met hers, they were dark and thoughtful. The hangover was evident from his wince when the girl in the next room slammed her door.

"You look like hell." Lily pushed herself away from the door and plopped down in her desk chair.

He ran a hand through his hair. "I feel worse."

"Getting shit-faced will do that to you."

He fell back on her bed and started up at the ceiling. "Lily, we need to talk about…well…"

"What you said last night?"

"Yeah." He still didn't move. "I know blurting that stuff out at you when I'm drunk wasn't the best idea."

"Ya think?"

"I may have been drunk, but I meant every word I said, Lily."

Lily closed her eyes and counted to ten. A month

ago, this conversation would have meant the world to her, but not now. Now, it only meant she had to hurt the one person who had always been there for her through everything.

"Adam, you don't mean that…"

"Yes, I do." He sat and looked her in the eye. "I love you, Lils. I've loved you my entire life. I just didn't think you'd ever get better…"

"So you're only interested in me now that you think I'm getting better?" Anger leaked out of her voice. She couldn't help it.

"That's not what I meant." Adam rolled his shoulders. "I tried, Lily, I tried so hard to help you, but I couldn't. I don't understand why Nikoli could, when nothing I did worked. That is what I meant."

Either way, the outcome was the same. He hadn't shown any interest until Nikoli. It still stung a bit, but she'd forgiven him somewhere along the way. Didn't mean she wasn't pissed he only told her this after Nikoli.

"Adam, I love you. God knows, for the longest time, I thought I was in love with you, but I've only recently discovered the difference. You're my best friend, and you did help me more than you know. Just being there for me, never letting me push you away. That kept me from going off the deep end. You will always be my best friend, and I will always love you, but I'm not in love with you."

"You love the campus manwhore." Adam's eyes dilated, his anger evident in the way his body tensed. "He's going to break you into little pieces."

"Then my best friend will be there to put me back together again." Lily offered him a small smile. She knew it was true. Nikoli was going to hurt her, but she'd take the hurt for the way she felt right now.

"But, Lils, if you'd only listen to what I'm saying, you won't be broken." Adam stood and started to pace. "I love you, Lily. We can be so happy together, if you'll just trust me and let me show you."

"Adam, what about Sue?"

"What about her?"

"You're supposed to be getting married in a few weeks. What would that do to her?"

He stopped pacing and sat down on the floor. His face was torn, confused.

"I think you're only saying all this now because of Nikoli. You love Sue, don't you?"

"Yes."

"Then why would you even consider leaving her?"

"*Because I love you!*" he shouted, his frustration pouring out. "You're not listening to me, Lily. I love you more than I could ever love Sue. I want to marry you, have kids with you, and grow old with you. Only you. I've always wanted that. You are my heart, Lily. It's killing me watching you and Nikoli, thinking that should be me with you. Every time I see you two together, it feels like someone is stabbing me in the heart. What can I say to make you understand, Lily? I love you."

Tears blurred Lily's vision and she wiped them away. He sounded so broken.

"Why, Lily? Why do you trust him and not me?"

"Because I was afraid, Adam." Her words were

hesitant, uncertain. "I've been seeing Rebekha again, twice a week for the last few weeks. We've been talking about that. I was afraid that if I let myself touch you, you'd die, just like Daddy. I couldn't do that. My mind refused to even contemplate it. Nikoli had no ties to me. He was a stranger and I wasn't afraid of hurting him like I was you."

"Do you still think you can hurt me?"

"No. I understand my fears now, and between Nikoli and Rebekha, I'm getting better."

"Then why not give us a chance, Lils? Let me show you how much I love you, how good we can be together."

"Because I don't love you like that, Adam." Her voice was quiet, somber. She watched him recoil in hurt, and it nearly made her double over from the pain. "I do love you, but I love you like a brother, like my best friend. I don't know what I'd do without you in my life, but that's all I feel for you, Adam."

He stood, his movements stiff and slow. His eyes were haunted when he looked at her, but there was a determination in them too. "When he breaks you, Lily, I will be here to pick up the pieces. Then I'll show you what you mean to me, and maybe you'll give us a chance."

"Adam…"

"No," he cut her off. "Don't say anything, Lily. I'm not going to give up on you. I'm the one who will be here for you when he's gone. Remember that." Adam walked over and planted a quick kiss on her head. It was so fast, it reminded her of

Nikoli's sneak attacks. It was over so quickly she didn't have time to freak. He gave her a crooked smile and let himself out, closing the door behind him.

Lily closed her eyes and let her head fall to the desk.

Damn you, Nikoli Kincaid, for ruining any chance I had with Adam.

She cried, cried for the life she could have had, for the happiness that might have been, but mostly she cried for the hurt she'd caused the one person who she never wanted to hurt, but had.

Chapter Seventeen

Lily blinked at the bright sunshine as she walked out of the Miami-Dade airport. To her left, Luther looked ready to fall down and kiss the ground. He didn't fly so well. Even liquor didn't do the trick. Nikoli had laughed and told him he should have slept. Lily didn't think that was an option for the poor guy. Flying truly terrified him. She'd plugged in her headphones and watched a movie on her tablet, and then opened a book she'd bought to bring with her. Nikoli had taken his own advice and slept the entire flight. She had a feeling he didn't like flying either, only he handled it better than Luther.

They waited for the bus that would take them to the car rental facility on the property, and once there, Nikoli rented a new Lexus. Lily would have taken the less expensive Ford Focus, but as Nikoli kept reminding her, he could afford it. Since she'd told him she knew who he was, he seemed almost irritated with her for not asking him for things, but she didn't want anything from him. Except for his

263

love, and that was something she wasn't going to get.

The hotel was expensive too. Lily cringed thinking about the room service bill Luther was sure to run up. He loved room service. He'd spent all day yesterday telling her about the wonderful room service the hotel offered. It was their favorite place to stay when in Miami. Nikoli reserved two rooms, one for them and one for Luther. The front desk clerk was overly helpful when he saw them, which made Lily realize they must have stayed here quite a bit over the years for the staff to know them. She shouldn't be surprised, though. They were into racing, and Miami was a racing city.

Luther declined going out for lunch. He wanted to pass out. Poor fella looked like he needed it. Nikoli shook his head and carried their luggage down the hall, motioning for Lily to unlock the door. The room was gorgeous. There was a sitting room with a very comfortable looking couch and a wall-mounted TV. A small fridge and sink were tucked into the corner next to the bathroom. Nikoli opened a set of double doors that led to the bedroom and dumped their luggage in front of the dresser that sported a TV sitting on it as well. The massive king sized bed was covered in a lovely gray comforter.

"Do you like it, Lily Bells?" Nikoli asked, coming up behind her and wrapping his arms around her.

"It's beautiful," she said, turning her head to meet his wandering lips, and she sighed when his mouth finally landed on hers. His kiss was soft, gentle. It left her breathless.

"Want to try out the bed?" he whispered against her lips before pulling back and staring down at her.

"Nice try." She leaned her head back against his chest. "Ellie is mine."

"Not after this weekend," he promised. The determination in his voice sent a full body shiver though her. "What do you want to do first? Rest, grab a bite to eat, or go see your mom?"

Lily smiled. He hadn't forgotten that she wanted to see her family. They'd flown out early so he could take her, since they'd be busy tomorrow. She wasn't quite sure what time the race began. Nikoli said they'd text the time and location to him.

"Can we go see my mom?" she asked. "I called her last night to tell her we were coming. I'm sure she'll cook a massive meal that no one can finish."

Nikoli laughed. Lily had grown up in the mountains, and he'd learned that they tended to try and feed people into complacency, or so she'd threatened.

"Sure, baby. Go freshen up, and I'll go down and program the GPS with the address. Meet me down there when you're ready."

He was being so sweet. This was the Nikoli she'd grown to love, not the person he was around everyone else, even Luther. She was going to miss him. Even though he hadn't said anything, she had a feeling this was their last weekend together. Call it intuition or instinct, but she knew she wasn't wrong.

She went to the bathroom and took care of her business before she grabbed her purse and the kids' presents and headed downstairs. She refused to be sad. If she only had him for this weekend, then she was going to enjoy it.

The drive to her mother's took them about an hour. She lived right outside the city, but with traffic, it took longer than either of them had expected. Lily saw two orange groves on the way. Her mother always raved about the fresh orange juice she got from one of them. She and Lily's stepfather had moved from North Carolina to Florida right after Lily graduated high school. They loved it, and the kids loved living close to the beach. What kid wouldn't, though?

When Nikoli slowed the car and pulled into the Spanish style home, Lily got nervous. This was her first big test to see if Nikoli really had helped her deal with her phobia, or if it was just him she could tolerate touching her. What if she started screaming? What if she terrified the twins? What if…

"You'll be fine, Lily Bells," Nikoli told her, his eyes calm and reassuring. "You're better now. You can do this."

"I don't know," she whispered. "If I can't…"

"You and I have been together for months now, Lily, and nothing bad has happened to me, has it?"

"Well, no."

"Then have a little faith," he said. "You aren't cursed, you aren't responsible for anyone's death, and you're not going to cause anyone to be hurt or to die. You can do this, Lily. I have faith in you, so how about having a little in yourself, *Milaya*?"

His words wrapped around her, like a cool balm on a hot summer's day to her rattled nerves, and she returned his smile. She still felt nervous, but the panic that had tried to overwhelm her disappeared. Vanished. Nikoli had that effect on her. He was her woobie. She almost laughed at the thought. She'd had a ratty yellow blanket she'd clutched whenever she was afraid when she was little. Her mama called it her woobie. Nikoli felt like that right now, her own personal woobie.

Her mother stepped out on the porch, and she studied her from where she sat. Lily didn't look a thing like her mother. Joanna Stanton was a short bundle of energy. Blonde hair was piled up on her head in a messy bun, and she wore a pink tank top and blue jean shorts that showed off her sun kissed skin beautifully. Her mama looked good. The Florida climate suited her.

"Daylight's wasting," Lily said.

"What?" Nikoli asked, never having heard her speak like that.

"It's something my Dad used to say whenever he dreaded doing something. It was his way of reminding himself when something had to be done, there was no point in putting it off."

"Your father was a wise man," Nikoli said. "Ready to go?"

Not really, but she got out of the car anyway. She stood staring at her mom. They hadn't seen each other in a long time. Her mother stared back at her just as intently. Nikoli came over and gently nudged her forward. She glared at him. He needed to give her time. He shook his head no and pushed her forward again. The man was insufferable. He never let her just take a minute and think.

She gave him one more glare and started walking. When she reached the porch, her mother took an automatic step back. She knew Lily's phobia intimately.

"Hi, Mama," Lily said, her voice hesitant.

"Lily." Her mother's voice was just as soft as hers. Lily used to love listening to her read to her when she was little. "Welcome home, sweetheart."

Lily closed her eyes and took a deep breath, her thoughts focused on what she was about to attempt. She waited for the panic, for the overwhelming fear to consume her, but all she felt was the warmth and the love she associated with her mother. And Nikoli. She could feel his presence behind her, and she took strength from that.

She walked over to her mother and wrapped her arms around her, hugging her tight. "I love you, Mama."

Her mother let out a strangled cry and hugged her back just as hard. "Oh, my baby…"

Lily felt her mother's tears fall down and splash her face. She heard the wonder in her voice. It made her heart cry and swell with love at the same time. She'd deprived herself and her mother of this for years, and now instead of panic, she felt a deep sadness. She'd caused them both so much pain.

"I'm so sorry, Mama," she whispered, her own tears joining her mother's. "I didn't mean to hurt you…I just…I…"

"Hush now, sweet girl." Her mama stroked her hair like she had when she was a little girl. "Hush and let me hold you."

Behind her, Lily heard the trunk pop, and she

knew Nikoli was getting the gifts she'd bought for her family, but it was only a distant thought. Right now, all she was concerned with was that she was in her mother's arms with no fear, no panic, no need to start screaming.

And that was all because of Nikoli Kincaid.

They spent the afternoon lounging by the pool while her mother cooked them enough food to feed three armies. The twins were ecstatic to see Lily. She hadn't spent a lot of time with them in person, but she did Skype with her mom and the twins at least two or three times a week. They tore into their gifts like little fiends and squealed with delight. What really broke Lily's heart was when they were so shocked she hugged them. She spent two hours just sitting on the floor playing with them, smiling like she hadn't in a very long time.

Once everyone had been fed, Lily offered to help her mom with the dishes. Nikoli was content to sit and talk about baseball with her stepfather. She helped her mom gather up dishes and took them into the kitchen, where she started scraping them. Her mom ran some dishwater for the pots and pans. She always refused to put pans in the dishwasher, proclaiming that was where all the nicks and scratches came from.

"Tell me about this young man of yours," her mother said without preamble.

"He's my saving grace, I guess you could say. I would never had learned to control my phobia without him."

"How did he do it?" her mother asked curiously. "What did he do that we didn't?"

269

"It's not that, Mama. You did everything you could. It was more me. I wanted to change, to be able to let someone touch me. It wouldn't have worked if I hadn't needed to change so badly. Nikoli just...he never let me give up. He pushed and pushed and pushed. Sometimes I wanted to strangle him, but he never pushed too far. He knew when to stop. But mostly, he was just there when I needed him."

"He pushed you?"

Lily snorted. That was putting it mildly. "He pushed my limits, never let me give in to my fear, never let me give up, Mama, even when I wanted to. I never thought I'd be able to let anyone touch me ever again, but I can now, and it's all due to him. I'm mostly healed because of that man."

"Oh, baby, I'm so happy for you. I only wish I could have helped you more, gotten you better sooner. I'm so sorry."

Lily put down the plate she was scraping and took her mother's hands into hers. "Don't be sorry, Mama. This phobia of mine wasn't your fault, and you did do everything you could to make me better. You're a good mother, and I love you so much. No more tears, okay? Only smiles from now on."

"It's good advice, Mrs. Stanton."

They both turned to see Nikoli lounging in the doorway. Lily felt her heart skip gleefully at the sight of him and cringed a little inside. Not out of fear, but the beginning of pain. This was their last weekend together. She knew it deep down. She couldn't shake the thought. Intuition. She wanted to curl up and cry.

Lily's mother went over to Nikoli and wrapped him in a bear hug. He laughed and hugged her back. "What's that for?"

"For giving me my baby back," she said, a tremor in her voice. She was fighting not to break down. Nikoli smiled down at her.

Nikoli now understood where Lily got her kindness from. Her mother was one of the sweetest women he'd ever met, coming in a close second to his own mother. He saw the gratitude in her eyes and felt himself blush a little. She had no idea why he'd wanted Lily cured, and looking into her eyes now, he almost felt like a heel. Almost.

"Don't thank me," he told her. "Lily is a beautiful woman who deserves to be happy. I only helped a little."

"You are welcome in this house, young man," her mother said, wiping her eyes. "Always."

"Thank you," Nikoli said and then turned regretful eyes to Lily. "We need to get going, Lily Bells."

"So soon?" Joanna asked. "It's barely seven."

"I have to be up early tomorrow," Nikoli explained. "I have a race."

"Race?" Joanna asked sharply.

"Yes, ma'am." Nikoli nodded. "I came down to Florida to enter a race."

"You race cars?" Nikoli watched Joanna's eyes fill up with some emotion he couldn't explain. She had to be thinking of Lily's father.

"I do," he said, keeping his voice calm. "Lily has been helping me get the car ready for the race."

"Those damn cars." Joanna shook her head.

"Lily was forever under the hood of a car, even after her father died."

"It kept me sane." Lily smiled.

"Yes, yes, it did. Have you seen my daughter drive, Nikoli?"

"Yes, ma'am. I let her drive the car I'm entering back to campus when I bought it. She smoked me."

"That's my girl." There was an edge to Joanna's laughter. Nikoli knew she wasn't at all happy about Lily in a race car.

"We really do have to go," Nikoli said gently. "We still have to feed Luther, my partner in crime."

"Oh my, let me fix him a plate." Joanna went about doing just that on a paper plate they could take.

He went over and slipped an arm around Lily, loving how she snuggled into his side. He leaned down and whispered, "Happy?"

"More than I could ever tell you," she whispered back. "Thank you, Nikoli Kincaid."

He brushed his lips over her hair and caught her mother staring at them. She looked so full of hope he couldn't meet her eyes. He was, for the first time in a while, starting to feel guilty about his own motives. Lily truly was a beautiful person inside and out. She deserved better than to be used the way he wanted to use her.

"Here you go." Joanna handed the plate to Lily. It was overflowing under the plastic wrap. She was a good cook, and Luther would be groaning with food orgasms before he'd finished the plate.

"Thank you, ma'am," he said. "It's been a pleasure to meet you."

Lily handed Nikoli the plate and hugged her mother. "Love you, Mama."

"I love you too, baby," Joanna murmured, and Nikoli smiled, knowing how much this meant to Lily.

"Can you start the car while I tell the twins goodbye?" Lily asked him, and he nodded, telling her mother goodbye once more before walking out into the humid Florida night. He started the car and rolled the windows down before turning on the air conditioning. He blew the heat out and then rolled the windows back up to cool the car off. Carefully putting the plate of food in the back seat, Nikoli leaned back and let the cool air hit him in the face.

She'd been on his mind all week. Ever since she told him about Adam, he knew it was the beginning of the end of their arrangement. He'd gotten a little attached to her, but that wasn't a bad thing. It just showed him he could eventually care for someone.

The little voice in the back of his mind snorted at his own idiocy, but he ignored it. Lily was an arrangement. That was all. He'd done his part, he'd helped her get past her fear of anyone touching her. She'd gotten Boy Wonder. Now it was time for him to get his half of the deal.

He winced just thinking about it like a deal, something dirty and sordid.

The passenger door opened, and Lily slid in and buckled her seatbelt. "Thank you for bringing me."

"Of course," he murmured and pulled out of the driveway.

Lily turned on the radio and surfed a few radio channels before settling on one. She didn't say

273

anything else the entire ride back to the hotel. Not that she needed to. He could see the thoughtful expression on her face. She had to be thinking of the afternoon. He'd seen the wonder on her face when she first realized she could give her mother a hug, and it had nearly undone him, truth be told.

When they parked the car and went upstairs, just as Nikoli had predicted, Luther drooled at the sight of the food presented to him. He grabbed it and shut the door, as if afraid they'd ask him to share.

Shaking his head, Nikoli steered Lily to their room. She said she wanted a shower, and he nodded. He opened his laptop and started going through some emails that needed attention while he waited for her to come out. Shoes and socks off, he settled himself in the chair and started scanning his emails.

He found one from Lily listing all her thoughts about his new zombie game. He just stared in amazement after he'd read through the very detailed report. She listed the good things, the things she hated, what needed to be improved, and finally her thoughts on fixing everything she took issue with. He'd never gotten such detailed feedback from any of his beta testers. The woman was amazing in so many ways.

Twenty minutes later, he heard the shower cut off, and he closed his laptop. He turned and faced the bathroom door, waiting for her to come out. Another fifteen minutes went by, and still no Lily. Maybe shaving her legs? After another ten minutes he got concerned and went over to the door. Even before he raised his hand he heard her. She was crying.

"Lily?"

No answer.

"Lily, what's wrong?"

Still nothing but her the sound of her crying. He tried the handle and found it unlocked. She sat in the middle of the floor wrapped in a bath towel, her head on her knees. Tears streaked her face and her eyes were so sad. He knelt down in front of her and stroked her hair.

"What's wrong, baby?"

She just shook her head. He pulled her into his lap. "Shhh, *dushka*, don't cry. Tell me what's wrong."

Instead of telling him, she wrapped her arms around him and sobbed harder. What in the hell? She was starting to scare him.

"Lily, tell me why you're crying." He put an edge into his voice, a tone that told her he wanted no nonsense. She would answer him.

"Kiss me," she said instead, and he looked down into her dark blue eyes, eyes so dark they looked black.

He wanted her to tell him why she was crying, but when she looked at him like that, it undid him. He lowered his head and kissed her softly, tenderly. Her arms crept up around his neck, her fingers tangling in his hair. She pulled him closer. He reveled in the feel of her lips against his, their breath mingling. He ran his fingers up and down her back, relaxing and seducing her at the same time.

When he pulled away, he left her breathless, and the haunted look had fled her eyes. Now they were sleepy with lust and desire. Nikoli gathered her in his arms, stood, and walked to the bed. Putting her down, he stripped off his shirt. She looked up at him, and the trust in her face was something he'd always wanted, and the one girl he didn't want it from was giving it to him. What the hell was he going to do about Lily Isabella Holmes?

Lily stared up at Nikoli and waited for him to do or say something. He had the oddest look on his face. She had distracted him earlier by asking him to kiss her. She couldn't tell him she was crying because she was losing him. He'd freak. She'd made up her mind on the drive back that she would lose their bet. If all she had with Nikoli was this weekend, then she'd savor it and tuck it away to bring out when she was feeling lonely.

She loved him. It was as simple as that.

He reached down and pulled the bath towel away from her naked body and sat behind her on the bed to dry her hair. He used slow, gentle movements, and she sighed. He always made her feel so safe, so cared for. He tossed the towel after a few minutes, and she felt his lips on her neck, nuzzling. She leaned back against him and relaxed as his lips made their way down to her collarbone, his tongue swiping quick tastes here and there. He was being so tender.

His hands traveled down her arms, slid over her thighs, trailed back up her stomach, and then brushed against the underside of her breasts. She moaned and pressed against him, silently asking him for more. His hands curled around her breasts, squeezing softly before rolling her nipples. Lily arched her back, thrusting her breasts out, demanding more.

"Nikoli…"

"Shhh," he whispered. "Don't talk, *dushka*. Just let me love you." He moved from behind her and pushed her down on the bed.

She fought her tears at his softly whispered words. She'd love him as best as she could for tonight.

"Don't cry, *Milaya*," he whispered. "Please don't cry."

She smiled through her tears and reached for him. "It's okay," she told him. "I'm happy in this moment, Nikoli. Let me love you tonight too. Please."

He stared down at her with wide eyes and then nodded. He stood and slipped his jeans off. Lily stared up at him. He was beautiful. His skin was a rich tone, reminding her of someone from Greece more than Russia. His black eyes and hair gave him that bad boy look, one he encouraged. His body was sculpted from hours in the gym, and she loved every inch of it.

Lily sat up and held her hand out to him. He took it without hesitation, and she tugged. He smiled and lay down next to her, turning so he faced her. "What do you plan on doing, *Milaya*?"

"Whatever I want." She ran her fingers lazily over his chest. "Whatever I want, Nikoli Kincaid."

Nikoli closed his eyes and let Lily have her way. He was so proud of her. She'd spent the entire day having her family touch her, and now she was here, naked and asking to touch him. He was so very proud of his Lily Bells.

Her thumbs circled his nipple and he let out a small gasp. No one had ever affected him like Lily. The feel of her hands on his skin was driving him crazy. He wanted to flip her, bend her over the bed, and take her, but he didn't. Instead, he lay here, letting her exploring fingers torture him. Something he'd never really allowed any other girl to do. But then he'd never trusted anyone like he did his Lily Bells.

Her warm, wet lips started to travel over his skin, and it was all he could do to hold back a moan. He opened his eyes and stared down at her. She was doing to him what he'd done to her, and he realized how hard it had been for her to stay still if she felt even an ounce of what he did now.

Her touch set off a fire inside of him, and before long he was pulling her up to meet his lips. He could only take so much of her sweet torture. She tried to protest, but he hushed her and rolled so she was beneath him. "No, *Milaya*. Any more of that and it'll be over before it begins."

She laughed, and he felt it go through every part of him. He closed his eyes and forced himself to regain some control over the urge to fuck her hard right then and there. She deserved better than that.

"Lily, I need to ask..." She shifted under him, inadvertently rubbing herself against him. "Ah, fuck, Lily, don't move."

Another small laugh escaped her. "What do you want to know?"

"*Are* you a virgin?"

"No, I'm not a virgin. Remember when I told

you I got caught up in the wrong crowd after my dad died? Lost my virginity way back then, but it's been a *long* time, Nikoli."

"Well, hell," he grumbled. That was just as bad.

"Nikoli?"

"Yeah?"

"You're thinking too hard." Laughter danced in her eyes.

He laughed; he couldn't help it. Lily's laughter was contagious. He'd never hesitated with a woman in his life, but here he was worried about hurting this one. She was warm, wet, and willing beneath him, and telling him to get on with it. No one had ever had to tell him that before.

He thrust two fingers inside of her, causing her to gasp. "Still thinking too hard?"

"No." Her voice was low, and deep, and breathy all at the same time.

She was dripping wet, but still he hesitated. He worked her with his fingers, thrusting them in and out, his thumb rubbing her clit, listening to her moan and mutter nonsense things.

"Tell me now if you want me to stop, *Milaya*," he said, his voice harder than he'd intended, but damn, he hurt with the need to get inside her.

Lily gave him the softest smile he'd ever seen and cupped his face. "I don't want to stop, Nikoli."

He groaned and buried his face in the crook of her neck, his tongue dragging over the sensitive skin. He slid his fingers out of her and she whimpered in protest. "You're sure about this?"

"Yes." The one word, full of so much want and need did him in. He grabbed a condom from the bedside table drawer and rolled it on. The hotel always stocked them there at his request. He pushed himself up and dragged Lily toward him, her legs spread over his thighs. Moisture dripped from her opening.

"Look at me, *Milaya*. Don't close your eyes."

Lily felt the shudder go through her at his command, her body automatically reacting to it. She pulled her eyes up to his and gasped at the burning desire she saw there. The hesitation on his face made her reach up, and he laced his fingers through hers. His other hand curled around her hip and pulled her to him as he slid inside her. Lily moaned at the unfamiliar burning sensation as he stretched her.

"Easy," he murmured. "Relax, *Milaya*, just relax."

Lily gasped when he pushed deeper and the burning turned to something else, something she couldn't define. He filled her, and she felt herself clench around him, reveling in the way he groaned every time she did. She squeezed the hand still wrapped around hers as he began to move within her. His pace was slow and gentle, letting her get used to the feel and size of him as he slid through her and back out. Fire ripped through her, its heat intensifying with every second.

She pulled on the hand she held and he came down, shifting his body to keep his weight off her. His eyes met hers and she reached up to pull his head down, her lips finding his. He kissed her like it was their first kiss and their last kiss all rolled into one. Her legs wrapped around him and she let herself get lost in the feel of Nikoli moving, the sensations cascading through her, and the way his lips ate at hers, like she was the only thing keeping him breathing.

His pace became faster, harder, and Lily groaned, the sensations in her body reacting to it, the pressure building. His lips left hers and his arms slid under her, wrapping his hands over her shoulder blades, holding her steady while he drove himself into her, his thrusts deep and hard. Lily cried out, the pleasure so intense she didn't know if she wanted to run from it or demand more. Nikoli held her in place, his hips slamming into hers.

"That's it, baby," he whispered in her ear, his tongue swiping the lobe as his fingers found her clit and rubbed it. "Just let go, *Milaya*, let go."

The pressure inside built and built with each hard press of his thumb against her clit, each thrust into her body. When the orgasm hit, she wasn't prepared and screamed, Nikoli's name leaving her lips as the wave crashed into and over her entire body. She was only vaguely aware of Nikoli shouting her own name as he reached his climax. His body sagged on top of hers, his breathing as labored as her own. Lily smiled and felt herself relaxing, her body heavy and sated. This was something she'd never regret or forget.

It was several moments before Nikoli was able to gain the strength to pull out of her and roll, bringing Lily with him. He didn't say anything, but then neither did she. Never, in all his years, had he felt anything like he had when he made love to Lily. She'd shattered him, barreled forward and knocked down every wall he'd ever put up to protect himself. Her kindness, her need to love him like he did her, had been his downfall. She'd given to him what he'd never expected any woman to give. She'd given him every part of herself, holding nothing back, and he'd done the same. Her touch had undone him.

Lily Holmes scared the hell out of him.

Chapter Eighteen

The sound of cars being revved up blanketed the night. Lily blinked and brushed the remaining sleep out of her eyes. Nikoli had shaken her awake at 3:00 a.m. and here she was an hour later, still half asleep. She'd been awake a long time after they'd made love, thinking and listening to the even sound of Nikoli's breathing as he slept. She was running on about two hours, but the sound of the engines, the smell of the gas, it all started to wake her sleepy mind.

It wasn't what she imagined it would be. Growing up watching *The Fast and The Furious* movies had permanently warped her vision of what a street race should be. It was the middle of the night, the only real lights were some drop lights scattered around, and they'd taken over the parking lot of an abandoned warehouse. She'd imagined some racetrack scenario, with spectators and fans everywhere. Not what she got.

Nikoli left her and Luther by the car while he went to check in. Luther popped the hood and busied himself inspecting the car for the thousandth time. It was ready. She almost said something, but she knew it was his way of dealing with nerves. Instead, she studied the people, their backgrounds from all over, judging from the diverse group around her.

The adrenaline and excitement on every face she saw was, however, just as she'd imagined it. People were huddled in groups around their cars, some shooting the breeze, others shit-talking each other, and she grinned. This was amazing. No wonder her father had always said he loved this more than NASCAR. She wasn't even driving, and her adrenaline was through the roof.

"Hey, baby." Nikoli slid his arms around her. "How are you feeling?"

"*Ohmygoshthisisamazing!*" The words came out in a rush, all jumbled together, and Nikoli laughed.

"That's not what I mean," he whispered. "I mean are *you* okay after last night? Sore?"

Lily felt her face flame up at the reminder, and she shot a glance to where Luther was still buried under the hood of the car. "I'm fine," she muttered.

Nikoli laughed again and gave her another squeeze. He could see the blush spreading like wildfire along her neck and cheeks. She was adorable when she was embarrassed. "So what do you think of your first underground race?" he asked, his hand brushing against the underside of her breast. Her small gasp made him grin wider.

"Well, I thought there would be more people here, more lights, more…everything."

Luther stood up and slammed the hood. "Oh,

there are plenty of those around, Lily. This race is invite only and very hush-hush. Got to keep it on the down low."

"Are we ready?" Nikoli let his chin rest on the top of Lily's head.

"If we're not, there's nothing we can do about it now." Luther checked his watch. "You got five minutes to get in the car and get it to the starting line."

"Luther, don't let her out of your sight." He turned Lily around and bent down to give her a quick kiss. "Wish me luck, baby."

"Good luck," she said, a ghost of a smile on her face. She seemed sad this morning, and Nikoli wanted to reassure her, but he couldn't. He had the feeling she knew, like he did, this was their last weekend together. He had no idea how to comfort her when he was having issues coming to terms with it himself.

Instead of dwelling, he released her and slid behind the wheel of the car they'd labored over for this race. He started the engine, revved it a few times, and then pulled out, leaving Lily and Luther in his rear view mirror.

"Come on, Lily." Luther took her arm and started to pull her closer to where the cars were lined up, despite the fact she stiffened up. She might be better, but she wasn't cured. "We'll wait up here so we can see them when they circle back and cross the finish the line."

"How long does the race usually take?" Her eyes took in everything as she disentangled herself from Luther's grip. A hint of her panic crept up her spine, but she took several deep breaths and made herself calm down.

"Depends," Luther said, eyeballing the other cars. "It could be ten minutes or it could be a couple hours. The route is preprogrammed into the GPS. Nikoli got it when he signed in a few minutes ago. No one knows the route until they get in the car and plug the GPS in. Last year it was a thirty minute race."

The engines revved up, and without warning they all squealed tires and sped off into the early morning darkness. Lily's eyes widened. She'd expected someone up front to be waving a green flag or something.

Luther laughed at her expression. "We are ruining your expectations, huh?"

Lily nodded, nonplussed. This was not at all what she'd expected.

"We'll take you to a race that will reaffirm all those expectations," Luther said, laughing. "This one is for major money."

Lily shot him a smile tinged with sadness. She highly doubted she'd be going to any other races with them, but she pushed those thoughts down and started counting the minutes.

Nerves ate at her. The last race she'd been to was the one that cost her father his life. He'd plowed into a wreck on the track, been hit by another car and pushed into the wall, trapped and unable to move when the next few cars slammed into the wreckage. Lily didn't like to dwell on it because then she'd start thinking of if he'd been unconscious or if he'd been awake and in pain as he'd died. It always ripped her to shreds imagining all the what-ifs.

She couldn't help but think about it now, though. Nikoli was racing, and even though this wasn't a track, it was still dangerous. Maybe even more dangerous than an organized race like NASCAR. Worry for Nikoli consumed her, but she tried to keep it from showing. Luther was nervous enough for both of them.

After forty-five minutes, the wait started to get to Luther. He'd taken to pacing, as had several other people milling around. He'd been nervous before, but now he was clearly getting worried. The later it got, the more the city started to wake up. Soon, it would be next to impossible for the racers to hide from the police and the helicopters. That was another worry of Lily's. They'd both impressed upon her how important it was to not get caught, given who they were. This was how they financed their business, and it would be bad for business to get arrested for being involved in an illegal race.

Another fifteen minutes went by before the sound of loud engines could be heard. Luther grabbed Lily and pulled her well out of the way. Before she could protest, she saw the first of four cars fighting for first place. They were all over the road, pushing each other, angling to try and get around the ones in front of them. Lily squinted and spotted Nikoli in third place. Her heart nearly stopped when one of the cars slammed into his, forcing him off the road, but he recovered and shot back up to where he was.

Luther cursed rather violently while they

watched Nikoli fight to gain control of the second position. He swerved and slammed his car into the same Dodge Charger that had forced him off the road. The Charger's driver lost control of the car and spun out, flipping, taking the fourth car down with him. All that was left was the Mach 1 and the 1974 Chevelle. Neither looked willing to give an inch, both ramming into each other.

Lily bit down on her knuckles to keep from shouting. Luther leaned forward as they got closer, muttering something she couldn't make out. She didn't care. Her eyes were glued to the battling vehicles, their intent to win clear in their aggressive driving.

Closer and closer they came, each pulling out into the lead for a brief few seconds before being overtaken. She knew how important this race was Luther and Nikoli, but she didn't think they were going to win. She'd been watching the other driver and knew for a fact he wasn't showing his hand. The car sat up just a little higher in the front which told her there were modifications that could boost the speed under that hood. No racer worth a grain of salt would do a speed boost until the very end.

"He's not going to win," Lily whispered, which made Luther glower at her. "Well, he's not. The other car still has a speed boost left."

"How do you know that?" Luther asked, a growl behind his words.

"I know cars, Luther," she said, still watching the fight. "Trust me on this."

Luther pulled out a small radio and started shouting into it. Lily's eyebrows rose. If he'd been able to talk to Nikoli before, why had he waited and worked himself up into such a nervous wreck?

Before Lily realized what was happening, Nikoli pulled ahead and then drifted right hard, forcing the other car to swerve. The Chevelle's rear end slammed into Nikoli, and both cars started spinning out of control. They were simply going too fast. Lily watched, horrified as both cars bounced off each other again. That final hard slam sent Nikoli's Mach 1 over the finish line, while the Chevelle hit the side of the building, smashing the front end up into the dash.

Nikoli's car came to a halt and Lily ran, despite Luther shouting for her to wait. She needed to see that he was okay, that he wasn't dead. The car took a beating, and she knew Nikoli had as well. The door was flung open, and she reached him just as he fell out onto the pavement. Dropping to her knees, she grabbed his face and pulled it up so she could see his eyes. He gave her a half smile before dragging her closer for a kiss full of fear, passion, and need. It left them both breathless. He stared at her in shock when he pulled away from her.

"I love you," she blurted out, and Nikoli blinked. She knew she'd shocked him. She could see the shock in his eyes. She hadn't meant to say that. God, she hadn't meant to, but how was she going to take it back?

Lily started to say something, but the smell caught her attention. It was a mixture of gasoline and nitrogen. Her father warned her if she smelled that to run as fast as she could. She looked over to the Chevelle and saw them struggling to get the driver out.

She stood up and ran over. "Luther, get your ass over here and help us get him out before this thing blows!" She pulled out her small pocketknife and concentrated on getting the seatbelt off him while others yanked the door off and pulled the seat back so they could drag the guy from the car. She felt Nikoli at her back and looked to see him struggling to help them with the seat. He only gave her a grin when she sent a glare his way. He should be sitting down, not trying to help.

The guys managed to pull the seat back and free the driver's legs. Lily took a step back so they could drag him out of the car. Luther tossed her the keys to the Lexus and then jumped in the Mach 1. Nikoli headed for the Lexus, and Lily stared after Luther for a minute before hurrying to catch up with Nikoli. He slid in the passenger seat, and Lily got in the driver's side.

"Drive," he bit out before she could say anything.

Lily did as she was told without another word. She knew the police would be here soon, and they needed to be gone. He directed her down several side streets and through two alleys before they emerged onto the main highway. Lily pulled over at a gas station about ten minutes later and turned to assess the damage.

Nikoli had several nasty bruises, and a cut on his forehead was still bleeding heavily. She popped open the glove box and took out the first aid kit they'd stored there yesterday. Nikoli grumbled when she cleaned the wound and then closed it up with butterfly bandages.

When she was satisfied she'd done as much as she could with what she had, she closed the kit and gave him a once over. She knew without asking, he wouldn't go to the hospital.

"Are you okay?" she asked. "Is there anything I can get you?"

"A bottle of water would be nice," Nikoli told her, seeing the worry in her eyes. She nodded and got out of the car to go into the gas station. He let out a small sigh of relief. He'd won. It had been close, and he owed that to Lily. Luther warned him the guy was about to launch a speed boost, and Nikoli would have been sunk if that happened. Thank God she knew so much about cars, especially race cars.

When she'd kissed him, Nikoli realized two things. She loved him, but more importantly, he loved her. He felt how much she loved him in the way she'd kissed him. She'd put everything in that kiss she didn't dare say out loud. Not only had he responded, but he'd put just as much into the kiss as she had. He loved her, and it terrified him.

Then she'd gone and told him she loved him. The kiss had told him that already, but then her blurted confession confirmed it.

He didn't know how to respond to that.

This road was a familiar one for him. Sure, Lily hadn't asked him for anything, but who was to say that down the road, as she got her claws sunk deeper into him, that she wouldn't become just like every other woman? He'd misjudged one woman once, and he wasn't about to put himself in that position again. He couldn't do that to himself, no matter how much he loved Lily. He couldn't take the risk of feeling that heartbreak again.

Lily opened the car door and gave him the water, along with a few wet paper towels. He cleaned up his face and then swallowed half the bottle in one long pull.

"You're sure you're okay?" she fussed. "You could have internal injuries. Maybe we should go to the hospital?"

"No." He shook his head. "They'll be checking the ERs and local clinics looking for injuries from a car accident. I can't go there. I'm fine, Lily, really. Just get us back to the hotel room so I can lay down."

She started the car and pulled back into the flow of traffic. Nikoli closed his eyes and winced when she hit a rough patch in the road. He didn't think he had any internal injuries, but he was sore and felt every bump. It would be a relief to just lie down in the bed for a while.

It took a little over an hour to reach the hotel because of early morning traffic, but Luther was waiting when Lily parked the car. He helped Nikoli out and started to lead him through a side door Lily hadn't seen before. It was a back entrance only the staff used, but there was an elevator a few feet in front of the door. Once they got Nikoli to his room and settled in bed, Luther headed out, saying he needed to make arrangements for the car.

Lily sat down on the chair across from the bed and watched him sleep. He'd fallen out minutes after his head hit the pillow. Lily worried about a concussion, but he hadn't shown any signs of one. He wasn't dizzy or seeing double, and his eyes had been focused. Still, she worried, so she watched him for any signs of trouble.

She still couldn't believe she'd been stupid enough to tell him she loved him. The look of shock in his eyes worried her. Even though she hadn't meant for the words to slip out, she was glad they were out there. Sometimes, she thought Nikoli loved her as much as she loved him, but she couldn't be sure. She loved him enough to risk her heart being broken.

It was a risky bet and one she didn't know if she'd win.

When Nikoli opened his eyes several hours later, he saw Lily curled up in the chair she'd dragged close to the bed. She smiled softly when she saw him staring at her. His heart clenched, knowing what he was about to do to her. She didn't deserve it, but he couldn't risk his heart again. He just couldn't.

"Hey, sleepyhead," she said. "I was starting to get worried about you."

"I'm fine." He sat up and ran a hand through his hair. "Give me a few minutes, Lily Bells. Then we need to talk." He got up and headed to the bathroom. He slowed down as soon as his injuries caught up to him. He'd been slammed into the car door more times than he could count. Sure enough, once he took his shirt off, he saw the bruise that ran the length of his arm and wrapped around his shoulder.

He turned on the shower and then slipped in a

minute later, letting the hot water hit the bruises on his body to help soothe the sore muscles. How was he going to break her heart? How was he going to look into the eyes of the woman he loved and tell her he didn't love her? How had he gotten into this mess in the first place?

All because he was determined to have the one woman who not only ignored him, but inspired a hunt like no other. She ran, and he chased. When he caught her, he found not a sly fox, but a sweet and innocent young woman who truly epitomized the meaning of a good person. He hadn't been prepared for her. She made him laugh, made him question his own sense of self. She made him want to be a better person.

And despite all that, he was still going to break her.

Shutting off the shower, he dried off and put on the clean pair of jeans and t-shirt he'd left in here this morning for his after-race shower. He took a deep breath and opened the door. Lily was still sitting where he'd left her, but she was staring off into space, deep in thought.

He walked over and sat down on the bed. "We need to talk, Lily."

She smiled up at him, and it nearly did him in. There was so much hope on her face.

"Yes, we do," she said. "I didn't mean to blurt it out like that, but I was scared, and then you were safe and I couldn't help it. I do love you, Nikoli. I have for a long time."

"No, Lily, you don't love me." He shook his head. "You just see what everyone else does, and you only think you love me…"

She reached up and put a finger to his lips. "Stop right there, Kincaid. I do see what you let everyone else see—the fuck you, I don't care what you think man, and then I see you. The man who is gentle, and takes care of those he cares about. The man who stopped what he was doing to buy a little girl a sucker because her mama didn't have the money for it. I see the man who laughs, the man who can be kind and loving. I see the man I fell in love with, I see *you*."

Nikoli didn't know what to say. Lily really did see him, the man he hid from everyone, sometimes even Luther. How had he let her get this close?

"It doesn't matter, Lily."

"Of course it matters," she argued.

"No, it doesn't. I don't love you, Lily."

Her eyes. Dammit. He watched them go from so full of happiness to horror, and then to a deep and abiding hurt. It was as if someone had sucked all the joy out of them and left nothing but a broken and beaten landscape behind. Her face paled and her hands clutched the chair arms in a death grip.

She blinked, and he watched the tears pool in her eyes. More than anything, he wanted to pull her into his lap and tell her he was wrong, that he loved her too, but he didn't. Instead he just sat there, his face expressionless.

Lily got up, and he watched her cautiously. She rummaged in her luggage until she found her tablet. She turned it on and made several swipes. What was she doing? Once she was done, she put her tablet back and then called the front desk for a taxi.

"What are you doing?" he asked, getting a little alarmed. She hadn't said a word. He stood up and followed her.

"I'm going home." Her voice shook. "There's a noon flight back to Boston, and I was able to swap my ticket for it."

"You don't need to do that Lily," he said. "You can ride back with me and Luther…"

"No, that's not a good idea," she interrupted. "I don't want to see Luther's pity. I've seen it on his face for so many other girls. I couldn't bear it."

"At least let me take you to the airport."

"No," she said adamantly. "You are in no shape to be driving. You need to rest."

Another sharp pain ripped through him. He'd broken her heart and she was still more worried about him than her own pain.

She finished packing and then opened the door, looking at him one more time. The depth of her pain made him take a step toward her, but she put out a hand as if to ward him off.

"Goodbye, Nikoli."

Then she closed the door, and Nikoli stumbled as he walked over to the chair she'd just been in. He sank down and put his head in his heads, knowing he'd probably screwed up the best thing that ever happened to him.

It only took a moment for the pain of losing her to sink in. He stood, his fists clenched, and stared at the door. She was gone. Really and truly gone. Anger at himself, at the situation, at Lily for just leaving swamped him, and his fist hit the wall. He let out a ragged groan, but he welcomed the pain his body was experiencing. After what he'd just done, he deserved to hurt.

Images of her flashed in his mind, laughing, joking, and the way she smiled at the simplest of things. His heart argued with him, the pain it caused so deep, he fell down to his knees as it wrenched through him.

How was he going to survive this?

***

I don't love you, Lily.

Those words kept echoing in Lily's mind, each one a stab into her heart. It was as if he'd taken her heart, held it in his hands for a moment, and then started to squeeze, the pain worse with each passing moment. Lily felt as if she couldn't breathe, as if she wanted to hurl. Her heart ached, her body ached from the rejection. She wanted to cry, to wail, to shout at God, Fate, and any other entity she could blame for the pain she felt right now.

She called Adam and asked him to pick her up at the airport, and she begged him not to bring Sue. That witch was someone she'd hurt if she gave her one snide stare. Adam hadn't asked a single question, just said he'd be waiting for her. For that, she was grateful.

The flight home was difficult. She barely kept it together. When the plane landed and they all were hustled inside, she found Adam waiting in the baggage claim area. She threw herself at him and burst into tears. As soon as she saw his familiar face, the dam had broken. He wrapped his arms around her and pulled her close, murmuring nonsense. She cried so hard, and he just stood there and let her.

"Come on, Lils," he whispered after a long time. "Let's get you home, okay?"

Instead of taking her back to the dorm, he took her to the small apartment Mike and Janet shared. They were both there when Adam opened the door, but she ran past them into the bathroom. Standing was too much effort, so she lay down on the floor, her cheek pressed to the white tile that smelled like Pine-Sol.

She couldn't breathe. She tried taking deep breaths, but she couldn't breathe. It hurt too much. Tears slid over her nose and landed to puddle in front of her eyes on the harsh tile of the floor. The door opened and Adam came in. He didn't say anything, he just lay down next to her. His hand found hers, and he laced their fingers together.

Her sobs shook her, and she couldn't stop them. Her entire body cried out in denial, her soul felt like it had been torn in half. She missed him, and he hadn't been gone for more than a few hours.

Adam rolled and pulled her into him, his stomach against her back, and he held her while she shook from grief and her sobs robbed her of breath. Adam held her while she cried, not saying a word, but just holding her to let her know he was there and she was loved. She appreciated that more than she could say.

Her sobs quieted, and she stared at the white plastic of the small tub in front of her. She wanted to feel numb, but she didn't. Every breath, every movement hurt. Never had she imagined losing Nikoli would hurt this much. She felt like she was the one who'd been in the accident this morning. Her skin felt raw, her lungs burned, and her heart…her heart was just broken.

She was broken.

***

"You look like shit."

Nikoli raised blurry eyes to see his brother standing above him. Kade took a seat across from him at the table. The waitress came over, and he asked for a beer. "What are you doing here?"

"Luther called me. Said you'd been drunk for the last week and you wouldn't listen to him."

Luther needed to mind his own damn business. Liquor numbed the pain.

"What has gotten into you?" Kade continued. "You've never been much of a drinker."

That was before he lost the one person who really mattered to him.

"Go home, Kade."

"No, I'm not going home." He thanked the waitress as she set his beer down in front of him. "What the hell is wrong with you? Are you seriously binge drinking because of some chick?"

"You don't know a thing about Lily." He winced at the slur in his voice. "You don't understand what I did to her."

Kade's eyes sharpened. "Nikoli, you didn't do anything that can get you in trouble, did you?"

Nikoli snorted. "No."

Relief swept over Kade's face. "You need to pull yourself together, little brother."

"I love her."

That made Kade shut up. His mouth opened and closed, but no words came out.

"Then why the fuck are you sitting here, drunk off your ass, instead of with her?"

"You know why."

Kade flinched. He did know why.

"She's not Jessica." Her name still brought a scowl to both their faces.

Jessica Frasier. Her name still left a bad taste in Nikoli's mouth. The summer before he started Boston University, he'd gone to spend the summer with Kade in Virginia. Jessica had been his brother's girlfriend. Blonde, beautiful, and a manipulative bitch at heart. She'd started to flirt with him the day he'd arrived. Kade had told her how proud he was of Nikoli for what he'd accomplished, had told her about Nikoli's business.

His brother had been in love with her.

It hadn't mattered to Nikoli. The woman had convinced him that she loved him after a few weeks there, and he'd believed her. He'd been young and stupid, and he'd almost ruined the relationship between him and Kade. It still wasn't what it was, but they'd both realized soon after who Jessica really was at heart. Nikoli had hurt his brother, had taken what was his and never looked back. Maybe the pain he felt now was karma's way of paying him back.

She'd demanded things from Nikoli from the beginning, and he'd obliged her by buying anything she wanted. He'd left his brother's apartment and had been staying with Jessica. He'd come home one day and overheard a conversation she was having with someone on the phone. She'd been gloating about landing the rich brother, laughing while she told whoever about how she'd convinced Nikoli he loved her and about how she was now set for life.

Realizing what she'd made him do, he'd simply walked out and gone to find his brother. It had hurt, sucker punched him. At the time, he'd thought he loved her. He'd been so ashamed of what he'd done to his brother. He'd confessed to Kade what he'd overheard, and Kade had forgiven him. Jessica had manipulated them both. It had skewed both of them in their expectations of women. Neither had had a relationship that lasted longer than an hour since then.

Jessica had ruined him. Nikoli had loved her, or at least he thought he had at the time. He understood the difference now. He understood the difference between lust and love. He loved Lily, but he'd lusted after Jessica, and in the process had almost lost his brother. It would cause any sane man to pause.

"Nikoli, you know I'm the first person to advocate bachelorhood, but I think you need to get over it and go get your woman back."

Nikoli's head snapped up. Kade sat there sipping his beer. Looking all sage and wise.

"The day I met her, I knew you were sunk. The way the two of you were together…there was a connection there. I went home thinking my little brother found his one."

Nikoli was shaking his head before his brother even finished speaking.

"I can't."

"Little brother, you're sitting here so drunk, I don't think you can stand up. Luther says you've been like this all week, blowing off classes, and angry at the world. If you love the girl, you need to own up to it."

"I told her I didn't love her." Nikoli downed the shot of tequila he'd just poured. "She said she loved me, and I sat there and broke her. Her face…" He closed his eyes at the memory.

"I'm sure if you talked to her…"

"No," Nikoli interrupted his brother. "It's better this way."

Kade didn't say anything after that, but the look of disgust he gave Nikoli spoke volumes. Yeah, he was stupid. He knew that, but he was afraid.

Kade asked for his bill and paid Nikoli's tab as well. "Let's get you home. If you want to destroy your chance at happiness, man, go for it, but I'm not letting you binge drink anymore. If I have to call every bar in Boston to cut you off, I will."

Nikoli barely remembered Kade hauling him up. All he could think about was Lily.

It *was* better this way.

Chapter Nineteen

Nikoli tossed his empty beer can in the direction of the table and studied the crowd. His frat house was packed with drunken hot chicks, and he was finding it difficult to even look at one. He kept thinking about Lily. Her eyes haunted him. He hadn't been back to the penthouse since their night there. God knew he'd tried, but the thought of going there without her was too much. Maybe it was time to put it up for sale. He was graduating this semester and leaving Boston. He and Luther were setting up their corporate offices in New York. They'd decided on that two years ago, but now Nikoli was rethinking the location. Lily was moving to New York after graduation.

Fuck. She shouldn't be able to do this to him. He was seriously reconsidering relocating to a different city. She was just a chick. He tried to tell himself that every day, but he knew better. Lily Bells was special. She was kind, beautiful, full of love and joy, and she made him *feel*. Feel so much more than anyone ever had. She made him feel in a way that touched him to his core. It scared him. Enough that he let her walk away from him. Even after she told him she didn't want Boy Wonder, that all she wanted was him. He'd broken her heart. Her eyes...fuck, he could still see the pain in her eyes. It cut him to his core, and he hated that she could do that to him.

Hated that he loved her.

At least he'd stopped drinking himself into oblivion every day.

He needed to get laid. One good hard fuck and he'd forget her. She was just a chick, after all. Same as the rest of them. Same as the other girl he'd thought he loved. She'd been easily forgotten, and so would Lily. His inner demons laughed at him, but he ignored them. Tonight he'd find a girl, take her to one of the rooms, and forget Lily Holmes existed. His eyes scanned the room and zeroed in on the blonde getting a beer. Nikoli appreciated the way her dress clung to her curves and the way her hips rolled suggestively when she moved. Here was a girl meant to be fucked. With a grin, he stood up and swaggered over to her, his only intent to take her upstairs into one of the rooms and get her naked.

Lily sighed. She'd finally relented to Janet's constant demands that she come to a party. It was at Nikoli and Luther's frat house, but she was pretty sure Nikoli wouldn't be there. He hated these things. He'd rather be in a bar. At least she hoped he wouldn't be there. She wasn't sure she was ready to see him yet. It had been almost a month since he told her he didn't love her. Every time she thought about him, her heart shattered all over again. No one except Adam knew how badly broken she was. She'd learned over the years to hide her pain well. They all thought she was fine about breaking up with Nikoli.

Breaking up. She laughed a little bitterly at the words. They had never been together, not really. It was all just a stupid bargain. A bargain Nikoli had come out of smelling like roses. Lily came out the other end a broken mess—no Adam, no Nikoli, and she didn't even get the damn car. All she ended up with was a broken heart and the need to cry every five minutes. Which was why she gave in about the party. She needed to stop moping around and wallowing in her own pain. The only way to get past it was to go out and make herself do normal things. Like this party, even if it was Nikoli's frat house.

Mikey saw her first and rushed over to give her a hug. He grinned from ear to ear when she returned it. "Hey, Lils, you made it."

"Not like Jan gave me a choice," she said ruefully. "I don't think she was going to budge from my room until I came."

"Well, you know my girl," Mike said, a smile breaking free. "She's bossy and always gets her way."

"Hey!" Jan playfully punched him in the arm and then snuggled up to him.

"There's my girl." Adam wrapped an arm around her and hugged her tight. He gave her his one hundred watt smile and dragged her outside to the balcony where it was quiet. One other couple was making out in the corner, so he led her to the opposite end.

"Are you sure you can be here?" he asked. "Nikoli's here somewhere."

Lily's face blanched and her heart twisted. Her flight or fight instincts kicked in, and she wanted to run far, far away.

"I'll take you home," Adam said softly.

"No." She shook her head. As much as she wanted to run, she couldn't. It was inevitable that she'd see Nikoli, and she'd rather do it here with her friends around her than somewhere else. "Jan will freak out if I leave, and then everyone will think I left because of him. I'm not going to run away like a scared little girl, Adam. That's not who I am."

Adam gave her a rueful smile. "I like this new more confident you, but sometimes I wish the old Lily would rear her head up when you're about to get hurt again for no reason."

Lily knew what he was referring to. Women loved Nikoli, and she'd heard he'd had women hanging off of him everywhere he went. Tonight would be no different, but she had to suffer through it. Not only for Jan, but for herself. She needed to prove she could get through the pain. That she'd be able to breathe again one day without feeling the burn of the ache scorching her insides.

"You know how much I love you, don't you?" she asked, giving him another hug. She didn't know how she'd have gotten through those first days without him. He'd lain with her on Janet's bathroom floor for two days. They hadn't said anything, he'd just comforted her. He'd been her best friend, and it had helped more than anything else.

"I love you too, Lily." He hugged her back, and she made up her mind to talk to him, but she didn't want him to take it the wrong way.

"Adam, I need to talk to you." She leaned against the balcony railing. "I've wanted to say this for a long time, but I didn't because I thought you were happy."

"Have you reconsidered my proposal?" The hope in his eyes hurt. She didn't want him to hurt like she was hurting.

"No, Adam, it wouldn't be fair to either of us, and you know it, but I do want to talk to you about Sue."

He sighed and settled down beside her.

"The only thing I want is for you to be happy, you know that."

Adam nodded.

"Are you happy, though? The very fact that you were willing to dump her for me says a lot. Are you marrying her because you want to, or because you feel it's what's expected of you? Are you going to be happy with her five years from now, ten?"

"I honestly don't know, Lils," he said. "The closer the wedding gets, the more nervous and anxious I get. I start to question myself. Sometimes I think she manipulated me into asking her. I felt so pressured."

"Promise me that before you stand before God and all our family and friends, you'll think about what you're doing. Promise me you'll call this off if it's not going to make you happy. Please, Adam."

"I promise." He leaned over and kissed the top of her head. "Let's get back inside. Janet wants to show you all her wedding stuff. She has it all over here for some reason. I'm not sure why."

Janet attacked as soon as they came back into the main room. "I'm so sorry, Lily, I didn't know until Mike told me. I swear I didn't know."

"It's okay, Jan." I laughed. "It's fine, really. Now what's this I hear about wedding stuff? And why is it all at a frat house?"

Jan looked madder than a wet hen. "Mike was trying to fix the sink and ended up flooding the apartment. We're both staying here until it gets fixed."

"Oh, my," Lily murmured. That sure sounded like something Mikey would do.

"Come on, I'll show you everything I've picked out so far. I need help with the flowers and the bridesmaids dresses..."

"It's a party, Jan!" Mike shouted from across the room. "Let's party!"

She shot him a death glare, and Lily giggled. Janet started muttering about stupid men on the way up the stairs. The three drunken guys who stumbled down the stairs past her suffered the same look. They didn't waste time in getting out of her way. Lily laughed as she followed Jan down the hall, listening to her ramble on about colors and flowers.

Nikoli had his lips plastered to the blonde when he heard them. He'd know Lily's voice anywhere. He tore his mouth from the girl's and stared in horror as the door slowly opened. Jan looked up, her expression going from shock to outright rage when she saw him with his hands under the girl's shirt, his knee pressed up against her. It was Lily he saw, though.

Her eyes widened. They went from him to the busty blonde he'd shoved up against a wall. Her eyes, while they had been shuttered, now pooled with pain and hurt. A single tear escaped before she turned around and walked away.

Nikoli cracked. Seeing her again, after all these weeks, all the lies he'd told himself laughed in his face. The pain he'd seen in her eyes, the pain he'd been responsible for putting there not once, but twice, was a the slap upside the head he needed. He loved her. He'd tried so hard to convince himself he didn't, but she haunted him. He loved her, and dammit, it was time he told her. It was time he put them both out of their misery.

If she'd have him after this.

He started cursing and detached himself from the girl, meaning to follow Lily, but the little bit of fluff in the doorway stopped him.

"How dare you!" she shrieked. "Do you know what you did to her? Do you even care that she laid on my bathroom floor for two days? Do you care that she sobbed so hard she lost her voice? Who the fuck do you think you are, Nikoli Kincaid? You're nothing but a worthless, no good..."

"First this is *my* frat house, and I didn't expect her to show up here. Second, I sure as hell didn't mean for her to see that. Now get out of my way so I can check on her!"

"Check on her?" Janet yelled. "You stay the hell

away from her! She doesn't need you causing her any more pain."

Nikoli simply picked up the pixie-like woman and set her aside, ignoring both women shouting at him as he ran down the stairs. He looked and didn't see her anywhere, but everyone was staring at him.

"Where?" he barked, and several people pointed to the front door. He wasted no time and ripped the door open to bound down the steps. He knew exactly where she'd go. The small gazebo up the street in the center of the outlying buildings. She loved it there, said it was peaceful.

He stopped dead about twenty feet from the gazebo. There was a cell phone on the ground, with a trail of blood leading from it to the street. He took several more steps, and dread and panic froze his heart.

The phone was Lily's.

***

A wave of nausea woke Lily up. She groaned and rolled over, but found she was in a small, tight place. She opened her eyes to darkness. The first thing she noticed was that she was moving. *Calm down*, she told herself. *Calm down and focus*. She listened and heard the sounds of the highway. She was in a trunk and moving. They weren't going fast, probably under the speed limit.

Her head was killing her. She closed her eyes and tried to remember what happened. She'd been running, running away from Nikoli and the girl he'd been with. She'd run smack into someone. She'd mumbled an apology and tried to go around him, but he'd caught her arm and pulled her around. He'd told her to be quiet and come with him or he'd cut her. Her upper arm started to sting as soon as she remembered him saying that. She'd tried to get away, and he *had* cut her. That hadn't quieted her down. Adam's dad had taught her to scream and fight like hell if she ever got in this kind of situation, and that was exactly what she'd done. The last thing she remembered was the guy's fist barreling down at her, and then it had been lights out.

If she panicked now, she'd end up dead and missing instead of just missing. She ignored the pain in her arm and started feeling around the trunk. The first thing she looked for was a trunk latch. All new cars had them in case someone got locked in. There wasn't one, which said this was an older car.

Next, she examined the taillights, and this was her first bout of good luck. She turned and kicked the taillight several times as hard as she could, and it knocked the light out. Wiggling around, she managed to turn so her head was now looking out of the broken taillight. They were surrounded by cars. How to get their attention?

She searched the interior of the trunk as best she could but found nothing. It was completely empty. *Think, Lily, think*, she told herself. Her bra! It was white. She rolled so she could unsnap it, and then worked until she got it off. She wrapped one strap around her wrist so the wind couldn't rip it out of her hands. Then she thrust it out the taillight's now empty hole and started waving.

She prayed to God someone would see it and call the police.

***

Nikoli called Luther and explained what was going on. He asked Luther to call 911. The campus police were not the ones to handle this. His thoughts kept running to the one place he didn't want them to. The serial killer. He'd been getting closer and closer to the Boston Campus for months now.

Kade. He'd call his brother.

"What?" Kade barked into the phone when he answered.

"It's Lily." Nikoli's voice cracked, but he didn't care. "She's gone, Kade. Someone took her."

"Tell me."

"I came outside to find her, and all I can find is her phone…"

"She might have accidentally dropped it," Kade soothed.

"No, you don't understand," Nikoli said. "There's blood leading from her phone to the street. Someone forcefully took her, Kade."

"How long ago?"

"Maybe five minutes."

"Stay where you are, I'm coming. Text me the address."

Nikoli did as he was told, but he knew enough about these kinds of situations to know every second counted. He looked up when he heard running steps. Luther, Mike, Adam, and several other guys were barreling toward him.

"Stop!" he shouted. "We can't track the area up in case there's a clue."

"What happened?" Adam growled, getting right up in his face. "You piece of shit…"

"Look, now is not the time for this," Nikoli cut him off. "We can bitch slap each other later. Right now we need to find Lily."

Adam nodded, but his eyes promised Nikoli a world of pain.

"How many people do we have sober enough to drive?" he asked.

"Not enough," Mike said grimly, "but we can get more here."

"We need to all spread out and start looking. I know it's probably not going to do anything, but at least if we're out there looking and she's trying to get away, we might see something, anything that can help us find her."

"I'm on it." Mike took off toward the house, Adam hot on his heels. Less than a minute went by before people started to stream out of the fraternity, some climbing into cars, others on foot, to look for Lily.

Kade arrived about the same time the police did. Campus security showed up bursting with indignation the police had been called first. Nikoli repeated his story to countless people before he finally got fed up and stalked over to his brother.

"They have my statement, and they can question me all they want after we find Lily. I'm going to go look for her."

"Nik, just slow down. You don't even know where she is…"

313

They both hushed when news of a bra waving out of the broken taillight of an old sedan was reported on the highway. "With me," Kade said, and they climbed into his FBI issued SUV. Nikoli gave him directions, and before long they were on the highway, breaking every speed limit they came across, sirens wailing and lights flashing.

It took them twenty minutes, but they caught up with the unmarked car following the sedan. Nikoli spotted Mike and Adam closing in as well. He'd forgotten Mike's dad had installed a police scanner in his truck. They would have heard the call too.

The sedan sped up, weaving through traffic, having seen the police lights. Nikoli cursed when the car started to cut in and out of traffic. It was dangerous, too dangerous. He was going to crash. Kade came to the same realization and barked an order for ambulances to start heading their way.

Mike's truck was even with the SUV, and Nikoli rolled down his window. "They're gonna crash!"

"We know!" Mike yelled back.

Kade sped up, twisting the SUV in between cars in a way the poor thing had never been meant to. He sideswiped two vehicles to keep the sedan in sight. The old, gold colored Saturn made a sharp turn to the left, and the momentum was too much. It couldn't stop the force that plowed it into the car in front of it, and then went rolling, landing on the other side of the median where a tractor trailer hit it head on.

They all stared in horror as the car came to a stop against the guardrail, mangled into a mess of metal and plastic.

Kade came to his senses first and drove over the median to get to the other side. Nikoli had the door open and was running before he'd even come to a stop. This reminded him of the day Lily had run to him in Miami, but this was so much worse. His wreck had been minor. This was...she could be dead. *God, please don't let her die.*

He skidded to a halt, looking for the trunk. He saw a tiny piece of white material and said a prayer of thanks. His hands roamed until he found the seam of the trunk and pulled. Nothing. It wouldn't budge. Adam, Mike, and Kade joined him, and together they forced the lid up.

"Nonononono," Nikoli whispered, looking at Lily's lifeless body lying as twisted and mangled as the car. He reached for her, and Mike and Adam grabbed him.

"Don't," Mike said. "We need to wait for the paramedics. We could hurt her more if we move her."

"I need to know if she's alive." Tears streamed down his face, and he didn't care. All he saw was Lily, bleeding and so still.

Kade leaned in and put two fingers to the pulse point on her neck. "She's got a pulse. It's weak, but it's there."

They could see more lights in the distance. Nikoli tuned it all out. All he saw was Lily. He knelt down in front of the trunk and prayed. He hadn't prayed to God since he was a small boy, but he prayed now. He promised God that if he let Lily live, he'd spend every minute of the rest of their lives making it up to her. He promised so many things if only God would let Lily live. He was barely aware of the tears running down his cheeks or the sobs torn out of him. All he saw was his Lily Bells.

Kade gently pulled him away so the paramedics could go to work.

"What the hell?" Mike muttered. Nikoli's head whipped around to see Mike staring at the driver. He went over to see what had Mike so startled.

Brian Greggory.

Brian Greggory from the football team.

A slow rage built in Nikoli, and he ripped the door from the hinges. Kade tackled him before he could grab him.

"Let me go!"

"You can't beat the guy up, Nikoli. You'll get charged with assault and battery!"

"After what he did to Lily?" Nikoli shouted, enraged. "They can arrest me!"

"Lily needs you right now," Kade reasoned. "What is she going to do when she wakes up and you're in jail? Think, Nik. Just think for two seconds. What's more important? Lily, or beating an unconscious guy who won't even realize the beating he's getting?"

Nikoli stalked back over to where the paramedics were loading her into the ambulance. Adam climbed in behind them, and the paramedic said they could only take one passenger. He didn't argue the point, just headed for Mike's truck. Mike was waiting for him.

Mike pulled out behind the ambulance, and they both sat in grim silence as they followed the flashing lights.

Chapter Twenty

The wait seemed to go on forever. Nikoli kept staring at the clock. She was in surgery. Three hours. She'd been in surgery for three hours with no word. The nurse said the doctor would come out as soon as they knew anything. Adam had called Lily's mom and his own parents. They were all on their way. Nikoli had already arranged for a car to meet them.

His mind kept flashing back to the look in her eyes when she'd seen him with the blonde. It defied words to describe the pain in them. He'd give anything for her not to have seen that. He had been about ready to call it quits when the door opened. No matter who he was with, he couldn't see anyone but Lily.

She had to be okay. She had to forgive him.

He kept remembering all the laughter they'd shared. The times they'd just lounged on the couch watching horror movies, the debates they'd gotten into over food at one of the endless diners he'd introduced her to. He remembered the way her eyes

318

would go sleepy and darken to a shade of black when desire ruled her. He remembered the deep, husky sound of her voice when she gave in to the passion he stirred within her. Mostly, though, he just remembered Lily, the girl who loved her penguin pajamas and books. God, she loved books. He'd build her her own library.

If she'd just live.

He was the biggest fool God had ever created. The one person who saw past the front he put up and dug deeper to find the real him, he'd tossed out like she was no better than day old garbage. He'd been given a most precious gift, something that was worth more than all the money he had, worth more than any car he owned, something worth more than his own life...and he'd thrown it away. All because he hadn't been man enough to accept the risk of getting hurt.

And now he was hurting worse than he'd ever hurt, and Lily was fighting for her life. All because he was a fool.

"Can we go now?"

Nikoli opened his eyes at the familiar whine of Adam's girlfriend's voice. She looked irritated and impatient. She'd come to the hospital less than thirty minutes ago, and already she wanted to leave? Selfish bitch.

"No, we can't leave yet, Sue. Lily's still in surgery."

"Adam, it's not like being here is helping her in any way. Let's go home where you can relax..."

"Relax?" Nikoli exploded. He stood up, his eyes cold and mean. Sue took a step back. "You really are the most selfish bitch I've ever met."

She gasped and looked to Adam for help.

"You've known Boy Wonder what, three years or so? He's known Lily all his life. She's his sister, his best friend, a part of his soul. Do you really think he's going to fucking go home and *relax* while she's in surgery fighting for her life? And why the fuck would you ask him that? Other than the fact you're a jealous, selfish she-bitch. Sit your ass down or go home, but do not say one more word about Adam leaving."

He walked back over to his chair and sat. Sue stared at him, her mouth working while she tried to find words to respond. Finally, after a full minute, she turned on Adam. "Are you just going to let him talk to your fiancée like that?"

"If he were still talking to my fiancée, no, I wouldn't, but since you and I are done, then he can talk to you any way he wants."

"*What?*" she shrieked.

"You are a selfish bitch," Adam told her. "I just ignored it before. But asking me to leave Lily when she needs me? That's going too far. I've put up with your bullshit for a long time, Sue. I haven't loved you for a long time. We're done. Before you make a scene, think of where we are. Most of the football team and everyone who loves Lily is here. You'd best get yourself moving without a fuss."

Adam stood up and then sat down next to Nikoli. Mike and Janet followed. Nikoli raised his eyebrows. What brought that on?

"You love her, don't you?" Adam asked after a long while.

"Yeah, but I fucked it up. If she'll forgive me, I'm going to marry her."

"You ever hurt her like that again, and I'll put the barrel of a shotgun between your eyes and hide the body in one of the countless mountain breaks near the coal mines we grew up with. They'll never find your body. We clear?"

Nikoli nodded, and they both turned their attention back to the clock. What was taking so long?

Thirty minutes later, a tired-looking surgeon waded out into the waiting room and called out Lily's name. Nikoli and Adam pushed to the front.

"How is she?" Nikoli demanded.

"Is she okay?" Adam asked, his worry plain in his voice.

"Are you family?" the surgeon asked.

"I'm her fiancé," Nikoli announced and then pointed to Adam. "This is her brother."

"I'm Doctor Kerev. It was a bit touch and go. We had to remove her spleen and repair some damage done to her kidneys and lungs. She's got four broken ribs, a fracture of her left femur, and small cranial fracture."

They all gasped at the extent of her injuries.

"She'll pull through," the surgeon hurried to assure them. "We're going to keep her sedated while her body heals. She needs rest more than anything right now. She's being moved to the ICU."

"We're staying," Nikoli said, and his tone brooked no argument.

"Only immediate family," the surgeon said. "Everyone else should head home. There's nothing

321

more to be done for her right now except to let her rest."

After much grumbling, the waiting room cleared out, and Mike took Janet home. A nurse led Adam and Nikoli back to the ICU ward and into Lily's room. She was hooked up to so many machines. She looked helpless and small. They dragged chairs to her bed and stared at each other, just waiting.

The police came and took both their statements about the car chase. It wasn't long after that before Kade showed up. He'd been down to see Greggory.

"How is she?" he asked.

"Stable," Nikoli said. "The doc's keeping her asleep so she can heal."

"That's probably for the best." Kade nodded.

"Has Brian woken up yet?" Adam asked, his voice full of the same rage Nikoli was trying to keep under control.

"I talked to him," Kade replied. "We thought at first he might be our serial killer, but he's not. He doesn't fit the profile, and his apartment confirmed his statement. His place is a shrine to her. He's been stalking her for years, and I'm guessing she never knew?"

They both stared at him blankly.

"It's not uncommon for a stalker to never make contact with his victim until he's ready to strike. Or to never confess his obsession, in this case, since he claims they were friends. He saw an opportunity, and he took it. She was alone and upset, no one was around, and he grabbed her. He was taking her to small house he'd purchased with the funds from an inheritance from his grandfather. If Lily wasn't a smart girl, there is a good chance we'd never have found her. He took her in a dead zone—no cameras, no witnesses, nothing."

Fear gripped Nikoli's heart so hard, he nearly bent over. He'd almost lost her, he would have lost her if that bastard had managed to get her to his house. His hands shook at the thoughts of what might have happened to her.

"What's going to happen to him?" Adam asked, his hand clutching Lily's in a death grip. "He's not going to get out, is he?"

"With the charges that boy racked up tonight, there's not a judge in Boston that'll give him bail. He's going away for a long, long time. Especially with the atmosphere now. Women being kidnapped, murdered, and then dumped? That boy will be lucky if he sees freedom anytime in the near future."

"Still no luck on the serial killer?" Nikoli asked.

"I'm not supposed to discuss an active investigation," Kade said quietly, "but given what's happened tonight, and we think he's going to strike at one of the college campuses soon, I'm warning you. Any female you care about, don't let them out of your sight."

"You told me yesterday you guys were wrapping up," Nikoli said. "When are you leaving?"

"I'm not," Kade said. "My supervisor asked me to stay here in Boston until we catch this psycho. I'll be here until the case is solved."

They talked for a few more minutes, and then Kade left, telling them to call if they needed anything. Adam settled down next to Lily, her hand still clutched in his.

All they could do now was wait.

Chapter
Twenty-One

Lily hurt, everywhere. She tried to open her eyes, but they were heavy. She did manage to crack one eye partially open and saw Nikoli asleep in the chair beside her bed. He looked tired and his clothes were worn, like he'd slept in them for days. She closed her eyes again when the harsh light started to make them burn. How long had she been out?

She heard the steady beeping of machines and realized she was in a hospital. Why was she in a hospital? Her memory was foggy, but she vaguely remembered a car crash. Had she been in an accident?

She opened both eyes this time and looked around. Definitely a hospital. She was hooked up to more machines than she could count. She looked back over to Nikoli. Why was he here? Her last memory of him was all hugged up with some blonde ditz. She'd run from the house and then...then...ohmygod. She'd been attacked and woken up in a trunk. Someone had kidnapped her. She remembered kicking out the taillight and using her bra as a distress signal.

Then what happened? She thought hard, and her heartbeat started to race when she remembered the car going crazy fast, then they'd tipped over, and something must have crashed into them, but she wasn't sure. She'd passed out before she could register much.

She'd woken up here with Nikoli Kincaid sitting beside her bed, asleep and looking like he'd been through hell.

Her mouth was full of cotton. She needed water. The nurse's call button wasn't anywhere to be seen, and besides, she was so sore, she didn't know if she'd be able to reach it. She let out a tiny sigh, but it was enough to wake up the man sitting across from her. Nikoli's eyes sprang open, and his worried gaze found her face.

"You're awake," he whispered.

Lily nodded and winced. Her head hurt something awful. "W…wat…"

"Water?" he asked, and Lily nodded. He poured water into one of those little plastic hospital cups and held her head up so she could drink. "Just a few sips at first," he warned.

The cool ice water was the best thing she'd tasted in her life. It soothed her dry, parched mouth and the burn in her throat. When Nikoli pulled it away, she tried to protest, but he shook his head. "No, *Milaya*, you must sip it a little at a time or you'll get sick."

He reached over and hit the call button. "They'll

need to check you out, *dushka*. Just relax and let them work."

A few minutes later a nurse came in and smiled. "She's awake, I see. You've had us worried." She picked up Lily's chart and nodded. "You're in luck. Your doctor happens to be the one on call today. I'll page him as soon as I take your vitals."

For the next twenty minutes she was poked and prodded. She'd always hated hospitals, even when she was little. There was just something about the sterile smell that disturbed her. Cleaning fluids mixed with the stench of sickness. The only thing she really wanted to know was when she could go home. The doctor said they'd take it day by day, which caused her to scrunch her nose in disgust.

Adam came rushing in about the time the doctor left. He made a beeline for her and grabbed her into a hug. All the breath went out of her at the pain that lanced across her ribs. Before she could say a word, Nikoli had hauled him off her.

"Her ribs," he said before Adam could open his mouth. "You were hurting her."

"Hell, I forgot." Adam ran a hand through his hair. "I'm sorry, Lils."

"It's okay," she said, her throat still a little scratchy.

"I'd have been here sooner, but I fell asleep in the cafeteria and didn't see Nik's message until just a few minutes ago." He grimaced and shot an apologetic look Nikoli's way.

Lily frowned. They were acting like friends. Since when were Adam and Nikoli friends? They hated each other.

"How are you?" Adam turned his attention back to her, walking over and sitting down in the chair Nikoli had vacated.

"I'm sleepy," she said truthfully. She was having issues keeping her eyes open.

"Sleepy?" Adam laughed. "You've been asleep for almost five days, Lils."

"Five days?" she gasped. No way!

"Yeah, you had some pretty serious injuries, and then there was a complication." He glanced over at Nikoli, and he nodded. "You had some bleeding in your brain and they had to relieve it almost right after your first surgery. You scared the hell out of us."

No wonder she had such a horrible headache.

"You mom and my parents are here. Don't be shocked when they show up later today," Adam warned her. "I'm going to try and keep them from visiting until tomorrow, but there's no way your mom is staying away. We had to strong-arm her to get her to go to the hotel and get some sleep."

She gave Adam a once over and noticed his clothes were as rumpled as Nikoli's, and he hadn't shaved in a couple days either, by the looks of it. Had they both been here the entire time?

"She needs to sleep," Nikoli said. "Now that she's awake and talking, why don't you head home and get some sleep yourself?"

"That's not a bad idea. I need a shower too. Want me to bring you dinner back?"

Nikoli nodded, and Lily glanced between the two of them, nonplussed. Had she died and gone to some remote region of hell, perhaps?

Adam laughed at the confusion on her face. "Don't worry, Lils, Kincaid and I came to an understanding. We're all good." He leaned down and kissed her forehead. "Get some rest, and I'll be back in a few hours. I'll call your mom too."

Nikoli nodded to him and then dragged the chair closer to the bed and sat down. He stared at her, not saying a word. There were so many emotions flickering in his eyes, it was hard to define them all.

"I'm sorry, *Milaya*," he said after a long moment. "I'm so sorry."

"It's not your fault someone attacked me, Nikoli."

"Yes, it is. If I wasn't such a stupid ass, you would never have been put in that position. You wouldn't have walked in on me and then run out so that bastard could take you."

She sighed and started to say something, but he put a finger to her lips.

"Quiet, *Milaya*," he said, his voice deep and gruff. "When I saw your face that night…God, it cut through me, and I realized then what a selfish bastard I was." He ran a hand through his hair. "I lied to you, Lily, when I said I didn't love you. I do. More than my own life, but I was so scared when you told me in Miami. I kept thinking of the girl who'd broken my heart before, and I couldn't do that to myself again. So I lied."

He lied? A flutter of hope sprang to life inside of her, but then she remembered all the women he'd been with since they broke up. "Nikoli…the last month…all the women…"

"Not a damn thing happened," he swore. "I tried,

Milaya. Trust me, I tried *hard* to forget you, but I couldn't. I kept seeing your eyes, all broken and haunted. That girl you found me with? She was my last ditch effort to try and be the old me, but I couldn't. I was about to take her back downstairs when you walked in. I don't blame you if you don't believe me, but it's the truth, Lily. You've seen me with girls, but how many have you heard talking about fucking me?"

She thought back over the last month, and she'd heard rumors he'd been playing hard to get and it was driving the girls insane, but she couldn't think of a single person who claimed to have slept with him.

"I love you, Lily Isabella Holmes. I fucked up and let you walk away once, and I'm not doing it again. I'm an ass, but I'm an ass who loves you. Will you forgive me, Lily? Will you forgive all the hurt I caused us both and marry me?"

Marry him?

"I swear to all that's holy, *Milaya*, I will spend every damn day for the rest of our lives making it up to you if you'll forgive me. I promised God I'd take care of you if he'd give you back to me. You'll never know the hell I went through when I found your phone lying there on the sidewalk, and the blood…God, Lily, I almost lost it. Then when I saw that car flip with you in it, I almost died myself."

He reached down and grabbed her hand. "Please, *dushka*, forgive me. I'm so fucking sorry, Lily. Give me a second chance? Please?"

Lily stared at him, shocked and dazed. She'd heard nothing but *blah, blah, blah* after the words *marry me*. He'd really asked her to marry him? Hope refused to be pushed down again as she gazed into his onyx eyes. They were open and honest, full of pain, regret, and love.

Could she forgive him for everything he'd done? He'd broken her so badly. He'd healed the damaged person she'd been, only to break her into a million tiny pieces that were still sobbing on Janet's bathroom floor.

"Nikoli," she said softly. "You don't understand what you did to me, what I went through…"

"Jan told me," he said just as softly. "I'm sorry, Lily. I know it doesn't mean anything, but I am truly and deeply sorry, and I will never hurt you like that again. I swear it."

Could she trust him again? She loved him so much, her very soul ached without him, but could she go through that again if he decided he didn't want her? Her mind shied away from the thought of that pain, the pain that still sometimes woke her up in the middle of the night, and she'd cry until she went to sleep. The only person who could fix the broken mess she was sat staring at her, his heart in his eyes. She took a chance once, and she'd take it again, even given what happened, because she would never regret Nikoli Kincaid. He was her heart and her soul.

"What does *dushka* mean?" she asked instead of answering right away.

"It means sweetheart." He ran a hand through his short hair. "I've never called a girl sweetheart before. It's why I'd never tell you what it meant. I didn't want to explain it even to myself."

He'd been calling her sweetheart for months and she'd never even realized.

"You're killing me Lily." He leaned forward, resting his elbows on the bed. "Please say you forgive me."

"I forgive you, Nikoli."

He brought her hand to his lips and placed a kiss lightly on her palm. "Thank you, *Milaya*. I don't deserve it, but thank you."

"No, you don't deserve it," she told him. "And you are a selfish bastard, and if you ever make me hurt like that again, I swear I will shoot you where you stand."

He chuckled. "You still haven't answered my question yet, Lily Bells."

"I don't know if I want to marry an ass or not," she said, but there was no heat behind the words. She did want to marry him.

"Yes, you do," he countered, a wicked grin spreading across his face.

"I do, do I?"

"Uh-huh." He nodded. "Who else is going to put up with your prudish tendencies?"

"I am not a prude!"

He gave her the patented Kincaid stare.

"Well, if I'm a prude, then you're a manwhore."

"Did we or did we not agree to never use that word again?"

"As long as you continue to call me a prude, then I'll call you a manwhore."

"I love you," he said, laughing.

"I'll marry you, Kincaid, on one condition."

"What?"

"I want your car."

"Ellie? You want Ellie?" He looked stricken, and Lily nearly laughed out loud.

"Yes."

He got up and started to pace. "I can buy you any car you want, Lily Bells. Just name it and I'll have it sitting in the hospital parking lot today."

"I want your car, Nikoli."

Nikoli took a deep breath and came over to sit on her bed. He leaned down until all she could see were his eyes. They were warm, and she could see the love in their dark depths. "If it means I get you, then fine, *Milaya*, you can have my car."

Her mouth dropped open. He'd give her the car? He loved that car…he loved her. He really loved her if he was willing to hand over the one thing he loved more than anything.

"Well, how about you just let me drive the car once in a while?"

He grinned. "Is that a yes?"

"Don't you think it's too soon, though?" she fretted as he leaned back. "We've only known each other a couple of months."

"My father married my mother a week after he met her. Kincaid men waste no time in staking a claim when it matters. I love you, Lily. Not for a week or a month or a year. I will love you when I'm old and gray, when I'm too senile to remember your name, but I'll still remember that I love you. I don't need months or years to know I want you to be my wife. You're all I need, all I'll ever need. Marry me, Lily. Please."

"Yes, Kincaid, I'll marry you."

He leaned over and placed a butterfly kiss on her lips. "I love you, Lily."

"I love you too, Nikoli."

He smiled and kissed her softly once more, but her eyes were drooping shut.

"Sleep, sweetheart, just sleep."

Epilogue

The Christmas tree was a mess. They were all gathered at Adam's family home for the holidays, and his mother had left them in charge of decorating it. She, Nikoli, Adam, and the twins were staring at the lopsided tree with both horror and awe. All the ornaments were on, the lights twinkled at them, but it was the Leaning Tower of Pine.

"Maybe we should tie it to the wall?" Luther suggested.

"You put a hole in my mother's brand new living room, and she'll shoot you," Adam said. "Don't think she won't either. That woman has a mean streak wider than the Mississippi."

"That's the God's truth," Lily said. "You remember when we brought snowballs in the house and they melted all over the hardwood?"

Adam shuddered. "Don't even think about it."

"It gives it character," Nikoli said thoughtfully. "Kids, do you like it?"

The twins jumped and down, their shouts of 'yes' all that Nikoli needed. "See? They love it.

That's all that matters."

Lily slipped an arm around him and laughed at his logic. She had no doubt as soon as the parents saw the Christmas tree nightmare, they'd make them redo it. Her mom loved Christmas, and it had to be just perfect. Her mother had swooped in like a hurricane and descended on the Christmas decoration bins like a tornado. Now the quaint farmhouse was decked to the nines and looked like they'd stepped into some kind of holiday showcase home.

"Promise me you'll never make us live in a place where Santa threw up," Nikoli whispered in her ear, and she laughed out loud.

"I never make promises I can't keep," she teased.

He groaned.

"Duct tape!" Adam shouted, and they both looked up, startled.

"Duct tape?" Nikoli asked, staring at them like they'd lost their minds.

"Duct tape fixes everything," Lily said, and he looked down at her in amusement.

"Well, it does," she said defensively.

Adam went running and came back a few minutes later with one of those heavy duty Command hooks and a roll of duct tape. He put the hook on the wall, and then wrapped duct tape around the trunk near where the tree started to lean, and then pulled until it was straight. Luther held it in place while Adam tied off the end of the tape to the hook. Then they maneuvered the tree so you couldn't see the tape, and Nikoli burst out laughing. It had worked. The tree stood straight, and Adam looked like he was going to strut around the living room.

He looked at Lily, and then Luther, and then his gaze took in Adam and the twins. One thing struck him. If he hadn't met Lily, he'd be the same old Nikoli, spending Christmas at Luther's, feeling like he was a third wheel. Instead, he had friends and family to spend the holiday with, and he owed it all to the woman wrapped around him. She'd made him whole and given him back his ability to love someone other than himself. She was his home, and would always be.

Lily's phone rang, and she pulled it out of her pocket. A small gasp escaped her, and he looked down at the screen. Suzie Daniels. It was her literary agent.

"Hello?" she said. "You did? Really? How much? Wow. Merry Christmas to you too, Suzie, and thank you so much!"

She ended the call and looked up. Her eyes were wide and excited. "Joanna sold my book to *Simon* and *Schuster*!"

"Congratulations!" Adam grabbed her and swung her around. "You deserve it, Lils!"

Luther took his turn next before Nikoli reclaimed her and planted a kiss on her mouth. "Congratulations, *Milaya*."

Adam started laughing.

"What's so funny?" Nikoli demanded.

"Ask her what the name of the book is," he said, chortling.

Nikoli quirked an eyebrow at her. "Well?"

She shook her head and grinned. His eyes

337

narrowed. "What *is* the name of the book, Lily?"

It was Adam who answered.

"Manwhore."

Lily burst out laughing and took off running.

"*Milaya*!" he roared and chased after her, happier than he'd ever been in his life.

The manwhore had found his peace at last.

The End

Acknowledgments

There are so many people I have to thank. This book wasn't one I thought I could write, as it's a romance novel, but you guys pushed me, and I did it. So thank you to everyone who made me leave my comfort zone and write something so unfamiliar, but so endearing to my heart as well.

Jennifer Hewitt deserves a big thank you for all she has done for me this year. She has been such a huge help to me with social media and just telling the honest to God truth when my writing sucks and gives me ideas on how to fix it. I don't know what I'd do without you! You are a blessing, my friend. This novel would not be where it is right now without her listening to me, reading, and complaining until I fixed it. Gracias, chica!

As always, a huge shout out to my girls, Ang, Susan, and Delsheree. Without your help, this book would still be collecting dust in the WIP folder. You gave me so much help in the beginning of this endeavor. So, thank you, ladies.

I have to say thank you to my friend Layth. You showed me how to be silly again and gave me back my laughter. Thank you for being my friend. I'm glad I met you, and despite your asshat gene, I still love you.

Thanks to everyone at Limitless for being so patient with me while I struggled with this. You guys rock.

My editor, Lori, has had to put up with me during this process and I know she's had to count to ten a few times, so thank you for all the hard work you do and for putting up with me.

Huge shout out to my family for putting up with me when I write and forget the rest of the world exists.

Last, but not least, thank you to all my wonderful readers. You guys are why I write, and I just want you to know how grateful I am for your support. Thank you all so much.

About the Author

So who am I? Well, I'm the crazy girl with an imagination that never shuts up. I LOVE scary movies. My friends laugh at me when I scare myself watching them and tell me to stop watching them, but who doesn't love to get scared? I grew up in a small town nestled in the southern mountains of West Virginia where I spent days roaming around in the woods, climbing trees, and causing general mayhem. Nights I would stay up reading Nancy Drew by flashlight under the covers until my parents yelled at me to go to sleep.

Growing up in a small town, I learned a lot of values and morals, I also learned parents have spies everywhere and there's always someone to tell your mama you were seen kissing a particular boy on a particular day just a little too long. So when you get grounded, what is there left to do? Read! My Aunt Jo gave me my first real romance novel. It was a romance titled "Lord Margrave's Deception." I remember it fondly. But I also learned I had a deep and abiding love of mysteries and anything paranormal. As I grew up, I started to write just that and would entertain my friends with stories featuring them as main characters.

Now, I live Huntersville, NC where I entertain my niece and nephew and watch the cats get teased by the birds and laugh myself silly when they swoop down and then dive back up just out of reach. The cats start yelling something fierce...lol.

I love books, I love writing books, and I love

entertaining people with my silly stories.

Facebook:
https://www.facebook.com/authorAprylBaker

Twitter:
https://twitter.com/AprylBaker

Wattpad:
http://www.wattpad.com/user/AprylBaker7

Website:
http://www.aprylbaker.com/

Blog:
http://mycrazzycorner.blogspot.com/

TSU:
http://www.tsu.co/Apryl_Baker

Goodreads:
http://www.goodreads.com/author/show/5173683.A
pryl_Baker

Linkedin:
http://www.linkedin.com/pub/april-
baker/44/6b9/3a4

CPSIA information can be obtained
at www.ICGtesting.com
Printed in the USA
BVOW07s0145020516
446382BV00001B/3/P